BLOOD SHOT

A JOHN JORDAN MYSTERY BOOK 15

MICHAEL LISTER

PULPWOOD PRESS

Paperback ISBNs:

ISBN-10: 1-947606-00-X

ISBN-13: 978-1-947606-00-5

Edited by Aaron Bearden

Designed by Tim Flanagan

Join Michael's Readers' Group and receive 4 FREE Books!

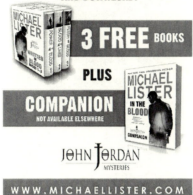
Books by Michael Lister

Sign up for Michael's newsletter by clicking here or go to
www.MichaelLister.com and receive a free book.

Blood Work
Cold Blood
Blood Betrayal
Blood Shot

(Jimmy "Soldier" Riley Novels)
The Big Goodbye
The Big Beyond
The Big Hello
The Big Bout
The Big Blast
In a Spider's Web (short story)
The Big Book of Noir

(Merrick McKnight / Reggie Summers Novels)
Thunder Beach
A Certain Retribution

(Remington James Novels)
Double Exposure
(includes intro by Michael Connelly)
Separation Anxiety
Blood Shot

(Sam Michaels / Daniel Davis Novels)
Burnt Offerings
Separation Anxiety
Blood Oath
Blood Shot

(Love Stories)
Carrie's Gift

(Short Story Collections)
North Florida Noir
Florida Heat Wave
Delta Blues
Another Quiet Night in Desperation

(The Meaning Series)

Meaning Every Moment
The Meaning of Life in Movies

Sign up for Michael's newsletter by clicking here or go to
www.MichaelLister.com and receive a free book.

ACKNOWLEDGMENTS

Thank you for all your incredible, generous assistance in the creating of this novel"

Dawn Lister, Aaron Bearden, Mike Harrison, Donnie "Spanky" Arnold, and Bobby "Banjo" Whitehurst

For Sheriff Mike Harrison

Your generosity with your time, expertise, and great ideas makes each of my books immeasurably better.

You honor the badge, your family, our community, and the WHS Class of '86. Go Gators!

AUTHOR'S NOTE

Blood Shot is a sequel to both *Double Exposure and* the John Jordan series. The book alternates between "Then" and "Now" chapters. "Then" chapters contain selected passages from *Double Exposure*. The "Now" chapters contain John Jordan's current investigation of the events in *Double Exposure*. If you have recently read *Double Exposure*, you might prefer to skim or skip over the "Then" chapters—though, of course, I hope you won't. If you haven't read *Double Exposure*, I hope you'll not only read the "Then" chapters, but consider reading that novel after reading this one. Regardless of *how* you read this or any other of my novels, I truly appreciate *that* you are.

1

Then

E vening.
Fall. North Florida.
Bruised sky above rusted rim of earth.
Black forest backlit by plum-colored clouds. Receding glow. Expanding dark.

Deep in the cold woods of the Apalachicola River Basin, Remington James slowly makes his way beneath a canopy of pine and oak and cypress trees along a forest floor of fallen pine straw, wishing he'd worn a better jacket, his Chippewa snake boots slipping occasionally, unable to find footing on the slick surface.

Above him, a brisk breeze whistles through the branches, swaying the treetops in an ancient dance, raining down dead leaves and pine needles.

It's his favorite time of day in his favorite time of year, his family's hunting lease his favorite place to hide from the claustrophobia of small-town life increasingly closing in on him.

S creams.

He hears what sounds like human screams from a great distance away, but can't imagine anyone else is out here and decides it must be an animal or the type of aural illusion that occurs so often when he's alone this deep in the disorienting woods.

Still, it unnerves him. Especially when . . . There it is again.

Doesn't sound like any animal he's ever heard, and he finds it far more disquieting than any sound he's ever encountered out here.

It's not a person, he tells himself. It's not. Can't be. But even if it were, you'd never be able to find anyone out here.

The sound stops . . . and he continues.

O ne good shot.

Even closing the shop early—something his dad never did, particularly during hunting season—he has only the narrowest of margins, like the small strip of light from a slightly open door, in which there will be enough illumination for exposure.

The drive out to the edge of his family's land; the ATV ride into the river swamp; the walk through acres of browning, but still thick, foliage—all close the door even more, but all he wants is to check his camera traps and get one good shot with his new camera.

He'll trudge as far as he can, search as long as he can—capturing the image at the last possible moment, stumbling back in full dark if he has to. Given the circumstances of his current condition and the lack of choices he has, there's nothing he'd rather be doing, no way he'd rather spend his few short evening hours than in pursuit of the perfect picture.

L oss.

Emptiness. Numbness.

His dad dying so young has filled the facade of Remington's life with tiny fissures, a fine spider's web of hairline fractures threatening collapse and crumble.

Facade or foundation? Maybe it's not just the surface of his life, but the core that's cracking. He isn't sure and he doesn't want to think about it, though part of him believes he comes alone to the woods so he'll be forced to do just that.

He's wanted to be an adventure photographer for over a decade, but pulling the trigger now, making the investment, obsessively spending every free moment in its pursuit, in the wake of his dad's death, the wake that still rocks the little lifeboat of his existence, is a fearful man's frenzied attempt at mitigating mortality—and he knows it. He just doesn't know what else to do.

Heather could tell him.

2

Now

S ome unsolved cases are like unanswered questions.

Not casual curiosities, but obsessive, relentlessly repeated questions nagging mercilessly at the edges of everything else.

Others are like open wounds.

Seeping, susceptible-to-infection lacerations incapable of healing without intense treatment.

Who killed Robin Wilson, the previous sheriff of Gulf County, and four of his men-- with their own guns-- has always been the unanswered question type of unsolved case, but why Remington James was hunted down like an animal in the woods and who killed him in cold blood has always been more of the open wound kind of unsolved case.

Both haunt me. But in different ways.

One is incessant questions.

Who's the killer? Why'd he do it? How'd he do it? How'd he get away with it? Did he have help? Was there a cover-up?

For those of us charged with answering questions, with bearing witness, with giving some sort of narrative cohesiveness to the seemingly arbitrary and accidental elements of an unfinished story, the unanswered questions of an unsolved crime stalk us, mock us, gnaw at us.

The other is an open, unhealed wound.

Since I joined the Gulf County Sheriff's department, I have been obsessed with one unsolved case more than any other. What exactly happened out in the unforgiving swamp during Remington James' long, dark night of the soul troubles me in a way that few mysteries have.

Who killed Remington James? Not who pulled the trigger. Who was behind it? And why?

One possible answer—and one that only adds to the enigma —is that he witnessed the murder of a young woman out in the swamps where he had his camera traps set up—something he claimed to have happened in a message he left behind—but no evidence of such a crime has ever been found.

Did Remington make up the story about the murdered woman? If not, why hasn't she been found? Or was she? If she was, who found her and what'd they do with her body?

E verything changes with a single phone call.

For nearly a year I have been pleading with Heather James, Remington's widow, to talk to me, to help me find out what really happened to Remington and who was really behind it.

She declined each and every request I made—politely at first, but later with forceful rudeness, and eventually with complete silence.

And then after ignoring me for months, she calls me.

"I'm in town," she says. "I'd like to talk."

"Okay. When? Where?"

"I'm emailing you a manuscript. I've been working with a local writer to tell the truth about what really happened to Remington. Take a look at it and we'll talk. How's tomorrow?"

"Fine," I say. "Why now? What changed?"

"I'll explain when we meet."

"Okay."

"The manuscript is based on everything I've been able to piece together from the evidence, the original investigation, and what Remington left behind. We don't have an ending yet. Not really. Not one that explains things in any satisfactory kind of way. I'm hoping you can help with that. I know you've been working on the case."

"I have, but the original investigation was . . ."

"A fuckin' joke," she says. "You figured out whether it was ineptitude or cover-up?"

"I have some ideas."

"I look forward to hearing them," she says. "Talk to you tomorrow."

Without saying goodbye or anything else she hangs up.

3

Then

H eather.
Like longing for home while being lost in the woods, all his thoughts these days lead back to her.

She had called when he was driving the ATV off the trailer, preparing to venture farther in the forest than his dad's truck could take him. Like the truck and trailer and the life he's now living, the ATV belongs to his father. Had belonged. Now it's his.

He was surprised by the vibrating of the phone in his pocket, certain he was too far in for signal. Another few feet, another moment later, and he would've been.

When he sees her name displayed on the small screen— Heather—he feels, as he always does lately, the conflicting emotions of joy and dread.

—Hello.

Light, photography's most essential element, is bleeding out;

the day will soon be dead. Time is light, and he has little of either to spare. Still, he has no thought of not answering the phone.

—You okay?

—Yeah. Why?

—For some reason, I just started worrying about you.

With those few words, the day grows colder, the forest darker. Heather gets feelings—the kind that in an earlier age would get her staked to the ground and set afire—and they're almost always right.

—You there? she asks.

—I'm here.

In his mind, she is wearing lavender, and it highlights her delicate features in the way it rests on the soft petals of the flower she's named after. She smells of flowers, too, and it's intoxicating —even within the confines of his imagination.

—Where are you? I can barely hear you.

—Woods. We're hanging by a single small bar of signal, he says, thinking it an apt metaphor for their tenuous connection.

He pictures her in the small gallery just down from the Rollins College campus in Winter Park, the sounds of the Amtrak train clacking down the track in the background, the desultory sounds of lazy evening traffic easing by her open door, and it reminds him just how far away she is.

—I'm sure you think that's some kind of metaphor.

—You don't?

—I don't think like you. Never have.

—Never said you should.

—You're okay?

—I'm fine. Just here to check my traps and try out my new camera.

—Well, be careful.

—Always am.

—Good.

—Got one of your feelings?

—I'm not sure.

—Either you do or you don't.

—Not always. Sometimes they have to . . . how can I put this . . . develop.

—Funny.

—Just trying to speak a language you understand.

He needs to go, but doesn't want to.

—Be extra careful, she says, and I'll call you if anything develops.

—I won't have signal.

—'Til when?

—'Til I get back. Hour or so after dark.

—Maybe you shouldn't go.

—You tell me. I don't have a feeling one way or the other.

—I'm so glad you're lensing again. Don't want to stop you.

She had always been encouraging of his photography, including letting him take nudes of her starting when they met in college and continuing into their lives together. Even when he wasn't taking pictures of anything else, he was taking pictures of her.

They are quiet a beat, and he misses her so much, the day grows even colder, the vast expanse of river swamp lonelier.

—We gonna make it? she asks, her voice small, airy, tentative.

—You don't have a feeling about that?

—I'm not ready to let go. I can't.

—Then don't.

—But . . .

—What?

—I don't know. We're not gonna figure it out right now, and you're losing light. Call me when you get home.

As is her custom, she hangs up without saying goodbye.

He smiles. Glad. Grateful. Goodbye is something he never

wants to hear from her. Back when they first started dating, he'd asked her why she never said it. Because, she'd explained, we're in the midst of one long, ongoing conversation. I don't want that to end.

She didn't say amen after her prayers either.

4

Now

"I want to reopen the Remington James case," I say.

"I thought you already had," Reggie says.

We are in her office in the back of the sheriff's department, which is behind the Gulf County Court House in Port St. Joe, on a laid back Monday morning in early April, the AC on.

Reggie Summers is the sheriff of Gulf County and my boss. She was appointed by the governor after Robin Wilson, the previous sheriff, and four of his men were murdered. She is smart and tough and honest and the reason I took this job. A natural beauty, no drama cowgirl, she has smooth skin the color of river clay that she never ever covers with makeup, long, straight brownish hair perpetually in a ponytail, and mesmerizing eyes.

"I mean really reopen it," I say. "Give it priority until we solve it or something comes up that pulls us off of it."

"What else are you working on right now?"

"Not much. Testifying in court in a few upcoming cases,

looking for Daniel and Randa, still tracking down records on the Alison fraud case. It'd be a good time for me to really dig into it."

She purses her lips and seems to consider it, her gray-green eyes narrowing in focus on things I can't see.

For reasons that remain a mystery to me, she has always seemed reluctant to let me really investigate this case—though not half as reluctant and actually resistant as she is about the Robin Wilson case, which is why I'm not even going to mention that I plan to investigate both of them together because I think they could be connected.

"Is there some reason you don't want me to?" I ask.

She shakes her head. "Why would there be? Just comes down to managing the department and its resourses."

Reggie's office remains bare, only half-moved-in, and I wonder if it's an expression of her oft-stated feeling that this is a temporary gig, that she really doesn't feel at home here. I know she believes the citizens of Gulf County won't elect a female sheriff, and she may be right, but something about her refusal to really move in and make this her office and her department makes it seem like she's not sure she'll even make it to her first election.

"You're my best investigator," she says. "Is this the best use of your time?"

I nod. "I think it is."

"Do you? Or do you just want to do it?"

"His wife has finally agreed to talk to me," I say.

"Whose?"

"Remington's."

"Really?"

I nod. "Even sent me the manuscript of a book she's writing about the case."

"She's writing a book about the case?"

"Not the case. What happened to her husband."

"Does she know?"

"Not everything. She's working with a ghostwriter. They've written it as a story, filling in what she doesn't know with imagination, best guesses, and conjecture."

"God help us."

"Give me one week," I say. "Anna and Taylor are at her parents' in Dothan for the week. Sam's in rehab. And Johanna's with her mom in the North Georgia mountains for spring break. I can devote every waking moment to it."

"Who're you kidding?" she says. "You know good and damn well you'll dream about it, too. Probably how you'll solve the damn thing."

I smile.

In addition to my family being away, I have even more time on my hands than usual because when I turned in my resignation as a chaplain at Gulf Correctional Institution, the warden offered me a part-time position if I would stay—something I gladly and gratefully agreed to.

"We've got an opioid epidemic on our hands—or haven't you heard?" she says. "Tourists driving into our little county in droves, local beekeepers fighting with ones coming in from out of state for tupelo season, an influx of people and a buttload of activity with Deseret. Can't interest you in something actually happening here today?"

"If I don't uncover any new evidence or get any kind of break in it inside of a week, I'll put the folder back in the filing cabinet for a while."

"And if you uncover something new?"

"If it's significant enough you let me keep working on it."

"For how long?"

"Another week with the same deal."

"And you won't let any current cases slide?"

"I won't."

"Okay. One week. That's it. And you better not wind up in some damn true crime book, either."

5

Then

More screams.

Or what sounds like screams. Surely they're not. Surely they're just—

Unbidden, unwelcome, he hears Heather screaming in his mind. Screaming in pain. Screaming for him. It's something he never wants to hear, something he didn't think he could bear.

Is there anything worse in the world than hearing the woman you love screaming in pain and being unable to do anything about it?

Closing the shutter on such thoughts, he refocuses his attention on his surroundings, on the task at hand.

Moving.

The forest grows thicker—tiny, barren branches buffeting his upper body, scratching his hands and face, as dead leaves, limbs, fallen trees, and bushes hinder him from below.

The temperature is sinking with the sun. A wet North Florida cold is coming, the kind that creeps into a man's marrow—especially when he's alone, unable to contact the outside world, uncertain about exactly where he is.

The cold air carries on its currents the faint smell of smoke, as if a great distance away an enormous forest fire is raging, running, consuming.

Home.

He wouldn't have chosen to come back to this place, but it feels right to be here—here in the real Florida, not the manufactured or imported, not the tacky or touristy, not the Art Deco or amusement park, but the great green northwest, Florida's millions of acres of bald-cypress swamps, dense hardwood hammocks, and longleaf and slash pine forests.

Here, in addition to taking care of his mother and keeping his family from ruin, he can hone his craft, practice his art, lens the rare and the beautiful, film Florida's most exotic and elusive wildlife.

Suddenly, startlingly, the thick forest opens up, giving way to a pine flatwood prairie. Several acres in circumference, surrounded by thick hardwood forests and cypress swamps, the small area is comprised of scattered longleaf pines, saw palmetto, cutthroat grass, gallberry, fetterbush, and fallflowering ixia.

Thankful for the temporary respite from the abrasive, nearly impenetrable hardwood forest, he moves more quickly through the thick but low-lying foliage on the soggy soil.

Lifting his feet high, in part to avoid the palmettos, in part out of his phobia of snakes, he lopes across the small flat plain within a few minutes, wondering why in all his previous trips out here he's never seen this particular one before.

—You lost?

The voice startles him, and he jumps. Turning, he sees a

gaunt old man with grizzly gray stubble, holding a large wood-grain shotgun, having just emerged from the cypress swamp Remington is about to enter.

Taking a moment before answering, Remington gathers himself.

—Only in the most existential sense, he says.

—Weren't meanin' to frighten you.

—It's okay. I just didn't expect to see anybody this far in.

—Me neither.

The man, younger than he first appears, is wearing grimy green work pants, scarred boots, a red flannel shirt, and a soiled baseball cap with a local logging company logo on it. His swimmy, slightly crossed eyes seem to float about, impossible to read.

—You a grower?

—A what? Remington asks, but then realizes he means pot.

—You ain't huntin'. What's in the bag?

—My camera.

—Camera? You with Fish and Game?

Remington shakes his head.

—Some sort of cop?

—No, sir.

He wants to say he's a photographer, but can't quite get it out.

—You hear someone scream a few minutes ago? Remington asks.

—Scream? The hell you talkin' about? Ain't no one out here but us.

—Probably an animal. I heard something.

—Ain't from around here, are you?

Remington starts to shake his head, but stops.

—Used to be. Am again, I guess.

—People what own this land don't take much of a shine to trespassers. Best go back the way you come in.

—This is my family's land. My dad is—was Cole James.

Remington realizes that the land he's standing on now belongs to him.

—I's sorry to hear about his passin'.

—Thanks.

—What're you doin' out this far?

—Taking pictures.

—Of what?

—Animals, mostly. Some trees.

—What kind of animals?

—Deer, gator, fox, bear, boar, and the Florida panther.

—Ain't no panther this far north.

—So everyone keeps telling me, but I've seen it.

—The hell you say.

—I have. When I was younger. And I've seen its tracks since I've been back.

—Well, you best be gettin' back. Be dark soon. Easy to get lost out here.

—Thanks, I will. I'm almost done.

—Wouldn't wait, I's you. Want me to, I'll take you in.

—Thanks, but I've got a compass.

The man cackles at that.

—Suit yourself. I jest hope the panther don't git ya.

He then turns and continues walking in the direction Remington has just come from.

Remington stands and watches the man until he crosses the small pine flatwoods plain and disappears into the hardwoods on the other side.

Unsettled by the encounter, he tries to determine why. Would he feel the same way had Heather not called and told him about her undeveloped feeling?

I would, he thinks. Though he can't quite identify what, there was something menacing about the man. Threatening. He's up to something illegal—and not just trespassing. It could be poaching or over-the-limit hunting, but it's far more likely that he's the grower.

He considers walking out of the woods right now, but is determined not to be scared off his own land. Besides, he's on a mission, and knows how depressed he'll be tonight if he goes in without accomplishing it.

Looking up, examining the quality and quantity of daylight left, he decides all he really has time to do now is check his traps, which is at least something. Something he can live with. But as he turns to enter the hardwoods, an indentation in the ground catches his eye, and he stops.

There in the soggy, sandy soil, as if in plaster, is a perfect paw print. And a little ways farther another. And then another. And another.

He's fairly certain the tracks are those of an adult Florida black bear, but searches the nearby trees for confirmation. He smiles as he sees the territorial scratch marks that Florida black bears make in the tree trunks. His smile broadens when he realizes that the marks are nearly seven feet high.

C older.
    Darker. Deeper.
Remington's not exactly sure where he is. Lost.

Leaving the tip-up mound in the soft pink glow of sunset, he begins to walk in the direction of his inmost camera trap. Or so he thinks.

N octurnal noises.
    Crickets. Frogs.
Chirps. Hums. Buzzes.
Loud.

Forging on, he ventures deeper and deeper into darkness and

density. Black leaves crunching beneath boots as he follows a ridge line into a stand of hardwoods over five hundred years old.

Chill. Stalking. Frightened.

The feeling that he is being followed persists. Stopping, he listens carefully and shines his small penlight in all directions, but hears and sees only nature.

This deep, this dark, the woods seem haunted, as if alive with an ancient menacing force predating humanity.

Nearing it now.

Almost there.

As he closes in on the spot of his deepest camera trap, the cold and fear and weariness begin to fade, floating up like smoke from a night fire, breaking apart as if bits of ash and rising into invisibility.

Walking faster now. Excited. Energized. Renewed.

D ry.

Following a spring and summer of record low rainfall, autumn had continued the arid trend, the rivers' flood plains receding, the swamps shrinking.

Of course, it's not just lack of rain that causes the forest to crackle and evaporate, but overdevelopment in Atlanta and the overuse of water in Georgia and Alabama—people downstream are always at the mercy of the people upstream.

The only water in the area is a small spring-fed slough, which is normally just part of a tributary system that flows inland from off-shoots of the river to small lakes and streams, but is now cut off, forming a single standing body.

The sole source of hydration for miles, this small, black, leaf-covered pool is the perfect place for a camera trap. Every animal in the area must come here eventually.

Remington had set up his inmost camera trap in the hollowed-out base of a cypress tree across from the mouth of the slough. Equipped with an ultra wide-angle lens, the camera frames nearly the entire width of the water, but on the opposite side so it captures the faces of the creatures as they dip in for a drink.

By the time he reaches the trap, the last feathers of the flamingo sky have floated away. Now, only the tops of trees are illuminated, their empty, craggy branches black, backlit by a faint smoke-gray sky.

R emoving the memory card from the camera trap, he places it in his new camera and drops to the thick leaf-covered ground to view the shots. Pressing the display button, the first image appears. Spinning the selection wheel, he scrolls through the eerie images.

E ven on the small screen, the burst of light against the dark night gives some of the frames an otherworldly quality.
Moonlight.
Overexposure fading to faint pale pallet. Ghostly.

G lowing red eyes.
Odd angles. Necks craned.
Sand-colored streaks, leather-colored flashes.
Night. Beyond the slough and its track-laden muddy rim, deer passing by trigger the trap, their eyes glowing demonically in the flash.

Day. Leaping, turning, darting deer break the infrared beam, leaving blurs of buckskin behind. Too fast. Ill-framed. Unusable.

The distant deer the camera captures are too far from the slough to do anything but trigger the trap.

B lack spots.

Red-gray coat. Triangular ears. Short, stubby tail.

Dusk, and the small cat prowls about, slinking, skulking, stalking. Head down, facing the frame, green slitted eyes staring into the camera.

Unlike the rare, endangered Florida panther, the Florida bobcat is much more common. Just three times the size of a large house cat, the sleek feline is stealthy and secretive, difficult to photograph, the kind of animal the traps were made for.

The bobcat shots are stunning. Simple. Subtle. Natural.

C ircle of light, dropping off to dark woods.

Empty frames.

S oft, diffused light. Liquor-like glow. Late afternoon.

Humans.

Shock.

Murder.

Handgun. Close range. Blood spray. Collapse.

Shovel. Dig. Dirt. Bury. Cover.

Remington is rocked back, reeling at the random horror his camera has captured.

In flip-book fashion, the staccato images show two people appearing in the far right corner of the frame. The distance and angle lead to soft focus, the small screen adding to the difficulty of deciphering details. Based on size, carriage, movement, and mannerism, Remington believes he's looking at a man and a woman, but their camouflage jumpsuits and caps make it impossible to tell for sure.

Jittery, random pictures record the larger of the two figures raising a handgun, though a rifle is slung over his shoulder, and shooting the slightly smaller one in the back of the head. A spray of blood, and the now dead person falls to the ground like the leaves she lands on. The murderer then removes a small, folded camping shovel, kneels down and begins to dig. Hundreds of shots later, the larger person rolls the smaller into a shallow grave. Removing his jumpsuit, he drops it into the hole with his victim, then douses both with liquid from a plastic bottle, drops a match, and steps back as the flames leap up out of the opening in the earth to dance in the dusk sky.

Nausea.

Clammy skin. Cold sweat.

Unaware his distress could deepen any further, Remington's panic intensifies when, thumbing through the images, he sees the murderer remove his jumpsuit to reveal a dark green uniform. Although unable to tell exactly what agency the man is with, he thinks sheriff's deputy or wildlife officer most likely.

Flickering flames.

For a long time—over thirty images—the man stands adding accelerant to the holocaust hole at his feet, eventually dropping the bottle itself in and refilling the grave with dirt, covering the mound with dead leaves.

All the photographs had been taken in the afternoon light, preventing the strobe from flashing and alerting the murderer to the presence of the camera trap and the frame-by-frame chronicling of his crime.

I ncapable of moving, Remington continues to press so hard against the backside of the hollow cypress base that it hurts his back.

Denial. Disbelief.

I didn't really just see what I thought I did . . . did I?

Turning slightly—his head more than anything else—he shines the penlight over across the slough to the back right corner. Even from this distance and with such a small beam, he can see the mound rising beneath the leaves.

Glancing down at his camera, he pulls up the information for the last image he looked at. According to the time and date stamp encoded in the picture, it was taken less than two hours ago.

The murderer had been finishing up about the time Remington was unloading the ATV and talking to Heather. And hearing what he thought were screams. He wonders if, like lost light, the horrific screams had been trapped in the swamp until someone had arrived to hear them.

It wasn't that long ago.

The killer could still be out here. I've got to—

Movement from the other side of the watering hole triggers the strobe of the camera trap, illuminating the area like heat lightning flickering in a dark night sky.

Seized with fear, Remington freezes. Full stop. Even his heart and lungs seem to quit functioning for the moment. Facing away from the flash, he makes no move to turn and see what sort of creature triggered the strobe.

—Did you just take a picture of me?

The calm, whimsical, slightly amused voice is unrecognizable, sounding like a hundred others he hears every week, indistinguishable in its southern uniformity.

Remington doesn't respond, just remains hunched down, his back against the cypress stump. What's left of the hollowed-out base of the tree doesn't offer much in the way of protection, but the man is across the watering hole, which provides a barrier and puts some distance between them.

—I bring her way the fuck out here to avoid all the cameras in the tree stands and you take a picture of me?

With the camera trap's memory card in Remington's new Canon for viewing, the man's picture had not been recorded when he set off the strobe.

But it's not a bad idea.

Adjusting his camera, Remington holds it up, and snaps a picture of the area across the water that the voice is coming from, then quickly pulls the camera back down.

—You keep taking my picture, you're gonna make me feel like some sort of celebrity or something.

Remington's quickly coming to hate the sound of the cold, laconic voice.

Switching the camera to view mode, Remington glances at the picture he took. The top edge of the frame cuts off just below the man's chest, revealing only that he is indeed a wildlife officer with the Florida Fish and Wildlife Conservation Commission.

—Waited just a little longer the first time I's out here, it woulda been dark enough to set off that flash and know it was here.

Remington quickly sets up the camera again and tries to figure out the best angle.

—The fuck you doin' out this far? I seen you about a mile back. Figured I'd follow you since you was headed this way. Sure glad I did.

Holding the camera up again, Remington attempts another picture. As he does, the man fires a shot from a rifle that whizzes overhead near the camera and hits a tree a few yards behind him, splintering the bark, lodging deep into the heart of the hardwood.

—I'm tired of having my picture took.

This time the picture is framed much better, but the man has moved.

—You might as well talk to me. Got nowhere to go. You do realize that, don't you? This is the end of the line, partner. Even if it was just the two of us. I'm more at home out here than anywhere. But I've radioed my buddies, so . . .

Remington's mind races.

What do I do? How can I get out of this? I don't want to die. Not now. Not like this. Heather. Mom. Pictures. Run. Hide.

—Sorry it has to be this way. I genuinely am. But no way I can let you leave these woods. If there was some other way, I'd be happy to . . . but there ain't. Some shit's just necessary. Ain't particularly pleasant, but it is, by God, necessary. Wouldn't do it if I didn't have to. That's the God's truth. Speaking of . . . You wanna say a prayer or anything, now's the time.

—Who was she? Remington asks.

—Huh?

—Who was she? Why'd you kill her?

He hadn't planned on saying anything. The two questions had erupted from him without warning.

—It doesn't really matter, does it? Not gonna change anything. Won't make any difference for her or you.

Something about the man's practical reasoning and unsentimental logic reminds Remington of his father, and he hates that. His dad shared nothing with this soulless sociopath, save a pragmatic approach to life.

A flare of anger.

His dad's sober sensibility infuriated him. It was so safe, so serviceable, so on-the-odds.

Heather.

What if that were her buried in that hole? It'd matter. Might not change anything, but it'd goddamn sure matter, it'd mean something. The shot and burned and buried victim means something to her circle, means everything to somebody.

—Still like to know, Remington yells.

—Just complicate things. Come on out and I'll make it quick. Painless. Won't torture you. Won't hurt somebody you care about.

Stowing his camera and its original memory card securely in his sling pack, Remington prepares to run.

Odds aren't very good. But there it is. It's who he is. Born without the practical gene.

Run.

His body hears his thought, but doesn't respond.

Now.

Pushing up from the cold ground, he stumbles forward. Bending over, swerving, attempting to avoid the inevitable—

Shots ring out from behind as rounds ricochet all around him, piercing leaves, striking tree trunks, drilling into ridge banks.

Run.

6

Now

On my way home, I stop by the Ambulance building to talk to the EMS director, Carter Peak.

My drive from Port St. Joe to Wewa was particularly slow today. I got behind both a loaded log truck and two flatbed trucks and trailers full of bee boxes. Agriculture in our area isn't what it once was, but it still has a huge impact on everything from jobs to land use to traffic.

Parking on the side near the front of the Ambulance station, I walk through the open bay between the two ambulances and into the back room where the on-duty EMTs work and rest while waiting for calls to come in.

The large, open room has a kitchen on one end and seating area on the other, and like the ambulance bay, is quiet. Unlike previous times I've been in here, the TV in the seating area is muted, and, except for Carter, the room is empty.

Carter Peak is a large, thick man with curly, longish hair. He is kind, good-natured, a little goofy, and one hell of a good EMT.

I find him over in the kitchen area, sitting at the table with a cup of coffee and a library book.

"What're you reading?" I ask.

He holds it up. It's Glyn Johns' *Sound Man: A Life Recording Hits with The Rolling Stones, The Who, Led Zeppelin, The Eagles, Eric Clapton, The Faces.*

In addition to being the EMS director, Carter is the front man for a talented local band called Mix Tape Effigies.

"How's the music career going?" I ask, taking a seat across the table from him.

"Better than ever," he says. "Got a new song on Youtube that's gettin' a lot of love, looks like we might get to open for Rick Springfield for the fundraiser concert he's doing for the college, and we just booked Gulf Coast Jam, but . . . I won't be quitting my day job anytime soon."

"Would you like to?"

I've encountered a lot of artists over the years—actors, writers, painters, musicians, nearly all of whom dream of *making it.* What that means to most of them has to do with finances and popularity, and even though chances of it happening are minuscule they continue to dream, continue to pursue, and that makes their lives richer and more meaningful. The things we care about, that drive us, that make up our dreams, are far less about making a living than making a certain kind of life.

"I'd love to play music full-time, plus . . . this gig takes a toll on you, you know? All the guys tell me I'm way too much of a pussy to be doing this. It does get to me. Anyway, what brings you by? I'm sure it's not to talk about my jukebox hero daydreams."

I tell him.

He shakes his head and his eyes take on a far off stare. I can see him accessing the unpleasant memories.

"I've never seen anything like it, John," he says. "I've been called out to some horrific wrecks where . . . what was there wasn't recognizably human, to some sad-ass suicides, but this . . . this was a massacre. Everybody was dead."

He has a slight lisp and a wet, whistley mouth when he talks, which only intensifies the more he talks—or the more excited he gets when he talks. Interestingly, his lisp and his over-salivated mouth vanish when he's singing.

"We were first on the scene," he continues. "Not that there was much we could do—but we got to see it all, raw, fresh . . . looked like something from a war zone. And it was so . . . isolated. Took forever for us to get everybody out there—most came by boat down the river. Took forever for FDLE to process the scene. We were there from almost sunup to well after dark."

"Robin Wilson was sheriff at the time," I say.

"Yeah," he says, shaking his head and letting out a harsh laugh. "If you want to call it that. More like a . . ."

"What?"

"I try not to speak ill of the dead."

"Make an exception just this once," I say with a smile.

"He was a thug with a gun and a badge and more power and authority than anyone in the county. Hell, the county paid him to do whatever the hell he wanted to. Made up his own rules, acted as if he and his little posse were above the law—and they were. Hell, they *were* the law."

"He worked the case himself, didn't he?" I ask.

He shrugs. "I guess. If you want to call it that. Was it ever solved? He and some of his men supposedly worked it. I know Dahl Rogers and Skip Lester were pretending to work it with him."

"Pretending?"

"Did it ever get solved?"

"No, but—"

"Only thing they worked at was a cover-up. Something was wrong with the investigation from the jump. He let FDLE process the scene but wouldn't really let their agents work the case. I don't know. I'm just glad you and Reggie are in there now."

"You think Robin and his men's deaths had anything to do with what happened to Remington and the others in the swamp?"

"Two groups of men being killed execution style," he says. "Only two groups of men to be killed like that in the history of this county—well, since the Indian-Settler days—and one group was investigating the deaths of the first group. What do you think?"

"I think what you obviously think," I say. "It'd be one hell of a coincidence."

"And who the hell am I? Just a glorified EMT, not a detective of any kind, but between you and me . . . I'd say somebody's still covering it up. I mean, come on. Neither crime has been solved. Really? In all this time. I don't know. Something ain't right. Says something for you and Reggie that you're looking into it. Really does."

"What was the talk at the time?" I ask.

"Which time?"

"Both. Start with the swamp massacre."

"Well . . . big shootout in the swamp like that and everybody assumes drugs, but none were ever found and . . . nobody believed Remington or Mother Earth would be mixed up in shit like that, so . . . There were some wild ass theories, though. None of 'em worth repeating. It's just a giant unsolved mystery. And those messages Remington supposedly left behind. Why was no girl ever found? Why would he say it if it wasn't true? But . . . still . . . no girl was ever found. And if there was one, why didn't anyone ever come looking for her? I don't know . . . It's just all so . . . But I knew Remington. Knew his dad, Cole, better, but the whole family was good people. If he said a woman was killed out there then there was a woman killed out there. If he said Gauge did it, then Gauge did it. And if he said he hid evidence of it then he hid evidence of it. But . . . fact remains no evidence of it has ever been found. And on the second one—Robin and them . . . take your pick. Jealous husbands, rape victims, drug related, or . . . most likely . . . whoever was behind what happened in the swamp. I mean . . . what if it was a big drug deal out there that went bad? What if they were involved? What if they took the money and the drugs and whoever they took them from . . . executed them? 'Cause it was like a statement. I mean . . . hell . . . they were killed with their own guns."

7

Then

R obin Wilson, the former sheriff of Gulf County, along with his inner circle of the men—lifelong friends—who worked for him, including Donnie Ray Kemp, Dahl Rogers, Skeeter Hamm, and Skip Lester, were executed one by one with their own guns.

Dahl Rogers was found in his locked car in a wooded area near an empty subdivision. There was some question at the time as to whether his death was suicide or murder, but FDLE ultimately ruled it a suicide, though they believed it was connected to the corruption and the murders of the others in the department. Donnie Ray Kemp was found in a nest of cypress tree roots in the Apalachicola River, a gunshot wound in his chest. Skeeter Hamm was found sitting in a ratty old recliner on his houseboat in a blood-soaked wife beater and blue jeans, bullet holes in his left cheek and the center of his chest. Eric Layton, Reggie Summers' brother-in-law, was found dead in his deep freezer on his back porch. Skip Lester was killed with his gun in his kitchen, the pot of gumbo he was cooking still simmering on his stove.

At the time of the murders, Wilson and his department were under investigation by FDLE for a variety of allegations relating to everything from the violation of the civil rights of citizens and inmates to criminal misconduct.

This reckoning, the methodical murder of each corrupt and compromised cop, took place quite a while after their department had conducted the Remington James case and around the time Reggie moved back to Wewahitchka to take care of her mother and become the chief of police of her old home town.

For many years the small city of Wewa hadn't had a police department, but instead fell under the jurisdiction of the county sheriff's department. As more and more came out about Robin Wilson's questionable, even criminal, conduct and the FDLE investigation began, the city commissioners decided to reinstate their own police jurisdiction and brought in Reggie to run it.

As the chief of police in a department of one (she was chief and the entire squad), she investigated the murders because many took place in Wewa—or at least on this end of the county. Eventually, she was appointed to the position of sheriff and the city of Wewa returned to being policed by the sheriff's department, like it had been before she was hired.

While still the chief of police in Wewa, Reggie arrested Robin and locked him in her cell in the old city hall building she was using for an office. Shortly after that, she was called out to search for her niece, Lexi Lee, who was missing at the time. While she was out searching and he was still locked inside his cell, Robin was shot nine times with his own .45.

Merrick entered the building a short while later looking for Reggie and found Robin dead. He was knocked out by whom he and others assumed to be the killer.

FDLE cleared both Reggie and Merrick of Robin's murder.

As far as I can tell, Reggie has kept the investigation into the murders open, but hasn't given it much priority and hasn't taken advantage of many of the FDLE resources on offer to her.

From what I can gather, FDLE couldn't make a connection between the Robin Wilson corruption case and his murder. Since it was two different investigations, the agency didn't automatically work the second one, only offered to help the new sheriff since it was her jurisdiction and her decision.

Many in the media have questioned both departments about the case, and how the murder of a sitting sheriff can continue to go unsolved, but so far no amount of pressure seems to be able to motivate Reggie to make the now-cold case a priority.

8

Now

Walking into my empty, quiet house makes me sad.

Closing the door behind me and kicking off my shoes in the mudroom, I step into the kitchen and stand for a moment.

Total stillness. Total silence.

And then I detect, ever so slightly, the hum of the refrigerator.

Usually Anna and Taylor and sometimes Johanna are here to greet me, to give me hugs and kisses and tell me about their days. Usually Sam is in her hospital bed in the corner of the living room smiling at me, patting my hand as I pat hers. But now, as if a body without a soul, my home lacks presence, lacks sound, lacks those who make coming back to this place each day the thing I look forward to the most.

It reminds me of how quiet and lonely my solitary life used to be.

Anna is at her parents' with Taylor, taking advantage of Sam being gone, getting away from her ex-husband who recently moved to town to torment us. She's also there to plan our wedding.

It's spring break for Johanna, my daughter, and she and her mother are on vacation in North Georgia.

And Sam, who is showing improvement that is surprising everyone, including her doctors, is in a special rehab facility in Tallahassee for additional evaluation and therapy.

I am alone.

My house is empty and it makes me feel empty.

Eventually the house settles and creaks and the central unit kicks on.

The kitchen is immaculate. I told Anna not to clean the house before she left, that I would do it when I got home, but of course, she couldn't leave without making it spotless first.

I step over to open the fridge, but pause to look at the pictures beneath the magnets on the front of its doors first.

Snapshots at various angles, their corners covered by the magnets holding them in place.

Anna and I in dress clothes at a friend's wedding, the two of us at our favorite restaurant in Panama City this past Valentine's Day, each of us with our daughters, the four of us together—at the beach at sunset, grilling at the Dead Lakes Campgrounds, hunting for Easter eggs at Dad and Verna's place.

These are among my favorite photographs, each its own world of life and meaning. It occurs to me that Remington died attempting and succeeding to capture just such images.

Mixed in among the photographs are the words of the refrigerator magnets. In addition to everything else, Anna has taken the time to leave me small poems expressing her love.

I open the fridge to find containers of food she cooked for me before she left and sweet notes that make me feel simultaneously less and more lonely.

As if a bachelor again, I drink orange juice thick with pulp straight from the bottle, return it to the fridge, and close the door.

Stepping even farther into the dark house, I can see the moon's reflection on the gently undulating surface of the lake through the French doors in the back. The moon is big and bright, but from where I stand inside, only its reflection on the water can be seen.

My plan had been to come in, get comfortable, and spend the rest of the night reading the novel manuscript Heather had sent me and the case files I copied and brought home, but something about the empty, quiet house makes me want to leave.

So I do.

9

Then

He runs as fast as he can, his boots slipping on the slick surface of the leaves.

Keep running.

Slamming into the thick-bodied bases of hardwoods, he absorbs the blows, spins, and continues. Tripping over fallen branches, felled trees, and cypress knees, he tucks, rolls, and springs, somehow managing to find his feet again and keep moving.

Eventually the shots stop, but he doesn't.

He runs.

The cold air burns his throat and lungs.

He keeps running. His heart about to burst, he keeps running. He doesn't stop.

Exhaustion. Fatigue. Cramps. Shin splints. Twisted ankle. Thirst. Lightheadedness.

He runs.

He runs toward the river. It's less than two miles away . . . or is supposed to be.

I should've reached it by now. Where is it? Where am I? How'd I get turned around? Why haven't I found anything?

Seeing the hollowed-out base of a cypress tree, he collapses into it. He doesn't check for snakes. He just backs in and falls down. A few minutes ago, he was more terrified of snakes, in general, and cottonmouths and rattlers, in particular, than anything else in the entire world. A lot has changed in the last few minutes.

Attempting to slow his heart and catch his breath, he listens for footsteps, blood bounding through his body so forcefully his eyes feel like they'll bulge out of his skull.

Full moon.

Freezing. Fog.

Why didn't you just go back? You had a choice. You knew what you should do and you didn't do it. You're gonna die out here and they'll never find your body. Heather and Mom—

Mom.

She'd be expecting him by now. Needing him.

Having waged a futile war against MS for decades, his mother is now in the final stages of peace talks with this foreign captor of her body. The only terms she can get are complete and unconditional surrender, which she's nearly ready to give.

He had promised his dad he'd take care of her, move back to the Panhandle to be with her, and here he is lost in the middle of a cypress swamp on a freezing night, hunted like one of the endangered animals he's been trying to help.

Sorry, Dad.

But it's not just about letting his dad down again. His mom can't take care of herself. It's dangerous for her to be alone. Each evening he feeds her, helps her with her medications, moves her from recliner to dining table, to bathroom, to bed.

Will she survive the night? Will I?

Caroline James had been a truly beautiful woman—the kind people stop to admire. Long before her diagnosis, she had a vulnerability that added to her attractiveness. As her disease progressed, vulnerable beauty became feeble beauty, but beauty nonetheless. It wasn't until her husband and caretaker abandoned her that the last of her attractiveness wilted.

As if a physical manifestation of the spiritual withdrawals Cole's absence produced, Caroline's body began to wither—drawing in on itself. Curling. Constricting. Clinching.

Like the petals of a flower closing, the aperture of her allure shut down completely, never to reopen.

He pulls out his phone to check for a signal.

At certain places along the river there's just enough reception to make a crackling, static-filled call.

He has no idea where he is. He thought he had been running east toward the Chipola River, but if so, he should have reached it. He keeps moving. Maybe he's closer than he thinks.

No signal.

Not the faintest trace. Where the hell am I? Lost.

Think.

How do I find my way to the river?

He thinks if he can just make it to the river, he can flag down a passing boat or manage to make a phone call.

F og-covered forest.

Cloud-shrouded orb. Diffused, intermittent light. Pale. Ghostly.

Smattering of stars.

He sits shivering after taking the last sip of water from the bottle in his sling pack. The full moon is bright enough to cast shadows, but diluted, knocked down several stops like studio lights with scrims, by scattered clouds and a thick, smoke-like fog.

Snap.

Breaking twig. Leaves rustling. Stop.

Approaching footsteps. Ready to run.

Willing to fight. Relief.

He lets out a quiet but audible sigh as a small gray fox prances out of the fog. The dog-like creature—gray-brown on top, rust and white underneath—is barely three feet long. Out foraging for food, the animal doesn't react to Remington's presence.

Instinctively, he reaches for his camera.

Stop. No. Too dangerous. Can't risk the flash revealing his whereabouts to the murderer or his friends—if they've joined him. If they're going to.

Fog thick as he's ever seen anywhere, the entire forest seems on fire, jagged outlines of trees etched in the mist, their tops disappearing as if into mountaintop clouds.

More footfalls.

The small fox darts away as a man steps out of the mist.

Remington sits perfectly still. Breaths shallow. Eyes unblinking. The broad, alpine man has long, unkempt brown hair, a burly beard, and lumbers along in enormous work boots, radio in one massive mitt, a blued Smith and Wesson .357 magnum in the other.

I'm about to die.

Though heading straight toward the tree base, the man seems not to have seen Remington yet—perhaps because of the darkness or fog, or maybe because of the leaves he has gathered around himself for cover, but most likely because of the man's height.

Pausing just before reaching what's left of the cypress tree, the man turns and surveys the area, his mammoth boots sweeping the leaves aside and making large divots in the damp ground.

Before Remington had moved away from home, he seemed to know everybody in the area. Now, he's continually amazed at how few people he recognizes, and though the giant standing in front of him resembles many of the corn-fed felons he grew up with— guys with names like Skinner, Squatch, Bear, and Big—he's distinctive enough to identify if he knew him.

Remington jumps as the man's radio beeps.

—Anything?

—Not a goddamn.

—Okay. Keep looking.

—That sounded like an order.

—Sorry big fellow. Please is always implied. I meant, would you keep looking please?

—We could do this all night and never find him.

—Yeah?

—Or we could get the dogs out here and make short work of this shit.

—Dogs mean involving more people.

—We don't catch him a whole lot more people will be involved.

—I hear you. Let's give it a little while longer, then we'll call Spider. Either way, camera boy won't leave these woods alive.

—Make sure Arl and Donnie Paul split up. We need to cover as much ground as possible.

That's four he knows of. The calm murderer, the big bastard in front of him, Arlington, and Donnie Paul. Are there others?

When the big man finishes his conversation, he pockets the radio, unzips his jeans, and begins to urinate on the ground, the acidic, acrid odor wafting over to find Remington's nostrils. Finishing, he zips, clears his throat, spits, and begins to trudge away.

At least four men.

Out here to kill him.

Dogs.

If they use dogs on him, the river is his only hope. Got to find it.

Where the hell am I?

He quietly pulls the compass out of his pocket.

It's smashed. Useless. Must have happened on one of his falls or when he crashed into the tree.

Know where you're going. Use a map and a compass.

Always tell someone where you're going. Never go alone.

Always carry the essentials. If you get lost, stay put.

Make yourself seen and heard.

He had to move, to find the river, and the only people out here he could make himself seen and heard to wanted to kill him.

Maybe I should try to circle back to the four-wheeler. Maybe I could outrun them, make it back to my truck, then to town before they did.

If he knew where the other men were . . . but he doesn't. He could walk right into them. And if they've seen his four-wheeler and truck, they've probably disabled them. Or might have a man watching them.

No, the river is his best hope. His only.

Time to move.

Carefully.

Quietly. Slowly.

Climbing out of the cypress stump, he avoids the damp ring of urine the big man left as he begins to make his way in what feels like the direction of the river.

Feeling his way through sharp, craggy branches and hard, twisting vines, his progress is plodding.

The dry, dead leaves crunch and crackle beneath his boots, undermining his attempts at silence. He tries shuffling his feet, then sliding, then lifting them high and placing them back down softly, but nothing he does makes any difference. Quiet advancement through the woods this time of year is impossible.

He has no idea exactly where he's heading. Just moving. He could be walking away from the river, could be walking toward one of the men hunting him. He has no way of knowing.

His breaths, backlit by moonlight, come out in bursts like steam from a Manhattan manhole.

His movements are awkward, unsteady, every shivering step a struggle in the turbid terrain.

Halting occasionally, he listens for the other men.

Body tight with tension, he can't help but believe a high velocity round will rip through him at any moment, the scorching projectile piercing vital organs and arteries. Bleeding out slowly, painfully like a gut-shot animal. Or his head exploding in Zapruder film-like fashion. Of course, he could be attacked from close range, brained with an oak branch or beaten to death by the big man.

Panic.

He wants to run, everything in him giving in to the flight side of his fight-or-flight response, but he realizes it would be suicide. Even if he could remain on his feet and not run into a tree or trip and bash his head on a cypress knee, and even if his frenzied, out-of-control run didn't alert his predators to his presence, he would soon tire, becoming even more dehydrated and disoriented.

Slow and steady. Careful and quiet.

He knows he needs to mark the trees he's passing, to be able to identify them if he comes this way again, but doesn't want to reveal his whereabouts to the others.

Gnawing.

Growling.

Grumbling.

He hasn't eaten since lunch, and his body pangs remind him.

Cold.

Hungry.

Tired.

Lost.

Lonely.

Afraid.

He wants to sit down, find a place to rest a while. Just a few minutes. But he keeps moving, stumbling forward in the foggy forest, not sure where his unsteady steps are leading him.

Rustling in a thicket to his right. He stops. Listens.

A large, dark marsh rabbit darts out of the bushes, stops, turns, speeds away. Its small, red, rodent-like feet carrying it beneath a fallen tree. It then disappears into the dense undergrowth beyond.

Exhaling, he begins breathing again, his heart thumping on his breastbone the way the rabbit's back feet do on the ground when sending out alarm signals.

Freeze.

Fear.

Panic. Inside.

He's taken very few steps before he hears—what? The approach of a man? Has to be. Sound's too distinctive to be anything else.

Hairs rise. Goose bumps.

Quickly. Quietly.

Ducking behind the base of a large pine and into the surrounding underbrush, Remington tries to hide and to still his racing heart enough to hear where the man is coming from.

Listen.

Heart pounding.

Deep breaths. Calm down. Relax.

Close. Footsteps. Forest floor.

Whatta I do?

Be still. But—

The steps stop suddenly.

Bracing.

Waiting.

Nothing.

Don't forget to breathe.

Crouching so low, clenching so tight, holding himself so still . . . his body aches from the tension.

10

Now

I'm driving down Highway 22, the road that connects Wewa with Panama City, returning from doing something I haven't done enough of lately—attending an AA Meeting.

The April evening seems delicate somehow. Stiller, cooler, its colors softer, more muted.

To my left, rows and rows of slash pines beneath the moonlight. Tall, straight, close together.

To my right, where once were endless straight lines of slash pines, empty fields as far as the eye can see, fenced in and awaiting the newly planted grass to grow and the arrival of tens of thousands of head of cattle.

The St. Joe Company recently sold most of its timberland— some 400,000 acres—to a Mormon Church-owned cattle company called Deseret Ranches.

For half a billion dollars Deseret Ranches has become the single largest private landowner in Florida.

Now when the slash pines are cut down, loaded on log trucks, and hauled away, they are not replanted. Instead, the land has been cleared, fenced, and grassed for pasture. Where once the planted pines stood in tall, stately silence there will soon be herds of bellowing cows grazing beneath the watchful eyes of cowboys —an image that harkens back to Florida's original cowman crackers, the horse-riding cowpokes named for the cracking sounds their whips made as they drove their herds across the flat, prairie grass plains of North and Central Florida.

The two lane highway straddles what used to be and what is still to come.

It's dark and a little foggy, the moon having ducked behind a bank of clouds.

I call Merrill. He answers on the third ring.

"What're you working on?" I ask.

"Right this minute or in general?"

"In general," I say. "This week."

"Couple little things besides looking for Randa and Daniel and keepin' an eye on Chris."

Chris is Anna's ex-husband who was recently released from jail. He is both dangerous and a disruptive force in our lives.

A few months back a friend of ours, Daniel Davis, went missing while Merrill was watching him. The significant other of Samantha Michaels, Daniel was doing a true crime podcast with Merrick McKnight, Reggie's significant other, at the time. We know or believe we know who he's with, but we question whether or not he went willingly—something hard to fathom given his relationship with Sam and her condition at the time.

Randa Raffield is a young woman who vanished off the face of the earth in the seven minutes between crashing her car on Highway 98 between Mexico Beach and Port St. Joe and the first deputy's arrival on the scene.

Merrill and I are looking into both cases, as well as keeping an eye on Chris and awaiting his next move.

"I really appreciate you doing all that," I say.

"Tol' you you don't have to tell me that every time."

"Can't help myself. I really appreciate all you're doing."

"So you keep sayin', but guess what? Nothin' to be grateful for. Ain't turned up shit on Daniel or Randa. You heard from her lately?"

"Not a word," I say. "Not since she broke our bet."

A couple of months or so ago Randa Raffield had bet me I couldn't solve the Angel Diaz case before she did, saying if I did she'd return Daniel safely to us. And though I had won the bet, she had refused to return Daniel.

"This shit draggin' out lot longer than I ever thought it would," he says. "Didn't think it'd take even half this long to find them."

"She's a talented, resourceful woman."

"Hope for Daniel's sake that's all she is. 'Cause those ain't the first words I'd've said about her. Dangerous, deadly, murderous bitch comes to my mind. Why'd you ask?"

"What you're working on? 'Cause I've got one week to work on the Remington James case and I may need a little help."

"Just let me know."

"I will. Th—"

"Bitch, don't thank my ass again," he says and hangs up before I can.

I drive slowly, in no hurry to return to my empty house, and think about Remington James and the dark night he spent some twenty miles and three years away from where I am now.

What were you doing out there? Was it really just to check your camera traps? How'd you wind up on the far side of Cutoff Island? Was there really a murdered woman? What happened to her? Who was she? Why hasn't anyone missed her? Come looking for her? Did Robin Wilson and his corrupt cop force cover it up?

When I get back into town, I drive by my house and continue

down toward the river to Byrd Parker Drive where Reggie and Merrick live.

I don't call or text, just show up unannounced.

Merrick McKnight, a former journalist and now true crime podcaster, lives with his two children in an old clapboard house not far from where Reggie lives with her mom and son in a single wide mobile home close to the landing. Though they don't live together, they night as well, and I'm far more likely to find them at the same place, so I start with Reggie's.

Reggie's mom, Sylvia Summers, opens the door.

"John," she says, "what a pleasant surprise. Come on in. How are you?"

"I'm good," I say. "How are you?"

"Not bad for a sick old lady," she says. "Not bad at all."

Reggie and Merrick are on the couch. Merrick pauses the movie they're watching—a Nordic crime thriller about a cop with insomnia I vaguely recognize—and they stand.

"Everything okay?" Reggie asks.

"Yeah," I say. "Sorry to interrupt. I just wanted to ask y'all a few questions."

"What's up?" Reggie says.

"Have a seat," Sylvia says. "John, would you like some coffee?"

"No thank you. Won't be able to sleep as it is."

"I don't sleep much anymore anyway," she says, "so I drink it day and night. It's my one remaining vice and I can't get enough of it."

I sit in a chair not far from where Merrick and Reggie are on the couch.

Sylvia starts walking down the hallway. "I'm going to finish the letter I was working on before. Call me when y'all are ready to start the movie back. It was good to see you, John."

"I won't stay long at all," I say. "Just a few minutes."

"Take your time. I'm in no rush. Got nowhere to be, nothing

to do. I already figured out who did it, just want to see the end for confirmation. Come back for dinner sometime soon."

She disappears.

"Do you have news about Daniel?" Merrick asks.

Merrick was working on the In Search of Randa Raffield podcast with Daniel when he went missing, and has actually been accused of staging his disappearance for ratings.

I shake my head.

"I wanted to talk to you about the Robin Wilson case," I say.

"John," Reggie says. "Really? Now? Like this? Why?"

"I think what happened to him and his little band of bad cops could be related to what happened to Remington James and the others killed in the swamp."

"Oh," she says, seeming to relax a little. "What makes you think that?"

"They were working that case or supposed to be when they were killed," I say. "Execution style. If they were involved . . . it would explain why it never got solved. And why a county as small as ours has two groups of guys killed so close together. Hard to believe it could be a coincidence."

"They were corrupt enough to be involved," Reggie says, "but . . ."

"I know you two worked the case," I say. "That's why I wanted to talk to both of you."

"I was the chief of police of Wewa," Reggie says. "Hadn't been back long."

"I was helping my dad with the local newspaper at the time," Merrick says, "sort of between things. Wasn't sure what I was going to do, then I met Reggie. Anyway, Robin was under investigation. There were all kinds of rumors swirling around. If even half of what was said was true . . . He was a very bent individual."

"And so were his little minions," Reggie says.

"You went to high school with him, didn't you?" I say.

She nods. "Unfortunately. He was an interesting guy. Transferred here from Cottondale. His dad was the coach up there when they won state. Cottondale Hornets. Haven't thought about them in a long time. Robin actually wore his CHS Hornets t-shirt to school on his first day when he first moved here in the seventh grade. Wicked-looking hornet. He was showing his disrespect and disdain for his new school. By the end of the year, he was running the class, maybe even the school. "

She went to high school with them, knew them for most of her life. Why wouldn't she want their murders solved? The fact that their murders haven't been solved reflects poorly on Reggie and our department, but she doesn't seem to care. She and her family—including Merrick, her niece Lexi Lee, and her brother in-law, Eric Layton, were all tangled up in the investigation. Is that why she doesn't want it solved? Or has she already solved it and is trying to protect whoever did it—Merrick? Lexi Lee? Or did she do it? Is it possible Reggie killed Robin and his men?

"Everything Robin did was manipulative," Merrick says. "I mean everything. So he had an ulterior motive, but he asked me to follow the Dahl Rogers investigation—that was one of his men who, I guess the first to . . . die—but at the time, he thought it was just going to be him and he didn't want to turn the case over to FDLE. Said they had it out for him. It looked like a suicide, but there were some suspicious circumstances and . . . So he gave me full access and told me to write about the case to show everyone it was investigated the right way with integrity and transparency."

"Then others of his little inner corrupt circle started getting knocked off one by one," Reggie says. "Neither Merrick nor I really investigated the case. Not really."

"But you were close to it, saw it firsthand," I say. "So was your family. Hell, your brother-in-law was killed by one of them. Any idea what that was about?"

She frowns. "No. I can tell you what I suspected, but . . . that doesn't get you anywhere."

"I'd still like to hear it."

"Eric and my sister, Becky, were having trouble. Guess the truth is they had trouble their entire marriage. Anyway . . . I think Becky was messing around with one or more of them, trying to get them to help her get away from Eric. I think Eric getting killed was unrelated to the rest. He went to Skeeter's houseboat to confront him, they fought, Skeeter killed him."

"But we won't really know until we conduct an actual investigation," I say. "You can help me with it. I think what happened to them could be connected to Remington's case and I want to work them together."

She shakes her head. "I said one week. Remington James case only. Then it's back to normal duty. We have too much going on to . . . I'm sorry, but no. You always push. Push, push, push. It makes you a good detective, but . . . give your boss a break. Quit pushing me on this. Work the Remington James case. Do that. And only that. For this week only. If something comes up that shows there's a connection, come back and see me. If not . . . One week. Okay? You're making me sound like a boss and I don't want to. I really don't. Don't make me. Okay? Take *no* for an answer on this one. You got the *yes* you wanted on Remington. Go with that."

11

Then

When he spies a man in the distance, standing among the trees, he thinks it's an illusion, a trick of light or an apparition conjured by his mind.

But then the man radios the others and raises his rifle.

—I got 'im. I got 'im. South edge of the big bay swamp. I'm gonna run 'im to you.

Before Remington can react, a round whistles by his head and thwacks the bark of a laurel oak beside him.

Turning.

Running.

Stumbling.

Remington spins and reenters the hardwood forest he had just stepped out of a few moments before.

Tripping.

Falling.

Rolling.

His boot catches on a fallen black walnut tree and he goes down hard. Tucking in on himself, he manages to roll, mitigating the impact—until he bangs into the base of a hickory tree.

—He's running. He's running. South end of the swamp. Heading west.

They know where I am, Remington thinks. I can't run toward them. Staying on the ground, he slides over and lies beneath the black walnut that had tripped him.

And waits.

—I don't see him, the man yells into his radio.

Running. Breathless.

—I've lost him.

—Maintain pursuit, the calm voice of the murderer replies. Run him toward us.

Though not much of a hunter, Remington knows the culture and practices well. If a group of men after deer go into the woods without dogs, they'll split up. A small group will make a stand while the others go upriver a few miles, get out, and walk the deer toward them. Why more men aren't shot using this practice he's never understood.

They're running me like a goddamn deer. Well, I won't let them.

Fight or flight.

I'm staying. Making my stand.

I'd rather die standing than running.

He finds this thought amusing since at the moment, he's lying down.

Remington had hoped the man would trip over the fallen tree the way he had, but coming in several feet farther to the south, he misses it completely.

—You see him?

—Not yet.

—Just keep moving toward us. Go slow. Take your time. Make some noise.

—Don't let him circle back and get behind you, a different voice says.

The man is in front of Remington now. He's got a bright light attached to the barrel of his rifle and trains the beam along the path he's traversing. As soon as he gets a little farther away, Remington can slip out and head in the opposite direction toward the river.

The man fires a round into the air. The loud explosion temporarily halts the sounds of frogs, crickets, and other nocturnal noisemakers. And Remington's heart.

He fires another round as he continues to move.

—You get him?

The man doesn't respond.

—Jackson? Jackson? Did you get him?

Jackson, Remington thinks. So there's at least five men after him. Maybe more.

—You said to make some noise.

—So I did. I've got Arlington setting up in the flats in case he doubles back and gets around you.

—He won't get around me.

—What I like to hear.

So he can't go back out into the pine flats. Where, then?

Just a few more feet and Jackson will be swallowed by the fog. I guess I can go south for a while and then turn east.

Jackson stops suddenly, turns, and begins to shine the light behind him, searching all around.

Remington lies perfectly still.

Unable to fit entirely beneath the fallen tree, part of his body is exposed.

The light passes directly over him, but is too high to reveal his whereabouts.

Then the man makes a second pass—lower to the ground this time.

Don't shine it over here. Go the other way.

—Anything?

—Not yet. I'll radio when I have something.

—How far in are you?

—Not far. I'm taking my time. Making sure he's not just hiding. Wait.

—What is it?

Suddenly, Remington is blinded by the beam of the light.

—I got 'im. I got 'im.

—Where?

—Don't move. Put your hands up where I can see 'em.

—Which one? Remington asks. Can't do both.

—Jackson?

—Crawl out of there very slow.

—Jackson are you there? Where are you?

Remington eases out from the black walnut, as the man rushes in his direction, gun and light leveled on him.

—Jackson?

—Yeah.

—You got him?

—Got him.

—Shoot him there and we'll come to you or bring him to me and I'll do it.

—I shoot him, I make more.

—Fine.

—How much?

—Double.

—Done, Jackson says into the radio, then to Remington, Get on your knees.

—I just got up.

—One shot to the head'll be painless. I gotta shoot you a bunch of times, it's gonna hurt like hell and take you some time to die.

—I reckon I'd like to live as long as I can.

—Suit yourself, but—

As the man shrugs, Remington lunges toward him. Going in low, beneath the rifle, he digs his shoulder into Jackson's groin, then raises up, bucking the rifle away, tackling him to the ground.

As he falls on top of the man, he rolls his shoulder and turns his arm, smashing his forearm into the man's throat.

Rolling.

Clutching.

Running.

Grabbing the radio, Remington rolls off the man, snatches up the rifle and starts to run.

Root.

Stumble.

Fall.

Hitting the ground hard after just a few feet, Remington drops the rifle, but manages to hang on to the radio.

Crawling toward the rifle, his hands and knees slipping on the leaves, Remington can hear Jackson slowly climbing to his feet.

By the time Remington has the rifle again, Jackson is lurching toward him.

No time.

Don't think.

Just shoot.

Instinctively, he pulls back the bolt, ejecting a bullet from the breech, then jams it forward, racking another round into the chamber.

Raising the rifle, he takes in a breath, aims, exhales two-thirds of his breath, holds the rest, and calmly squeezes the trigger.

Nothing happens.

Jackson's almost on him.

Safety.

He presses the safety button and tries again.

The deafening sound in the dark forest leaves his ears ringing.

—Is it done? the calm voice from the radio asks.

Ripping a hole in Jackson's chest, the round goes through and lodges in a maple tree behind him.

Blood.

Spreading.

Falling.

Death.

Dark crimson flows out of the hole. Jackson collapses. Dead in seconds.

—Jackson? Did you get him? Jackson?

Flashlight beam. Bright light washing out his face. Eyes open. Ghostly.

Remington shivers.

The lifeless man looks eerie in the small circle of smoky light, surrounded on all sides by darkness. The disquieting image disturbs him deeply, and he rushes to get away.

He doesn't make it far before he drops to his knees. Retching. Coughing. Vomiting.

Shock.

Numbness.

Headache.

Everything around him seems a great distance away.

Like a bad drug trip, he feels detached from his body, sick, lethargic.

Trembly.

Clammy.

Dry mouth.

Shallow breaths.

Dizzy.

Did I really just kill a man?

I had to. He was going to kill me. I had no choice.

Would you rather be dead? Is that what you want? Would that make you feel better? You dead and him alive—the man, who with his buddies, was out here hunting you like a goddamn animal?

Why're you so upset? He was one of the bad guys. A killer. You just killed a killer. You had to. He was about to kill you.

I killed a man.

You had no choice.

He dealt that hand, not you. You were here to take pictures. These men are killers. He intended to kill you. The others still do.

But—

They'll probably still kill you, so you won't have to feel bad for long.

12

Now

After John leaves and before they call Sylvia back in to finish the movie, Merrick and Reggie sit alone in the still quiet room, looking out the back windows at the moonlight on the river.

"You think he'll leave it alone?" Merrick says.

Reggie shakes her head. "No way."

"We knew this day was coming," he says.

"Yeah, I've kept him off of it as long as I could, but . . . it was just a matter of time. It's funny . . . I really want him to solve the Remington James case, but in doing that he's probably gonna find out what really happened to Robin and the rest of them."

"Whatta we do?" Merrick says.

She shrugs. "What can we do?"

"Surely not just sit around waiting to be arrested."

"Not a lot of other options."

"I can think of some," he says.

"Well, stop. No good can come of any of that."

He takes her hand.

"You know the worst part of all of it?" she says. "It's not everyone finding out what we all did, but why. The thought of all that coming out . . . of everyone knowing—about me and poor little Lexi Lee . . . just . . ."

"I can't just sit by and let that happen," he says. "I can't."

13

Then

—Jackson?
—Come in, Jackson.
—Where are you? What happened?
—You think he got Jackson?
—No way.
—Somebody shot something.
—Probably just lost his fuckin' radio again.
—Get over there and find out.
—Almost there.

He needs to go back and hide the body, but he's not sure he can.

You can do it.

I can't.

You've got to.

I can't. I can't go back there. Besides, they'll see the blood.

You've got to cover it up.

I just can't.

—Goddamn. Oh Jesus.

—What is it?

—Jackson. He's dead.

—You sure?

—I'm looking at his dead goddamn body.

—He fuckin' killed Jackson.

—Gauge, did you hear me?

—I heard you, the calm, laconic voice says.

—He's dead.

—Get his guns, radio, and supplies, then hide the body. We'll get it later.

—Jesus, we can't leave him. It's Jackson.

—We'll come back for him. Right now I need you to figure out which way he went. We've got to find him. Get this over with. Then we'll take care of Jackson.

—Oh God, his kids. His wife and kids. What will we tell them?

—We'll figure that out later. I'll take care of it. Just find the fucker that did it.

He had killed a man.

A man with a wife and children.

His life would forever be divided by the before and after line of ending someone else's.

He'd never even killed an animal like his dad had wanted, not in all his years of walking through these woods with a shotgun, but he had just taken the life of another human being. Just like that.

Killer.

—His radio's missing. And his rifle.

—You think that bastard's listening to us right now?

—Hell yeah.

—You got a name? Gauge asks.

—Just call him Dead Man.

—It's gonna be a long, cold, lonely night. You should talk to us.

Remington is tempted to say something, but remains silent.

—Suit yourself. We'll be seeing you face-to-face soon enough.

—Tell him who he killed.

Gauge doesn't say anything.

—You killed a cop.

—Jackson was a deputy—with a family. You might as well put that rifle in your mouth right now and blow the back of your goddamn head onto a tree trunk. That's the best case scenario for you.

I killed a cop.

Don't even think about it. Just survive. Concentrate on surviving. Deal with the ramifications later.

He continues walking south, staying in the hardwood hammock in case Arlington has already set up in the flats.

Soon, it would end, and he'd have no choice but to enter the flats.

Where do they think I'll go? How can I do something unexpected? Go in a direction they'd never guess?

You could walk toward them.

No, I couldn't.

It'd take ... what?

Something I don't have.

You could go west, toward the four-wheeler.

Probably somebody watching it.

You hid it. You always do. Just like Cole taught you.

They could've followed the tracks.

Maybe. You could kill them.

The thought makes his stomach lurch. How many rounds are in the rifle?

Four to begin with. Jackson fired one. I ejected one. I fired one. One left. But I'm not going to shoot anyone else. I can't do that again.

Don't say what you won't do. Think about Mom. Heather.

Or maybe there're two left. If he had one in the chamber and four in the magazine.

He stops and checks the rifle. Pulling back the bolt, he ejects the round in the chamber. As he does, another one takes its place. Ejecting the second round empties the gun.

Bending to pick the two rounds from the ground, he stands, blows them off, and reloads the weapon.

As he nears the end of the hardwood forest, he veers right, heading in the direction of the four-wheeler without making a conscious decision to do so.

Get to the ATV, then to the truck, then to town. Then what? Who do I go to? Who can I trust?

Pain.

Exhaustion.

Cold.

Fear.

Thirst.

Hunger.

Body cut, scratched, and bruised by the forest, every throbbing step bringing more discomfort.

Unsteady.

Moving slowly now, his shaking and shivering making him stagger and stumble.

Mouth dry, the taste of vomit lingering, he tries to swallow, to quench his thirst, but can't.

The frigid air causes his throat to feel like he's breathing fire, his ears so red-cold they feel raw and razor burned, his head so frozen it feels feverish.

Famished.

He's so hungry, his abdomen so empty, he feels as if his body is starting to consume itself, cannibalizing the lining of his stomach.

Opening his phone, he searches for signal.

None.

14

Now

The night is foggy now.

The town is empty. Appearing abandoned.

The single traffic light in town has switched, as it does every night, into a flashing caution light, its rhythmic, intermittent red glow splashing on the empty streets and closed businesses of downtown.

As I near our road, I see Chris Taunton, Anna's ex-husband, standing on the sidewalk of Highway 22 near the old hardware store looking toward our dark house.

I hit my emergency lights and pull over beside him.

The moment he sees me, he begins to walk back toward Main Street.

Throwing my car into Park, I jump out and tell him to stop.

He slows and turns toward me but doesn't completely stop moving. "Why, *officer?*" he asks, making a mockery of the word *officer*. "Sorry, I mean *detective*."

"I said stop."

He does.

"This is harassment," he says. "I can't even go out for a walk in my own town without you . . . accosting me."

"You'll know when you're being accosted," I say. "This is nothing like that."

"Why can't I walk without you bothering me?"

"You weren't walking," I say. "You were standing here watching our home."

"I certainly was not, but for the sake of argument let's say I was. There's no law against it."

"There is in this town," I say. "If you want to walk in the middle of the night, find somewhere else to do it. I don't want to see you around our home or street again."

"You really think you can tell me where to walk?" he says. "What to look at?"

"Tell you what I think. I think you're gonna keep pushing, keep aggravating and irritating in an attempt to get a reaction, the way all stalkers and psychopaths do, but you're not going to like the reaction you get. Promise you that."

"You threatening me?"

"Not at all. I'm telling you that this can all be avoided, but if you don't stop, you're going to get a reaction, but it won't be the one you're looking for."

"Oh yeah? What's that?"

"I'm not going to take the law into my own hands," I say. "I'm not going to beat you up or set you up. I'm going to do everything by the book. So keep provoking if you want to, keep stalking and harassing, but it's not going to end well for you. You're gonna find yourself right back in prison with even less of a life than you have now."

"Can I go?" he says.

I nod. "Just remember what I said. And don't let me see you around here like this again."

"Sure thing *de-tec-tive*. Whatever you say."

15

Then

—You out there, killer?

Gauge's voice is so calm, so flat and even, it chills Remington far more than the cold.

—I'm here if you need to talk.

Remington doesn't respond.

—You ever killed before? Not very pleasant, is it? But you had to do it, didn't you? See, there are times when you just don't have any other options. And when it's you or them, well, it's got to be them, right? Hey, I understand. I've been there. Earlier today, in fact.

Jerking the radio to his mouth, depressing the button, speaking—no thought, no filter, no way to stop himself now.

—Who was she and why'd you have to kill her?

He hadn't planned to. It just came out, as if independent of him, a rogue bypassing his decision-making process.

—Not knowing really bothers you, doesn't it?

—She wasn't trying to kill you.

—There's more than one way to die. And some shit's worse than death. A lot worse.

—Such as?

—Things that kill a man's soul.

—Such as?

—Well, I'm sure there're lots of things. Ruinin' a man's reputation comes to mind. Destroying his family. Taking away everything he's worked for. I suspect prison would damn well do it, too. But I'm just speculatin'. Who's to say what would kill a man—or cause him to kill?

—Bullshit justification.

—Don't be too harsh on me now, killer. You and I obviously have more in common than you'd like to think.

—We're nothing alike.

—We've both taken a life today.

—I killed a man, yes, but you . . . you murdered a woman. Self-defense is nothing like premeditated, unprovoked, cold-blooded murder.

Gauge doesn't respond.

Remington realizes he's said too much. He should've never started talking to him in the first place.

—Anybody hear anything? Gauge asks. Get a lock on him?

—No.

—Me neither.

—Nothing here.

—Keep looking.

—It's time to call Spider, the big man says. Get the dogs out here and finish this.

—I think we're closer to him than you think, Gauge says. Let's give it a few more minutes. That okay with you, killer?

Remington doesn't respond, and scolds himself for being stupid enough to do it before.

16

Then

She's never had someone look at her the way he does.

It's frightening and exhilarating at the same time.

He's so mysterious, so completely unknowable. What's going on behind those intense eyes of his? Is he thinking the same thing she is? Wanting to do the same things to her she wants him to?

In the past, when she's been noticed at all, it has been by men and boys she hadn't wanted to be noticed by. Drunk men way too old for her. Odd boys who saw in her a similar kind of pain and awkwardness and isolation.

He's not like any of that.

Sure, he's a little older, but not enough to be . . . Not too much. He's a man. He's not an old man. And he's stable. Secure. Strong. And so handsome. She's never had a handsome man find her appealing. Why would they?

She has nothing, is nothing. She's plain and poor and a little peculiar. Maybe more than a little.

But she's capable of love and loyalty. Capable of it in way the popular, pretty girls will never be.

Maybe that's what he sees. Maybe, just maybe, he can see something with those intense, mysterious eyes that no one else has been able to.

Could it be?

Could this really be happening?

Is it finally her turn to be happy?

She's not superstitious, but she rubs her bracelet for luck just the same.

17

Now

Bothered by my confrontation with Chris and still not ready to enter my empty house again, I drive out to the Salt Shaker Lounge on Highway 22.

A rural, roadside bar, 22 is a throwback package and lounge with the most colorful characters in town and a true sense of community. It's my favorite place in town to visit. Back when I was drinking I would've wanted to live here.

It's late on a weeknight. The joint is empty except for a few serious drinkers well on their way to oblivion scattered around the bar, and two heavily tattooed, scantily dressed, strung out young women over in the gaming area shooting pool.

By the time I reach the bar, the bartender has a tall glass of CranCherry juice waiting on me.

"Thank you," I say, raising the glass to her.

"Just don't overdo it," she says.

Chris Stapleton's *Whiskey and You* is on the jukebox and the muted TVs all carry the same program—a snowy hunting show in which women are celebrating shooting huge game they proudly mount on their walls.

As I was hoping, Hank Felty is here, sipping on his usual, face flushed, nose a deep red on its way toward plum.

I slide over beside him.

Hank Felty, who seems older than he is and is mostly retired, was once easily the largest grower in Gulf County and one of the largest in North Florida.

He turns toward me slowly, his eyes attempting to find focus, as he flicks ashes in the small glass ashtray in front of him.

"How's it hanging, Hank?" I say.

"These days it's only my balls that hang," he says. "And they stay around my damn knees."

He finishes off his whiskey and water and I buy him another.

I pepper him with small talk for a few, then work my way into what I really want to converse with him about.

"You remember Remington James and all those boys getting killed out in the swamp?" I say.

He nods. "Shit yeah I remember that shit."

"I'm lookin' into it," I say.

"No shit?"

"None."

"Well, I'll be damned, 'Bout damn time somebody did. Cole was a good man. So was his boy—or was on his way to be . . . coming one. Shame what happened to—well, both of them really."

"Everybody says you have that many dead men in a shootout, only one thing it can be," I say.

He nods.

"I just didn't think we had any operations that big around here by then," I say.

"Just 'cause I retired don't mean everybody did. You could say

. . . when I went off to . . . college, it created a sort of . . . vacuum. Somebody had to fill it."

I've heard him refer to his stint in prison as college many times before.

"Any idea who?" I ask.

He shakes his head. "Ain't just sayin' that 'cause you a law dog neither. I truly don't know. Everything's different now. Everything's changed. We used to keep it simple. Hell, we'd grow it out in the woods somewhere—usually on somebody's property who wasn't involved, but could keep an eye on it for us. If the shit was found, they'd act shocked somebody had done such a thing on their land. And we'd ship that shit. Wouldn't keep it on us."

He pauses to take a sip of his drink and a drag on his smoke, but when he finishes those he's forgotten what he was saying so just sits there silently.

From over in the gaming area, one of the young women knocks a ball off the pool table and they both yelp and laugh like it's the funniest thing they've ever seen.

"What do you mean?" I ask.

"Huh?"

"You said you wouldn't keep it on you, that you shipped it."

"Oh. Well, yeah. Hell yeah. You won't want to get caught with it, right? So you grow it on somebody else's land and then we'd double bag that shit up, put it in boxes and ship that shit Fed Ex or UPS."

His mention of Fed Ex makes me think of Laura Matthers, a young woman I dated when I first moved back to Florida from Atlanta. She drove into my life on a Fed Ex truck in what seems like a lifetime ago now.

The drive-thru bell dings and the bartender makes her way over to the window.

As I look back from glancing at her I become aware of a new song playing on the jukebox, and I wonder how many have played while I was listening to Hank and thinking about the illegal drug trade in this area. In a particularly sad and poignant song, Miranda Lambert is telling Mr. Tin Man how lucky he is not to have a heart.

"You grow and sell the shit around here, fine, you can make a little money, but you ship it to Tampa or Miami, Atlanta or Memphis, you make three times more—at least."

I nod and take another pull on my CranCherry.

"Had to make as much as we could on it," he adds. "Hell, we had to grow three crops every single time."

"Three crops?"

"Yeah, just to get one. Plant one for the cops. One for other growers watching you, wanting to steal your crop—they used to follow us around when they thought we were going to our field, so . . . you had to go a different way every time and really you needed to lead them to a fake crop. One you planted just for them. And the third crop was yours. Plant three to get one. Do business like that you got to make as much as you can off the one crop you actually get to keep."

I nod and think about the high price of doing illegal business.

"That many men out there, getting killed like that," I say, "have to be a pretty big operation, wouldn't it?"

He nods. "But . . . they could'a been out there for some other reason. Operation that big 'round here . . . Where? Where they growin' it? How they movin' it? How've they gotten away with it so long? 'Specially after a big shootout like that?"

"Think about who was sheriff at the time," I say.

"Fuckin' Robin Wilson," he says. "You're right. That would . . . explain it. Crooked bastard. You know why I went away to college? 'Cause he wanted a bigger piece of the pie and I thought I could negotiate with him. He showed me. My way or the highway, man—highway straight to damnation and ruination."

Miranda finishes telling Mr. Tin Man if he ever felt one breaking he'd never want a heart, and Keith Urban begins telling a sad woman alone in a bar that blue ain't her color.

"Could he have been behind it all?" I ask. "Pushed you out to take over? So when he was investigating what happened, he was investigating himself?"

He shakes his head. "Wasn't the type to do any actual work. Just wanted the skim—and a hell of a lot of it—from the work we did."

While we've been talking most of the patrons of the bar have paid their tab and slipped out into the night. Now it's just me, Hank, the bartender, and one other guy who appears to be sleeping between sips of his whiskey and soda.

"Could it be something besides weed?" I say. "Opioids or something?"

He shakes his head. "Won't grow around here. We tried. Needs like a damn tropical environment. Not hot enough up here."

"Any ideas where I should start? Who to look at?"

He shakes his head. "I'd tell you if I knew. Like I say, I liked Cole and Remington. I just don't think they's an operation that big around here. Must be somethin' else. 'Course what the hell else could you even do in the swamp?"

18

Then

L ost.
Again.

This tract of land that belongs to him now is so much larger than he realized before. Of course, he may not even be on his property any longer. Depending on where he is exactly, he could have wandered onto paper company land or state protected property or . . . Who owns the piece on the other side? A hunting club?

Occasionally, the cold wind carries on its currents the smell of smoke, causing images of the burning girl to flicker in his mind.

He wonders if his pursuers have built a campfire to huddle around, or if in the distance a raging forest fire is ravishing the drought-dry tinderbox of timbers.

Certain he should've reached the pine flats by now, he enters instead the edge of a titi swamp. Do the flats border the far side? All he can do is keep walking, shuffling his feet along the forest floor, scattering leaves, divoting the dirt.

He has no idea of the time, and though it feels like the middle of the night, he knows that even with all that's happened since he's been out here, not much time has elapsed.

It's probably between nine and ten.

—What time is it? he asks into the radio.

The question is addressed to no one in particular, but it's Gauge's languorous voice that rises from the small speaker of the walkie-talkie.

—You got somewhere to be?

—Just curious.

—We wouldn't want to keep you from anything.

Remington doesn't respond.

—It's 10:39.

—Thanks.

Is Mom okay? Is she lying on the floor after falling while trying to get her supper or medicine? Hopefully she's sleeping. Oblivious to how late I am.

Wonder what Heather's doing right now.

He had told Heather he'd call her when he came out of the woods. Did she grow alarmed when he didn't or angry that he had failed to keep his word again?

Did her bad feeling cause her to call Mom? Did she discover that I'm not home and call someone to come take care of her? Did she call the police? Even if she had, they wouldn't begin searching for him until morning. Would he be dead by then?

They haven't found my truck, he thinks.

It occurs to him that they'd know his name if they'd found his truck or four-wheeler. Or do they just want him to think that, get him to circle back, return to where he started and walk into a trap?

Will he reach his dad's Grizzly to discover it won't crank? Or will they let him get as far as the truck and find its tires are flat?

The thoughts of these men even touching his father's vehicles make him angry and sad. Since Cole's death, Remington had become both sentimental and protective over every one of his meager possessions—even those Cole cared nothing about and had discarded.

Dirty old hunting boots had become priceless, notes scratched on scraps of paper sacred texts, discount-store shirts Remington would be embarrassed to wear around the house invaluable because his dad's scent still clung to them.

19

Now

The moment I get home, I gather the manuscript and all the case files I have and go into my library-study. Sitting on the floor I spread them out around me and begin to read, check, and crosscheck my way through them.

It doesn't take me long to realize I need to stop.

All afternoon and evening I've been keeping myself busy, avoiding coming home alone, distracting myself with anything I could, including or especially the case.

I used to spend most of my time alone. Clearly I'm out of practice.

Before Anna and I finally got together, I lived a largely lonely life, but I also used my solitude to think and pray and meditate, to really listen to my life, to what it was trying to teach me. Lately, in my comfort and companionship and the fullness of family and work, I have done far less. And tonight when I had the opportunity to return to it, to take advantage of time and space and aloneness, I rigorously resisted it, I did everything else but what I should have done.

Pushing the case files aside, I move over to the altar I have set up in front of one of my walls of books.

Lighting candles and incense and turning on some Gregorian chant softly in the background, I sit up and begin to breath slowly, becoming mindful of my breathing. In and out, in and out, concentrating on my inhalation and exhalation and beginning to observe my thoughts that try to pull me away from my practice.

You can do this another time. You need to be reading the case. You only have a week until Reggie pulls the plug and puts you on something else. Why did he burn and bury her body? Why wasn't it found?

Breathe. Let go. Every thought is just that—a thought. Observe it. Release it. Watch it go the same way it came.

Flicker of candle flame animates the serene faces of the beatific figures and dances across holy cards and iconography, as smoke from the burning incense curls around the sacred objects and twists up into the dimness above, filling the room with the sweet scents of cherry and pine as it does.

It takes a while for me to get to a place of sending my thoughts on their way instead of letting each one stay and give rise to others.

I'm rusty, not as present as I have been in the past, not as sensitive to the realm that is beyond, below, and between, not as tuned-in to the subconscious, the spiritual, that which transcends.

The truth is I'm always rusty. My practice is never what it should be. At my best, I'm still neglectful of what I claim really matters to me.

But I feel the gentle pull back toward union, toward the best kind of oblivion.

I breathe.

I keep the case and other cares at bay.

I connect.

I pray.

I 'm still praying a few minutes later when my phone rings.
It's Anna. Her voice is dry and sleepy sounding. And by
far the best sound I've heard all day.

"You okay?" she asks. "Got worried when I didn't hear
from you."

"Sorry. Thought it was too late when I was finally able to call."

"It's never too late. You know that."

"You'd think I would," I say.

"With all that's going on with Chris and Randa . . . It really
worried me. I fell asleep and woke up panicked."

"I'm so sorry. I should've called. I should've called sooner. It
was thoughtless and inconsiderate, stupid—especially given
Chris and Randa and the work I do. Truth is . . . I'm out of sorts
without you here."

"I feel the same way," she says. "Why do you think I'm callin'
in the middle of the night?"

"I miss you," I say. "But it's not just that. I . . . I'm a little lost
without you."

"Always stay that way," she says. "It's the same for me."

Even though it's very low in the background, I pause the
Gregorian chant.

"Speaking of Chris and Randa," she says, "has anything
happened?"

I tell her about seeing Chris watching our house from the
sidewalk up on Highway 22.

"Be careful with him," she says. "Don't forget what he's
capable of, what he's already demonstrated he's willing to do."

"Willing to hire *others* to do . . . but I will. Taylor and your
folks okay?"

"Everybody's good. Mom and Dad said to tell you *hey*. They're so excited about the wedding. Really helping me with some great ideas. What would you think about having it up here? Make it sort of a destination wedding. Mom and I are going to look at a place tomorrow called The Grand. The pictures I've seen are . . . incredible."

"Anywhere. Anytime."

"I just thought it might be nice for all our family and friends to be in the same hotel. Make it a fun weekend getaway. Love the thought of every time you step out of the elevator you run into someone you know."

"Anytime. Anywhere."

"But what do you think?"

"I think it makes me miss you even more. Sounds wonderful."

"I know we've both been married before, but . . . I . . . I really want this to be the celebration it deserves to be, you know?"

"I do. It may not be the first, but it will be the last—and that's something to commemorate and memorialize."

"Exactly. That's exactly it. We're finally together and we're going to be, come what may."

"Come what may," I say.

The incense has burned out, but the sweet, woodsy aroma remains in the room.

"I want it to be just what you want it to be," I say, "but I agree it should be a sure enough celebration. And it will be. No matter where or when or what."

"Yes it will."

"How's the investigation going?" she asks.

"Investigations," I say. "Looking into what happened to Remington *and* Robin."

"Does Reggie know?"

"She told me to drop the Robin Wilson one and just concentrate on the Remington James case—and only for a week. But I think it's obvious they're connected. Can't really look into one without looking into the other, so . . ."

"So you're going to do it anyway?"

"Is that okay?" I ask.

"You mean because it might cost you your job?"

"I am down to only one and a half now," I say. "If I lose this one I'll only have a half and we can't live on half a job. I'm asking because it directly impacts you, our family."

"Thank you for asking, for considering me, us, but . . . do what you've got to do. We'll be okay. Just be safe. That's all that matters. We can figure everything else out."

I think about Remington not staying safe, about how lost and lonely Heather has been since then.

"I feel so bad for Remington and Heather," I say.

"I know. I do too."

"Makes me not want to take what we have for granted or miss a single second of it," I say.

"You'd think you would've called," she says.

I laugh. "Exactly. Just another way my aspirations don't match my actions. Unbelievable, isn't it?"

"Not so unbelievable, baby. We'll both keep those aspirations and keep working on making them match our every action."

"I feel like yours do," I say. "Far more than mine."

"That's only because you're more compassionate with me than yourself."

"You always see the best in me and make me better," I say.

"And you me."

"Get some sleep my love," I say. "I'll call you tomorrow."

"Don't forget to call."

"I won't."

"Night. Love you."

"Love you more."

"Not possible."

20

Then

F rigid wind whipping, whistling, biting.
Fog retreating.
Tiny ice shards like slivers of glass. Frozen dew drops sprinkled on limbs and leaves, grass and ground.
Shaking. Violently. Uncontrollably.
Too cold to think.
Body.
Dead.
Blink. Disbelief. Shock.
Beneath the base of a fallen oak, arm outstretched unnaturally, the gray-grizzled man he encountered when he first entered the deep woods lies dead.
Blood.
Tracks.
More blood.
Most of the man's blood appears to be spilt on the cold, hard

ground—splayed out along the path his body made while being drug toward the fallen tree.

Eerie.

Seeing a dead body out here, alone, on this cold, dark night disturbs him deeply. Frightening him far more than he wants to admit—even to himself.

Ghastly.

Ghostly.

Gray.

The man's blood-drained body is even more pale than before, the pallor of his face advertising a vacancy, the departure of the ghost, the emptiness of the shell.

Holes.

Mortal wounds.

The man has been shot—more than once, though how many times, Remington can't tell. Had he been with them? Is this whole thing about drugs? Poaching? More likely whatever he was up to out here was unrelated. He stumbled onto some men far worse than—

The man grabs Remington's ankle, turning his twisted neck, opening his mostly dead eyes.

Remington startles, yanks his leg back, trips, falls, comes up with his rifle.

—Why'd y'all shoot me?

—What?

—I ain't done nothin' to nobody.

—Who shot you?

—Were it 'cause of the bear? Y'all kilt me over a goddamn old bear?

—Who—

Remington stops. Feels for a pulse. The man is dead. Fully and completely dead this time.

So he did kill the bear, but he wasn't with Gauge and the others— and they certainly didn't kill him for killing the bear.

This is their way of silencing witnesses. A man like Gauge doesn't tie up loose ends, he cuts them off.

—Goddamn.

The sudden blast of voice on the radio makes Remington jump.

—What?

—It's cold as fuck out here.

For the second time tonight, Remington leaves the dead where they lay and begins moving again, holding the radio to his ear to hear what's being said.

—Coldest night of the year so far.

—Hey, killer, you okay? Didn't look like you had on a very warm jacket.

—Can you believe this is fuckin' Florida?

—It's thirteen degrees out here. Colder with the wind chill. This is the kind of hard freeze we have only once every so often that wipes out citrus crops.

—Do us all a favor and blow your brains out.

21

Now

With Anna out of town and not knowing Heather any better than I do, I decide it's best not to have her come to our home. Instead, we meet at Lake Alice Park on a warm, sunny Tuesday morning.

She arrives with Mike and Jean Thomas, a kind, white headed, late sixties, soft-spoken couple who own the most successful construction company in Gulf County. Mike is also a county commissioner for the district I live in.

"Morning, John," Mike says, extending his hand.

"Morning," I say, nodding to them both.

"Sorry to barge in like this," Jean says, "but we won't stay. We were having breakfast with Heather and asked her if we could come along for a minute. Hope you don't mind."

"Not at all," I say.

"Cole James was the best friend I ever had and one of the best men I ever knew," Mike says.

"Caroline was one of my closest friends," Jean adds. "Especially before she got sick."

"We wanted you to know how much we appreciate what you're doing and offer any assistance you might need."

"Thank you," I say. "I really appreciate that."

"It's a real offer," he says. "Both of any of our personal resources or those I manage of the county's. This case is a blot on our community and an embarrassment. We need to find the victim Remington mentioned and find out what really went on out there. I appreciate you helping Heather and will do anything I can to help you. That's all. Now we'll leave and let you two get to work."

"Just remember what we said," Jean adds. "Anything you need. Anything at all."

We shake hands again, he hugs Heather, and is gone.

"Hope you don't mind," she says. "I told them I was meeting you and they insisted on coming."

"I'm glad they did. Having their support in this is huge."

"Good. I don't think Jean was as close with Caroline as she now claims, but Mike and Cole were very good friends. I think he really will do anything he can to help us."

"Let's sit down over here," I say, leading her over to a wooden bench at the bottom of a gentle slope down by the water.

As we take a seat, she pauses to look at the name of the business that provided the bench, which is burned into the backrest.

"Wewa Outdoors," she reads. "It's funny. I forget that was the official name. Everybody just called it Cole James' or the pawn shop or the feed store. That's one of the things Mike is helping me with. Figuring out what to do with everything—the store, the home, the land. He and Cole were very close. I know he helped keep the business afloat when times were tough. Helped with Caroline's medical expenses, too. Anyway, I don't really care about property, about things—not compared to finding out what really happened to Remington and why, and proving he didn't make up the story about Gauge killing that woman."

"I'm really enjoying the manuscript," I say. "You've done a great job. It's riveting."

"Thank you."

"How much of is factual?" I ask.

"More than you might think. We researched all the men who were out there with Gauge hunting Remington. We found out a good bit about them. We used the crime scene notes and photos, the things Remington left behind. Things like the wrecked ATV, their tracks, forensics. Anything we could get our hands on. I'd say it's very accurate in spirit if not in letter, but pretty accurate in general."

Above us, the extending oak limbs form a canopy that blocks out much of the direct morning sun, but before us the surface of the lake sparkles with the soft gold light.

"Were you hesitant to talk to me before because you wanted to get your book done first?"

"No," she says, and seems offended by the question. "I . . . I was contacted. This was back shortly after it happened. We had an exhibition of Remington's work—the pictures he took that night, the ones we found anyway. It was spectacular. His mom was there with me—in a wheelchair. She was so proud of what he . . . accomplished. We both were. Are. I still am. Anyway, it was after the show . . . I was cleaning up and wrapping up a few things. Caroline was waiting for me. It was just the two of us.

"Then seemingly out of nowhere, two men showed up. All in black. Dark shades on. One held a gun on me while the other bent down and put a knife to Caroline's throat. The guy in front of me—I can still remember how he smelled, like coffee and country club aftershave—pressed the barrel of his gun to my forehead and cocked the trigger. I thought I was going to die, that we both were. With the knife at Caroline's throat, the guy over by her started groping her, fondling her breasts and . . . It was awful. Never felt so helpless and vulnerable in my life. Guy closest to me said if I didn't let everything go, stop looking into it, stop trying to find the answers to what really happened out there and who was behind it, he'd slice Caroline up, kill her slowly in the most painful way possible, and then after letting me live with the knowledge of that for a few days, would do the same to me. I knew he meant it, knew these were not men but monsters. Caroline, bless her heart, actually peed on herself sitting there in her wheelchair. She was so embarrassed, so scared and . . . I decided right then and there I wouldn't do anything else on Remington's case until . . ."

"Until when?" I ask.

"Until Caroline passed away and they weren't a threat to her anymore. She died recently. I had been working on the book this whole time—very discreetly and carefully, using the services of a private detective to get certain information so it couldn't be traced back to me. When she died I began working on it openly and agreed to talk to you. I want it solved. I want the truth to come out. I want whoever's ultimately responsible for it to pay. I want to clear Remington's name and find the other messages and info he left out there for us. I want to find the poor girl Gauge killed and return her to her family so she can be properly buried. And I don't care if they kill me for doing it. Part of me died when Remington did. A big part of me. Don't mind so much if they finish the job."

"Did they say or do anything that might indicate who they are, who they represent?"

She shakes her head. "I was trying to keep Caroline alive. Didn't notice much about them. Except . . . I genuinely truly believed their threat. Had no doubt they meant what they said."

"So you think whoever's behind what happened to Remington is still out there," I say, "wasn't one of the ones killed that day?"

"Those guys—even Gauge—were drones, worker bees, not the big boss."

Her use of *worker bees* makes me think of the upcoming Tupelo Festival, which takes place here in the park each year on the third Saturday of May, and reminds me that Anna and I have been in town nearly a year. It was at last year's festival that I caught my first case as an investigator with the Gulf County sheriff's department—the disappearance of Shane McMillan, a young man home on leave from Fort Benning.

"And you think they killed him because he saw what happened to the woman who was murdered?" I ask.

"Because he had evidence of it."

"No other reason?" I ask. "No other motive? Just that? He was at the wrong place at the wrong time?"

She shrugs. "It's what I've always thought. I guess there could be other motives. I don't know."

"Any idea why the evidence he had or the woman's body has never been found?"

"I was only able to search for them for a short while before the two men threatened us at the gallery that night. I stopped looking then. As far as Sheriff Wilson and his so-called investigation . . . it was either one of two things—corruption or incompetence."

"In his message, Remington said he was going to try to hide the photographs his camera traps took of the crime near a landmark on the river. Any chance he just wasn't able to do that?"

"I guess it's possible, but if that's the case, the memory cards should've still been on him."

I nod and think about it.

In our silence, I hear the sounds that were only desultory a moment before—the drive-thru teller at Centennial Bank, the light traffic on Main, a couple of kids playing on the jungle gym on the opposite side of the park, the occasional tractor-trailer piled high with recently felled pines gearing down as it comes through town.

"If it's still there," she says, "I'm gonna find it. I'll be here all week. Plan to search for it—for both of them, the body and the memory card—every day."

"If it's been out there all this time the chances of it working are . . ."

"I've got to look."

I think about the prospects of searching for a small memory card, not much bigger than a quarter in the vast, seemingly endless swamp, and the odds of actually finding it.

"The original crime scene and burial site had to be close enough to Remington's camera traps for them to capture it. Was that area searched thoroughly?"

She nods. "He actually had two camera traps set up. Both areas were searched thoroughly—and not by Wilson and his department, but FDLE. They used sonar and everything."

I think about that too.

A gentle breeze blows through the park, twirling bits of sand and leaves, waving the Spanish moss on the oak trees, and rippling the surface of the lake.

Heather clears her throat and swallows hard. "I can't explain why they didn't find her, but I know she's there."

"Could what he said be code for something else?" I ask. "Could he have been trying to get you or law enforcement a message that the men who were after him or their bosses wouldn't understand?"

She shrugs and seems to think about it. "I guess it's possible, but . . . I really don't think so."

"Then I can think of only two possibilities," I say. "Either his camera traps were moved or her body was."

22

Then

He wakes shivering, not sure where he is.
 —You still with us, killer?
The emotionless voice on the radio brings everything back: spray of blood, collapse, fire, run, chase, kill, hunt.
 —Don't be like that. Don't ignore us.
Remington remains motionless, quiet.
 —What about the rest of you? Anybody got anything to say?
 —I see him. I see him.
 —Where?
 —I've got a shot. I'm gonna take it.
Remington rolls, leaving both the radio and the rifle.
 —Anybody see anything?
 —What? I thought you had him.
 —I was just trying to get him to run. See if any of us seen him when he did.
 —Brilliant, Donnie Paul.

Grabbing the walkie and the weapon, Remington shakes himself and begins to walk.

—Did you run, killer?

Gauge is the only one to call him that, as if the others, without being told, know not to.

—I did, Remington says. But I was already. I can see the river. I'm almost—

—Almost what?

Remington doesn't respond.

—Did somebody get him?

—I didn't.

—Me neither.

—I didn't either.

—Wonder what happened to him.

—Killer? You there?

In the flats now, Remington turns west, back toward the ATV.

How long did I sleep? It's just as dark. I don't feel rested. It couldn't've been very long.

—Whatcha you think happened to him?

—Maybe a bear got him. Or he fell and broke his neck.

—Radio could've died.

—He realized he was telling us where he was.

—He's smarter than that, Gauge says.

—I don't know.

—I do.

—But he's freakin' the fuck out.

—He's heading in a different direction. Probably the opposite.

—So we don't need to cover the river?

—Unless . . . that's what he expects us to think.

—Come back.

—He may really be heading toward the river.

—Whatta we do?

—Everybody keep doing what you're doing. And remember he can hear us. Better use code from now on.

S tilted.
    Stiff.

Awkward, self-conscious.

Paranoid.

Walking through the flats, every tree is a man with a gun, is Jackson about to level his rifle and begin firing.

Move. Just keep moving.

He stays close to the edge of the hardwood hammock, crouching, turning, zig-zagging, trying to create a difficult-to-hit target for any would-be assassin.

What did I dream?

Fragments fall like confetti. Wisps. Snatches. Fading fast.

A bit of Shakespeare he had to memorize for a British Lit class somewhere along the way drifts up.

—To be or not to be . . . he whispers. Whether tis nobler in the mind to suffer the slings and arrows of outrageous fortune or take arms against a sea of troubles, and by opposing end them. . . . To sleep. Perchance to dream. . . For in that sleep of death what dreams may come. . . Shuffle off this mortal coil. . . Undiscovered country from whose bourn no traveler returns.

To be or not to be? That is the question.

It's being asked of him tonight. He's got to answer it. Suffer or take arms?

Answered that one once already, didn't you, killer?

Goddamn it. Gauge is in his head.

The thought of killing Jackson causes him to dry heave. He has nothing left to throw up.

Full moon.

Fog lifted.

Clear.

Cold.

Stars.

With the fog gone, the bright moon casts shadows on the frosty ground.

Walking through an herb bog, insect-eating pitcher plants, bladderworts, sundews, and butterworts slapping against his legs, he glances up to find Polaris and confirm he's heading in the right direction.

He is.

Just a mile or so to the ATV, then three to the truck.

He's beginning to believe he can do it, that he might actually make it, but he's so tired, so hungry, so cold.

Nearing the area where he had hidden the four-wheeler, Remington takes cover in a thick stand of bamboo.

Watching.

Waiting.

Listening.

The wind rustles the bamboo, clacking the shoots together, swishing the leaves. It rains down oak leaves and pine needles, sways palmettos, and makes the knocking sounds of palm fronds. And makes it impossible to hear.

He scans the area, searching for signs the men have been here —or are still here, but he sees nothing.

Cole had trained him to always hide his ATV when he came out here. You wouldn't want to really need it—be shot or snake bit—and not be able to get to help because someone vandalized or stole it.

Thanks, Dad.

The ATV is hidden well. They'd have to either stumble upon it, or, more likely, find its tracks farther back and follow them here. Marked, cut, carved, the small dirt road is layered by multiple tracks. The tire impressions left by his dad's ATV would be difficult to distinguish from the others.

Slowly.

Quietly.

Carefully.

Crouching, he eases toward the thicket that hides the vehicle. Nearly every inch of his father's Yamaha Grizzly is either camouflage or black, which when driven into a thicket of palmetto, bamboo, palms, low-hanging limbs, vines, and covered with fallen branches, makes it virtually invisible.

Gently pushing aside bamboo and pulling away branches, he uncovers the ATV, never so happy to see a vehicle in all his life.

After the four-wheeler is completely exposed, he ducks down behind it and surveys the area around him.

No men.

No movement.

No nothing.

Before rising, he reaches in his pocket for the key.

It's not there.

He checks again. It's gone.

He quickly checks his other pockets, jamming his hands in and feeling around in his jeans and his jacket.

He's still got the ring of truck, house, shop, and mail box keys, but not the small Browning fob with the buck outline that holds the single, small ATV key.

It must have fallen out at some point during the night, either when he was running, falling, rolling, or crawling.

Shit.

I can't believe this. *Fuck.*

How could I have lost it? *Think.*

23

Now

"Of course the shootout was drug related," Bryce Dyson says.

We're at Pepper's, the Mexican restaurant across from the Panama City Mall, eating tacos and burritos and talking about drugs and murder and corrupt cops.

Dyson used to work with Sam and Daniel at FDLE and our paths had crossed a few times over the years. He is now with DEA, working out of the Panama City field office.

He's a late-twenties-early-thirties guy with dark skin and wispy dirty blond hair that has receded to about the half way mark of his head. Beneath a large forehead and prominent brow, his light blue eyes seem to always be moving.

"I appreciate you talking to me," I say.

"You kiddin'? All you're doing for Sam . . . I'd do anything in this world I could for you. So glad she's doing better. Any word on Daniel?"

I shake my head and frown. "Not so far."

"Anything I can do to help find him, let me know."

"Thanks. I will. I can't believe we haven't found him yet."

He nods slightly and gives me a frown of his own. "Longer it goes the less likely a good outcome is."

No one is supposed to know where the DEA field office is, but everyone does. It's on Frankford not far from the old airport, so I offered to meet him on the other end of 23rd Street, but he wanted tacos. And not just any tacos. Pepper's tacos.

The building Pepper's is housed in was many other businesses before it became Pepper's, and its large open room of tiled floor and hard surfaces is echoey and loud, the sounds of the lunch crowd eating and drinking, talking and laughing, and piped in Mexican music bounces around the room, reverberating as if designed to do so.

Soccer is on the big screen TV behind the bar. Several men at the bar sit directly in front of it, fixated.

"For a long time now—since back before what happened to Remington—our Miami agents have been telling us that they're seeing huge amounts of product down there from up here, that North Florida is supplying South Florida in weed."

"Really?" I ask, unable to hide my surprise.

"I know, right, but . . . it's legit."

"And it's just marijuana?" I ask. "Nothing else?"

"Right. Which is smart 'cause it's not the priority it once was. Hell, everybody figures it'll be legal sooner or later, but in the meantime whoever's doing it is making a fuckin' fortune."

I nod and take another bite of my burrito.

"Thing is . . . we know about it, right? Been looking for it—for a long time now. Can't find shit. Don't know where it's being grown, who's doing it, how it's being shipped, nada. It's embarrassing."

"You sure it's still happening?"

He nods. "Positive. It did slow down a bit after what

happened with Remington and the others, which is another reason we think it was related, but then it picked back up again."

"What about where all the bodies were found?" I say. "Where they hunted Remington and his camera traps were set, doesn't it make sense that their crops are around in that area?"

"You'd think, but we searched it when they were found and since. And nada."

"You throwin' in all the Spanish since we're eating Mexican food?"

"Huh?"

"That's the second time you've said *nada*."

"Yeah? Bite me, *punta*."

"I'm gonna stick with the burrito and tacos, but thanks for the offer."

The waiter comes back and refills our drinks. We eat in silence as he does and thank him as he rushes away.

"What about the sheriff at the time?" I say. "Wilson. He ever under investigation related to drugs?"

He smiles. "Funny you should ask. We sent in an undercover agent. She set herself up in a little house trailer in the middle of nowhere, began to grow and sell weed and make and distribute meth. Ordinarily, we notify the sheriff when we send someone into his county, but we didn't say anything because the sheriff and a few of his men were targets of the investigation. So here she is investigating them and they start investigating her. Huge cluster fuck. Eventually, they arrested her and she had to blow her cover, but . . . she believed—well, everyone in the agency did—that they were only busting her to take out their competition. Wasn't long after that they were taken out, so . . . we never got to make a case against them."

Someone scores a goal and the guys in front of the bar erupt in cheers and high fives.

"Where is she now?" I ask.

He smiles. "She's not the woman Remington said Gauge killed. She's not missing. She's still an agent."

I nod. "Good. But whoever was killed could be another agent from somewhere. Can you check to see if any are missing—*have* been missing since back then? Gauge was from Franklin County. Maybe she was undercover over there."

"Or maybe there never was a woman," he says. "Pretty sure someone would've found her by now."

"You ever been out in those swamps?" I say.

"No, and I don't plan to."

"Well, even light gets lost out there. Not so hard to imagine a burned and buried body might not be found."

"So you think there is one out there?"

I nod.

"I'll see what I can find out about any missing agents for you."

"Thanks."

We finish the last of our food.

"Do you know how exactly the DEA in Miami knows the pot is coming from up here?"

He shakes his head. "I can find out. Probably all marked with the same mark. Growers brand their shit more than fuckin' car companies, but that would only let them know it all came from the same source. Not sure why they think it's from up here."

24

Then

The radio sounds and he jumps.

—Y'all remember that ugly girl Donnie Paul dated?

—The one with the real big tongue.

—Yeah.

—I remember her. Goddamn she was ugly as fuck.

—Remember how we used to talk about her, using that code we made up in school?

—Yeah. She never had a clue.

—Let's use that same code. As much as possible.

—We can do that.

Think, Remington reminds himself.

Where could it be?

No way to know. He had traveled too far, fallen too many places. It would take too long to backtrack even if he could, and with the way he's been navigating tonight, he'd be lucky to find even one of the locations of his many stops, drops, stumbles, falls.

How could he be so stupid?

Why didn't you protect it? Check on it? At least confirm it was still there before you walked all the way back over here?

He's so weary, so spent, his nerves so frayed, his taking of another man's life so recent, that he feels himself breaking down, about to cry.

Don't.

You can't. Not now. Later, okay, but not now. You don't have time. Take a minute. Take a breath. Clear your head. Pull it together.

He does.

After a moment, he says aloud, I'll just walk to the truck.

Patting his father's four-wheeler, he says, I'll come back for you when all this is over. He then stands and begins to walk down the small path toward his dad's truck.

He's only taken a few steps when a thought occurs to him.

Who's the most competent, careful, and practical man you've ever known?

Dad.

Which means?

He wouldn't've lost the key.

True, but what else?

What?

He would hide a spare key somewhere on the ATV. If not for himself, then for his son.

He would.

Turning, Remington rushes back and begins to search the machine.

Falling to his knees, he checks beneath the tire wells, under the suspension, around the motor. Looking for a small box with a powerful magnet, he scans all the metal parts first. What he finds instead is a hard blue plastic Stor-A-Key device with an adjustable cable and a built-in combination lock. Fastened to the chassis, the small box dangles down, but can't be seen unless you're underneath the vehicle looking up.

Three numbers.

One thousand different possible combinations. Just three little numbers determine his fate.

What would Dad use?

Of course.

For most of their marriage, Cole had told is wife he loved her with three numbers, writing them in rose petals on her bed, drawing them on napkins, the margins of magazines, newspapers, books.

1-4-3.

The number of letters in each word of I love you. 1-4-3. He tries it and nothing happens.

He was sure that would be it.

He spins the numbers, clearing and resetting the lock, and tries again.

1.

4.

3.

The cable releases and the small plastic box pops open. The key is inside.

25

Now

I meet Charles Masters at his family's bee business in Land's Landing.

Though there is an actual Land's Landing with a boat launch and small park next to the river, the entire area around and between Old Transfer Road and Land Drive is referred to as Land's Landing.

It's tupelo season and the Masters family is hard at work, getting ready to transport their bees to places along the river swamp near the soon-to-be-blooming tupelo trees.

Tupelo honey is a light golden amber honey with a slight greenish tint that smells of cinnamon and flowers and tastes like something they'd serve in heaven.

In addition to its distinct, delicate, and delicious taste, tupelo is popular for two additional reasons—it doesn't crystallize like other honeys, and because of its high fructose content, diabetics can use it as a sweetener.

Tupelo is also extremely rare.

It is only produced commercially in our little corner of Northwest Florida—and then only once a year for a very short time.

The tupelo tree, first discovered by William Bartram along the Ogeechee River in Georgia, is also sometimes called swamp gum, bee-tupelo, and tupelo gum.

Because tupelo trees grow in the river swamps along the Chipola and Apalachicola rivers, beekeepers have to move their hives as close to the trees when they're blooming as they can. Transported on barges and boats down the river, the hives are placed on elevated platforms along the banks or left on the barges, allowing the bees to fan out through the area that is pregnant with tupelo blossoms during a few short weeks each spring.

As soon as the tupelo flow is completed, the hives must be moved again and the honey harvested to avoid dilution with gallberry and other blooming flowers.

In addition to the annual festival, tupelo has been celebrated in Van Morrison's 1971 song of the same name, as well as featured in the critically acclaimed Victor Nunez film Ulee's Gold, starring Peter Fonda, which was shot right here in Wewa.

Hundreds of bee boxes in various states of disrepair are piled in front of the honey house where the tupelo will be slung from the hives once they return from their journey down the river. Beyond the unused bee boxes and the honey house, bees buzz and swarm around the stacks of boxes in the back lot, as Charles' father and brothers in full beekeeper suits use smoke cans to move the hives about.

Charles is not what I expect.

He's both short and small, his body resembling that of a boy instead of the thirty-something man he is. He has blondish hair and glasses and is dressed in clothes that look like they came from the boy's department at Sears.

I'm here to talk to him because he briefly worked for Robin Wilson, and I'm hoping he can give me some insight into the investigation into what happened to Remington, and who may have killed his old boss and coworkers.

"I appreciate you talking to me," I say. "I know how busy y'all are right now."

"Not a problem. Happy to help. Besides . . . weather's not cooperating this year. Looks like there's not going to be much of a harvest."

"I'm very sorry to hear that."

In addition to being so small, he's bookish and cerebral, and I wonder what made him want to become a deputy.

"What made you become a deputy?" I ask.

"Not what you'd expect, is it?" he says. "To be honest with you, I . . . wanted to be sheriff. Planned on living here my entire life and wanted to make a difference, take care of this area and people. Figured I'd start as a deputy and work my way up through the ranks. Do every job I could. Just didn't work out. I'm sure you're loyal to Reggie or may plan to run yourself one day, but the truth is . . . I haven't ruled out running for sheriff and may even do it next time around. If not, probably one day in the future."

I nod. "Well, I am loyal to Reggie, but you don't ever have to worry about me running. I've got the jobs I want. Have no interest in being a politician."

"Fair enough."

"I'm looking into the Remington James case and the murders of Robin Wilson, Donnie Ray Kemp, Skeeter Hamm, Skip Lester, and Dahl Rogers."

"You think they're connected?" he asks.

"Do you?"

He shrugs.

"You were there at the time both things happened, right?" I say.

He nods. "I was a deputy."

I would think his diminutive stature would disqualify him

from being a deputy, and I wonder if Robin Wilson, who seemed to do what he wanted to, regardless of laws or regulations or even public opinion, had made an exception for him for some reason.

"Which means I wasn't involved in the investigation—I mean as an investigator, but I was close enough to witness a lot. It's a very small department."

"Was it a real investigation—the one into what happened to Remington and the others involved in the shootout—or was it just going through the motions, pretending to investigate?"

"Can't say for sure, but . . . I'd say it was meant to look like an investigation but wasn't."

"Like maybe Robin and the others were involved somehow and were covering it up?"

"Maybe. I really don't know."

A noise from the backlot where his dad and brothers are working with the bees draws our attention and we both turn to look, watching without talking for a few moments.

Observing the beekeepers at work, I'm reminded how labor-intensive tupelo production is, how fragile the bees and the blooms are, and how often, in spite of all the effort, very little honey is produced.

Charles turns back toward me and I continue.

"I keep hearing how corrupt Sheriff Wilson was," I say.

"Don't believe what you hear," he says. "Whatever you've heard . . . what he did was far, far worse. Never met any career criminal that was a fraction as corrupt as that cop was."

"Really?"

He nods. "Never seen anything like it."

"I know he was under investigation by FDLE when he was killed. You have any idea what it was about or any conclusions they reached?"

He doesn't say anything.

"How were you able to work in such a corrupt department?" I ask.

"Didn't for long. When I first started I didn't know about any of it, and it didn't have a direct impact on me or the other deputies for a while. But as I began to see and hear more about what he was doing, how he and the others you mentioned were running the sheriff's department like an organized crime syndicate, I got out."

"I noticed you quit around the time the Sheriff was killed," I say.

He nods. "It was just before he was, but even then . . . I stayed longer than I planned."

"Oh yeah, why's that?"

"FDLE asked me to," he says.

"*FDLE?*"

"I was what Robin and his boys would call a snitch. I was the one who reported him to FDLE, and when they started investigating him, they asked if I'd stay to help gather more information. I didn't mind. I was happy to bring down that evil bastard. Of course, ultimately someone beat us to it."

"Any idea who?"

He shakes his head. "Wish I did. I'd buy 'em a beer. Like I said, that was after I left. But . . . it's not a coincidence that the ones who were killed were his buddies from high school who he hired after he got elected. They were all involved in the crime and corruption."

"What kind of crime and corruption we talkin' about?"

"You name it. Extortion. Kickbacks. Violating civil rights. Theft. Sexual harassment. Rape."

"*Rape?* You sure?"

He nods. "And not just inmates—though there was plenty of that. I'm not talking violent or brutal rape. Robin was the Bill Cosby of law enforcement—he used date rape drugs. It was found in his house when he was killed. Reggie can tell you all this. She was investigating him at the time. Hell, he died in her jail cell when she was still the chief of police of Wewa."

"I'll talk to her again. Who else should I talk to?"

"Merrick helped her I think. At least he wrote some articles about it. Don't know exactly how, but . . . Harvey Harrison, the big gay guy who lives in the church, and Reggie's high school sweetheart, Allen Maddox."

"Except for the date rape drugs, you didn't mention drugs in their list of crimes," I say, "and yet everyone keeps telling me that to have a shootout like that and law enforcement officers killed like that, drugs have to be involved."

"My list wasn't comprehensive," he says. "They were into everything. Things you can't imagine. Of course, drugs and drug money were involved. Sex, drugs, money, and power. All of it. You know how there are seven deadly sins? Before Robin and the rest of them, there were only three."

26

Then

S hoving the radio into his pocket and slinging the rifle strap
over his shoulder, he straddles the seat, pushes the key in,
turns it, presses the ignition button, and thumbs the gas.

Even in the cold, the motor coughs to life on the first try.

Giving it enough gas to keep it going and warm up the engine,
Remington is careful not to gun it, keeping the powerful motor as
quiet as possible.

Placing his boot on the brake, he shoves the shifter out of
neutral and into reverse.

Without turning on the lights, he backs up enough to turn
around. Brake, shift, gas, he's racing down the small dirt path
toward his dad's old Chevy, certain he'll be almost as happy to see
it as he was the ATV.

The four-wheeler feels powerful beneath him.

Cold wind.

Stinging face.

Watering eyes.

Hope.

It's the first time since Gauge triggered the flash on his camera trap that he feels truly hopeful—and that his hope just might be justified.

The path is narrow and overgrown, branches whipping at him, occasionally slapping him in the face.

Running with the lights off, he turns them on periodically to get his bearings and check the path. He can't do anything to lessen the sound of the machine, but by keeping the lights off, he can lessen his conspicuousness—something the full moon helps make possible.

Don't panic.

Stay in control.

He's tempted to leave the lights on and drive as fast as he can —more than tempted, a strong urge inside compels him to, but he reminds himself that even if the men weren't out there looking for him, it'd be a bad idea because of the condition of the path.

Part logging trail, part fire line; the woods that form the walls of the path encroach on the cramped opening, and he rides low, his head just above the handlebars, to avoid the branches and limbs of the drooping canopy.

The small lane is littered with stumps, limbs, branches, and fallen trees, uneven, and pocked with bumps and holes, but the Grizzly's traction, high clearance, tall tires, and double wishbone suspension make the brambly, cragged terrain seem almost like a smooth recreational path.

Reluctant to accept such a large gift from his son, Cole quickly came to love the Grizzly, grateful not only for the present, but Remington's knowledge of what he needed.

Over the years, as a child and as an adult, try as he might, for Christmas and birthdays, Remington had never found many gifts his dad liked or used. In the last few months since his father's sudden departure, he was often profoundly grateful that he was able to get him the Grizzly before he died.

Driving as fast as he dares.

Lights on.

Lights off.

Much of the brightness of the moon is absorbed by the canopy and walls of the overgrown path.

When the lights are on, they illuminate only a small area directly ahead, when they're off, he's flying blind through the blackness.

It'll be okay. The path is straight. Just hold it steady. Stay straight.

Still, what you're doing is dangerous.

More so than making a great big visible target for Gauge?

The intermittent light flashes, more often now, strobe the path, giving it a staccato, stop-motion, horror film quality.

I ncandescent.

Luminous.

Radiant rain.

Suddenly, the dark lane sparkles with the swarm of a thousand fireflies.

Shining.

Burning.

Minuscule Milky Way.

It's as if he is traveling at the speed of light through the universe, shooting past stars and planets inside an enormous black hole.

Darting about like arcing sparks and falling drops of fire, the Lampyridae flies give the enclosed area a surreal, magical quality.

These days, he sees far less of these phosphorescent flying beetles than when he was a child, which wasn't that long ago. Development of land causing loss of both habitat and food supply, use of pesticides, and harvesting for their luciferase has led to dwindling populations of the lucent lightning bug.

Are these fireflies left from summer? he wonders. It's been warm enough—up until tonight.

Or are they juveniles of the more mysterious and interesting winter firefly?

No way to know. And it doesn't matter.

He slows without stopping, pulls his camera bag around to the front, and withdraws it.

P ower.
        Lens cap.
Exposure.
Focus.
Click.
Click.
Click.

He can't help himself. He's got to capture this increasingly rare spectacle.

Click.
Click.
Click.

In a matter of seconds, he snaps several shots—some with the flash, others without, some with the Grizzly's headlamps on, others with them off.

Within moments, he has ridden past the lustrous, shining swarm. Replacing his camera in the bag, and spinning it back around, he glances over his shoulder. The fireflies are gone. Back to the hard, cold bark of the trees lining the lane.

They must have been responding to the intermittent illumination coming from switching the Grizzly's lights off and on, on and off.

Certain he got some good shots, he looks forward to showing

them to his mother, to finally fulfilling his promise to bring her the pictures she can no longer take. She'll love these—and those of the bears, and the ones from his camera trap.

This last thought reminds him again of the horrific images on the memory stick in his camera, and how far he still is from home and help.

Hopeful.

He'll soon reach the truck. He might just make it.

Continuing to turn his lights on and off, he's again tempted to leave them on.

Get a little closer first.

Okay. You can do this. You're gonna make it. Don't rush. Be cautious, but not hesitant.

He rides a little farther, branches slapping at him, one whacking him in the face, leaving a dotted line of cuts, the moist blood wet and cold on his skin.

Believing he's nearing the place where he parked his dad's truck, he slows the ATV and leaves the lights off for a few extra seconds.

When he turns them on again, the lights land on a man in dark camouflage overalls and a heavy black winter jacket, looking through a rifle scope at him.

27

Now

"Could I really have been married to a psychopath and not known it?" Casey Dalton says.

Her big blue eyes beneath her blond bangs really seem to want to know. The innocent eyes, blond bangs, and pale round face conspire to make her look far younger than she really is.

"It's more common than you might think," I say.

"Mask of sanity and all that, sure," she says. "I've read all about it . . . Still, it's hard for me to believe."

Casey was married to Gauge three years before what happened in the swamp that fateful day a few years back. I was surprised she agreed to meet with me, but as she explained when I spoke to her by phone earlier, she's still searching for answers.

She looks and sounds like a simple, small town girl, but I can tell there's more to her than her lack of education and sophistication suggests.

Was the woman her husband killed similar? Did he have a type?

"All this time and I still can't be sure," she says. "Still haven't found any real evidence that he was."

I nod.

We're standing in the large wooden gazebo out over St. Joe Bay because she didn't want to meet anywhere near her home in Eastpoint or anywhere official over here. She's wearing an inexpensive plain white cotton blouse and an unstylishly long denim skirt. Both the blouse and the skirt are thin and light and blow, not unlike her straight blond hair does, in the breeze coming in off the bay.

The fifteen-mile-long bay is formed by the mainland on the east, Cape San Blas on the south, St. Joseph Peninsula on the west, with a narrow opening out into the Gulf of Mexico on the north. At its widest point it is some six miles wide.

"I don't just mean I haven't found any evidence he was a sociopath," she adds. "I haven't found any evidence of any kind of illegal or even immoral activity. Think about that."

The same was true of the investigations into him—by the Gulf County Sheriff's office, the Franklin County Sheriff's office, and the agency he worked for, the Florida Fish and Wildlife Conservation Commission. I've read the files. No one had found a single piece of evidence to say that Gauge was anything but an upstanding citizen.

The men out there with him that night were a different story. Each one was crooked and corrupt in his own way, but the investigation showed that it was isolated to them and not a systemic part of the agencies they worked for—the Franklin County Sheriff's Department, St. Joe Police Department, Fish and Game, etc.

"But you're here," I say. "Talking to me."

"Yeah?"

"You're still searching."

"Yeah?" Her pale smooth skin furrows in confusion, but I can see in her eyes that she's genuinely asking, really thinking about it.

"Why?"

She shakes her head. "I don't understand."

"If in all this time you haven't found any evidence of . . . well . . . anything, why are you still looking?"

She starts to say something but stops.

Her eyes widen a bit and her mouth slowly falls open.

I can see the realization begin to spread across her pale round face.

I wait.

"If you had no idea back when you were together and you've searched for evidence in the years since and haven't found anything," I say, "why would you still be searching?"

"Because," she says, and pauses a moment, "some part of me . . . some part deep, deep within me . . . isn't completely convinced."

I nod.

"Wow," she says. "I . . . wasn't aware of that."

I can see she wants to think about that some, so I let her.

While I wait I determine to invite her over to the No Name Café and bookstore on Reid Avenue for a late lunch. She looks like she could use the food and the company—and one of their specialty coffee drinks.

She looks out over the bay and I follow her gaze.

The afternoon is overcast and foggy, pregnant with rain yet to fall, sky and water melting into each other where the horizon should be. Behind us, the planted palms lining the street and the park clack in the breeze, as tall pines stand by in stately silence, and it occurs to me that one definition of my part of North Florida might very well be where palms and pines meet.

As she turns back toward me, she sees the old lighthouse over my shoulder. "How long has that been there?"

I turn and look at it—the white tower supported by the steel structure and the black ball vent, dome, and service room—this centerpiece to the park next door that looks like it's always been here. But several lighthouses have been built and destroyed out on the narrow hurricane-prone point of Cape San Blas since 1847. The one that was moved here is just the most recent, the last lighthouse standing. And because it was moved here, it is likely to stand a lot longer than it would have out on the eroding tip of sand that juts out into the Gulf.

"About three years," I say. "They moved it over from the cape with the two Keepers' Quarters and that oil shed."

She studies it. "It's so . . . I know . . . it makes me feel so . . . I like having it here."

I nod. "Me too."

She looks at me again and our eyes lock. "Thanks for not treating me like trailer trash. Most people—men and cops especially—can't see past the dollar store clothes and Southern drawl."

"I hope I'd never treat anyone like that, but it's obvious you're very intelligent," I say.

"Don't know about all that," she says. "You helped me see in a few minutes what I hadn't in years."

"You saw it," I say. "I just asked you a couple of questions."

"I'll tell you what I am," she says. "I'm a hick who married a psychopath."

"In spite of not finding any evidence," I say, "you now believe you did?"

"Before this conversation I'd've said I didn't and there was no evidence, or if I was being real honest, I'd've said I couldn't be sure but there was no evidence, but now . . . well, now I think I was married to a psychopath."

I start to say something but wait to see if she'll expound on what she's said.

"There's no evidence that my husband was a psychopath," she says, "but there's no real evidence he was human either. It's like . .

. he wasn't really there. I was married to a shell, a body with no soul."

She looks away, shakes her head, and lets out a harsh little laugh.

"Been lying to myself about that for years," she says. "Trying my best not to see the truth. Then . . . after he was gone and people would ask about him, I'd . . . I was so defensive . . . thinking it was a reflection on me that I wouldn't even consider it. Not really. Now . . . it's like I've known all along—at least somewhere deep inside. I was married to a soulless, coldblooded animal. Wow. Feels so . . . freeing to say that."

She looks back at me. I give her an encouraging expression and little nod, but don't say anything.

"I don't know exactly what happened out there in those woods," she says. "I hope you find out, I really do, but . . . I'll tell you this . . . there is nothing in Gauge's background or life with me that I've been able to find that sheds the least bit of light on it and that's the truth. I wish it did, but it just doesn't."

"If anything comes up or you uncover anything that might be helpful," I say, "would you let me know?"

"I will," she says. "And who knows . . . now that I'm really able to stand the truth . . . maybe it will, but I doubt it. Would you do something in return for me?"

"What's that?"

"Will you let me know what you find out about him in your investigation? It would mean a great deal to me. I really, really need to know. Anything. Anything at all. I . . . I'm just so scared his son's gonna grow up to be just like him."

"Gauge has a—y'all have a son?"

"He was only one when all this happened," she says. "Is it nature or nurture? Is my little boy gonna grow up to be a monster like his daddy no matter what I do?"

28

Then

He squeezes the brakes so fast and so hard that the back end of the ATV lifts off the ground and he nearly sails over the handlebars.

The first round ricochets off the front bumper.

Boot on brake.

Shift down, past neutral and into reverse.

Gas.

Backing away as fast as he can on a path that was difficult in forward, he cuts his lights and ducks down on the right side behind the tire well.

Other shots whiz by, thumping into dirt and tree trunks.

Seeing a small opening in the thick tree line, Remington yanks the handlebars and throws the rear-end into the small gap.

Braking abruptly, he shifts into forward, turns the wheel sharply, and guns the gas.

Bullets continue to whistle by split seconds before he hears the crack of the rifle.

Racing down the way he's just come, he crouches low and zig-zags as much as the narrow lane will allow.

Leaving his lights off as long as possible, he flashes them occasionally to peek at the path he's bouncing down.

You're driving too fast.

No choice.

If you wreck, he'll shoot you for sure.

Not if I get far enough away first.

What if it's a wreck you can't walk away from?

He thinks about all the children in these parts who've been killed in four-wheeler accidents, some racing down dirt roads, rounding corners full bore, colliding head-on into cars, others running into trees or flipping the machines and breaking their backs.

What's more dangerous? Flying down a narrow tree-lined lane at deadly speeds in the dark or being shot at by a high caliber rifle? Before this moment, it wasn't something he ever imagined having to contemplate.

Don't think. Just react. Move. You've just come down this path, you know it's clear.

This time, he's in the middle of the field of fireflies by the time they light up and take to the sky, and he's driving so fast, several of them splat against the ATV, strike his jacket, and pop him in the head.

Sorry guys. I wouldn't do this to you if my life didn't depend on it. Shots continue to ring out, rounds piercing the bark of trees next to him.

How long before he hits a tire?

Fearful the fireflies reveal his position, he ducks even lower, moves even more, jerking the handlebars from side to side, trying to find the fine line between being a difficult target and turning over the ATV.

In another moment, he's through the swarm and the light-dotted sky dims again.

His radio crackles and he turns it up without removing it from his pocket.

—Is that you firing, Arl? Gauge asks. You got him?

—It's me. It's me. He's on a four-wheeler. Nearly made it to the truck. Now he's running down the little fire line.

—On foot?

—ATV. ATV.

—That's what I thought, but you said running. Have you hit him yet?

—Not sure. Don't think so.

—Don't let him get away.

—Then let me quit talking and get back to shooting.

A moment later, the shots start again.

—Anybody on the west side close to the fire line? Gauge asks.

Remington lowers his head, straining to hear.

—I can be at the end of the lane in a couple of minutes.

—Do it. Anybody else?

—I'm a mile or two away.

—Me, too.

—Well get moving. Head in that direction. Let's circle around and close in on him.

Lights off.

Rounds still ringing around him.

Distance.

Decision.

The farther away from the shooter he gets, the less accurate the shots become, but he's speeding toward the spot where another shooter will soon be.

I've got to get off the path, but where? How?

How about here?

Too dense. Wouldn't get far.

It's the same farther down. He flashes his lights.

Nearly to the end.

Slowing, he searches for any break in the woods big enough to squeeze into. Finding one, he turns the ATV to the right, heading back in the direction he had come from just a few minutes before. East. Toward the river.

If he can figure out how to negotiate his way through the dense timbers and thick undergrowth, the flats up ahead will provide ample room to open up the ATV and race to the edge of the river swamp.

The tree bases are big and close together, the understory high, concealing cypress knees, limbs, and fallen trees.

He tries flashing his lights periodically again, but the woods are just too thick.

Slowly, the large tires of the ATV climb over unseen solid objects, around massive trees, edging the machine and its rider ever closer to the flats.

—He's not here.

—What?

—I'm at the fire line and he's not here.

—He turned off. Heading east.

—Okay everybody. East side of the fire line. Don't just look for his lights. Listen for the engine.

Easing.

Crawling.

Inching.

Progress through the forest is so slow, it seems like he's not making any.

It'd be a lot faster just to run.

I know, but there's just a little more of this and then I can race through the flats.

But they're headed this way. Getting closer.

Just a little farther. If I have to stop, I will.

They'll be here by then.

The dense ground coverage is so thick as to be nearly impenetrable.

What should I do?

He wishes he could ask Cole. He might not be able to tell him what to do, but his answer would help calm him, clarify his thinking.

He remembers calling Cole from college once.

—If I take an extra class this semester and two the next, I can graduate in the spring. If not, it'll be December of next year.

—Well, we've got the money, if that's what you're worried about.

—Thanks, but I just wondered what you thought I should do?

His dad had not attended college, had never been faced with a decision quite like this one.

—I can't tell you what to do, he says.

Remington tries not to laugh. His dad had told him what he should do his whole life.

—It's like you're driving down the highway heading home.

Here it comes, Remington thinks. Conventional wisdom from the most practical man on the planet.

—There's a car in front of you. There's one coming in the other lane. You have time to pass. Do you? It's up to you. You'll get home either way. You can get there a little faster if you pass, but even if you don't, you'll get there just the same.

—Thanks, Dad.

—Whatta you gonna do?

—Pass.

—Let me know how much the other class and books are and I'll mail you a check.

Tell me what to do, Remington thinks now. Do I abandon your four-wheeler and run on foot or stick with it and try to make it to the flats?

No answer comes.

Cole is gone.

He's on his own.

The thought opens a hole inside him, ripping emotional stitches, tearing the inflamed tissue, reversing any healing his grieving had begun.

Gone.

Alone.

Stop it. Don't think. Just move. Just react.

—See him?

Remington leans down to listen to his radio.

—Hear him? Anything?

—Nothing.

—He's on a fuckin' four-wheeler for Chrissakes. Why can't we hear him?

—Big ass woods.

—Just keep looking. Listening. We'll find him.

Full stop.

The bottom of the ATV gets jammed on an old oak stump, lifting the wheels just enough to prevent them from finding any traction.

Stuck.

Fuck!

Boot on brake. Jamming the gear into reverse. Thumbing gas.

Spinning.

Stuck.

29

Now

The next morning, having skipped breakfast, Merrill and I climb into an old model Cessna Skyhawk, smaller than most SUVs, in a grass field on a farm up near the county line.

Merrill shakes his head. "The shit I let you talk my black ass into . . ."

The pilot is a gaunt half-Asian half-African man in his late sixties named Clipper Jones, Jr., whose dad had been a pilot in World War II.

"Buckle up, boys," he says. "Gonna be a little bumpy."

Evidently Clipper Jones, Jr. is given to understatement.

The small plane bounces and rattles across the ruts in the roughhewn and uneven farm field so violently it feels as if it will vibrate apart.

Merrill is up front with Clipper and I'm in the back in one of the two small seats, trying not to regret either the decision to take this little trip or my seat selection for it.

When we do finally lift off the hard, bumpy ground, the jerks and shakes, rises and falls of the little craft become even more pronounced.

My stomach falls and lurches several times, convincing me skipping breakfast had been the prudent thing to do.

We fly over the small town of Wewa, which looks even smaller from up here, the differing perspective disconcerting at first. Our house and yard and the lake they sit next to appear both larger and smaller than I expect, their relative sizes and relationships to each other odd and off.

In the far distance I can see thousands and thousands of acres of slash pines that once belonged to the St. Joe Company and are now owned by Deseret Ranches. Instead of uninterrupted acres of pines there are huge swaths of open, cleared cattle fields, mostly empty pastures where, one day soon, tens of thousands of head of cattle will roam.

We continue south toward Dalkeith and the swamp where Remington James had his camera traps and where the massacre took place.

As we near the place, Merrill says, "What we lookin' for again?"

The small cabin is loud. The three of us are wearing headphones with built-in microphones, but even with them it's hard to hear and understand what's being said.

"Anything," I say. "Got to figure what Gauge and the others were doing out here in the first place. Crops. Buildings. Anything suspicious."

"It's Dalkeith. Everything's suspicious."

"What kinda crops y'all lookin' for?" Clipper asks.

"Marijuana mainly," I say, "but anything worth killing for."

"Y'all cops?" Clipper says.

"He is," Merrill says. "I'm . . . sort of a private one."

"My folks were sort of like detectives," he says. "Started back during the war. Had some adventures, to hear them tell it.

Worked with a white PI named Riley. They's a book about 'em. If even half of what it says is true . . ." He shakes his head and smiles.

"Oh really?" Merrill says. "Like what?"

"For starters my mom was Japanese," he says. "Broke out of an internment camp with her family in California and came here—well, Panama City Beach. They helped catch a serial sex killer, stopped an espionage plot. My old man even fought in a heavy-weight bout for the chance to fight Joe Louis."

"That's very cool," I say. "I'd like to read about them."

"How long you been flyin'?" Merrill asks.

"Feels like all my life."

"But it couldn't be, could it?" Merrill says. "Didn't have planes when you's young."

"Brings up an interesting question," Clipper says. "Which one of you gonna land this little bitch if I have a heart attack and die?"

"You havin' chest pains?" Merrill says.

"Not so far, but . . . 'nother joke or two about my age just might bring on the big one."

"Slow your roll, Fred Sanford. I's just joshin' with you. You look young and spry and healthy, and more than capable of getting our foolish asses back on the ground safe and sound."

"Why foolish? For flying with me?"

"For flying at all. Nothing personal, Junior."

"None taken," Clipper says, letting go of the small steering wheel to turn toward Merrill.

The plane dips a bit and begins to nose downward.

Clipper extends his hand to shake Merrill's.

"Whoa, whoa, whoa," Merrill says.

"Shake to show no hard feelings," Clipper says, a big smile on his face.

Merrill shakes his hand quickly, then pushes it back toward the wheel.

"We've got a sayin'," Clipper says. "It's all fun and games until the plane goes down."

"We've got a sayin' too," Merrill says. "Keep your got-damn hands on the wheel and don't let the got-damn plane go down."

Clipper, continuing to smile, nods enthusiastically. "I like that one, too. Have to remember that. Reason I ask if y'all cops . . . I might be able to help you with what you lookin' for, but I wouldn't want to get all jammed up over it. And I wouldn't want y'all thinkin' I'm a grower or nothin'. I just picked up a thing or two from farmin' and flyin' 'round here over the years."

"We're investigating murder," I say. "Lookin' for possible motives. We'd appreciate any help you can give us and will leave you completely out of it. No one will ever know you said anything to us."

As we fly over the seemingly endless acres of woods and swamps, I wonder if Heather is down there somewhere searching for answers of her own.

He nods. Glances at Merrill. Merrill nods.

"If a guy's doin' it right," Clipper says, "not easy to see his crop from the air. He'll plant it in swaths beneath the pines or other trees, not in open fields. If it is in a field, it's usually planted alongside another crop like corn or something. They even tie it down so it runs along the ground beneath the corn. 'Course the shit keeps poppin' up so you have to keep retying it."

I nod.

"We'll fly over and see what we can see," Clipper says, "but best bet is walk the woods or go by boat down the river."

"Oh we doin' all that shit too," Merrill says. "This shit's like a redneck Planes, Trains, and Automobiles. Soon as we land—if we land—we gettin' in the car and driving out here and walkin' it. Site of a fuckin' massacre and John want to walk around in it. You an older brother. Bet you've seen some shit in your time. Let me ask you—you ever know of anything good happenin' to a black man in the woods?"

"Known plenty of bad shit," Clipper says, "but can't recall any good."

Merrill turns toward me. "See?"

"I've got snake boots for you," I say.

"*Boots*? Bitch, I want snake body armor."

He turns back toward Clipper. "After that we goin' down river to approach it by boat. Ever know of anything good happenin' to a black man on a boat?"

"You mean since the luxury liners we were brought over here in?" Clipper asks.

Merrill looks back at me. "See? We got history with this shit."

"Where do you want to go exactly?" Clipper asks.

"Around the tip of Cutoff Island," I say. "Would like to go across it to the Apalachiclola and then back to the Chipola and over the swamp between there and the upper Dalkeith Road. Then from Lister's Landing to the end of the road, but over the swamp, not the road."

"You got it."

He turns the plane abruptly and angles in toward the Chipola River and Cutoff Island beyond, my stomach dropping, my heart pounding, as he does.

"For fuck sake, man," Merrill says.

Nausea replaces whatever used to be at my core, my head starts to ache, my suddenly sweaty skin turns clammy, and I can feel myself about to throw up.

"Apologies," Clipper says. "I forget how hard this little plane is on passengers."

He levels out slowly and begins to fly more smoothly.

After my nausea subsides some, I start searching the area below us.

There are only shades of green, brown, and tan. Trees—the tops of which are all we see. Rivers—a wide, caramel-colored, watery border snaking around the trees.

Unlike other areas of North Florida where planted pines in

neat rows go on for what seems infinity, this thick, verdant, diverse garden is comprised of a wide variety of naturally occurring species of trees and what looks to be an impenetrable understory.

It doesn't take long to fly over the area—or to conclude that there is nothing to see but trees.

"Sorry to waste your time," I say to Clipper.

"But not mine?" Merrill says.

"Yours, too."

Clipper shakes his head. "Not a waste of time at all. Now you know. Truth is there could be several crops down there, hidden, only able to be found on foot. And if that's the case . . . you know somebody knows what the hell they're doin'."

"Somebody should," Merrill says, then shakes his head. "Lot of ground to cover on foot."

"Too much," I say. "It'd take us several months. I have a week."

30

Then

Jumping off the Grizzly, Remington jerks up on the handlebars as he thumbs the gas and the vehicle bucks off the stump, the front left tire rolling over his left foot.

Hopping on again, he shifts the machine back into forward and steers around the stump.

Get off and run for it or stay on and see if you can make it to the flats? Pass or stay in your lane?

Unlike college, he decides not to pass, but to stay put.

I've got to be getting close.

Up ahead, the thick woods appear to thin out.

Almost there. Come on. You can—

—Remember Vicky Jean? Gauge asks.

—Uh huh.

—Yeah.

—Hell, yeah.

—Remember what we said about her?

—She give good head.

—The other thing, something about her, but don't say it.

—Oh, yeah.

—I remember.

—Arl you stay where you are. Guard the path and the road. Donnie Paul you stay put, too. Everybody else set up on Vicky Jean.

Remington thinks about it. What else could Vicky Jean be but flat? Can't be voluptuous. Aren't any hills or mountains around here. No wetlands. They're going to set up in the flats and wait for me to come out.

Can't turn around. Arlington and Donnie Paul are back that way.

What do I do, Dad?

He thinks through his options. He can't go north or south. The woods are too thick and eventually he'd come out where the two men are waiting. Can't go back. Can't go forward.

The fact that he's telling them to set up in the flats, if that's, in fact, what he's telling them, means they aren't there already.

You could make your run now. Or you could hide and hope they pass by you.

He decides to hide.

As the hardwood trees give way to the longleaf pines of the flats, he goes back to using his lights intermittently. Turning them on just long enough to see a few feet directly in front of him, turning them off, traveling those few feet, then turning them back on again.

When he reaches the edge of the hardwoods, he finds a thicket and drives into it, cutting the lights and engine. Gathering leaves, limbs, and branches, he creates a makeshift blind, covering the ATV completely, then crawls beneath it to hide.

He warms his hands and face by the heat of the engine block, then pulls out the radio, turns the volume down, and holds it to his ear.

And waits.

And waits.

And waits.

—Everyone in position? Gauge asks.

—Ten-four, the big man says.

—Shit, all Little John has to do is be in the vicinity.

So that's his name. Little John.

—Yeah. Hey, big fella, would you mind bending down a little bit? Your head's eclipsing the moon.

—Bite me, Tanner.

—Okay, Gauge says, keep your eyes and ears open. Let's finish this and get the fuck out of here.

So, Remington thinks, at least five men left. Maybe more. Gauge, Arlington, Donnie Paul, Little John, and Tanner. He knows what Little John and Arlington look like. The others are just disembodied voices in the dark night.

—You think he came through here before we got set up? Tanner asks.

—No, Little John says. No way.

—Yeah, I don't think so either, Gauge says.

—Then where the fuck is he?

—Must be between here and the fire line.

—Unless he's on foot and snuck past us, Little John says.

—Arl, Donnie Paul, keep your eyes and ears open. We're gonna walk toward you and flush him out.

—Ten-four.

—We're ready.

—Okay. John, Tanner, maintain your positions and walk straight through to the line. Go slow. Look under every log, inside every hollowed out tree. Don't forget to look up, too. He could've climbed a tree.

—And don't shoot any of us, Donnie Paul says. Make sure you know it's him.

—Killer, you hearing all this? We're coming for you.

More waiting.

More thinking.

What a surreal situation I'm in. Is this really happening? I keep expecting to wake up.

Heather.

I miss you so much.

What if I never see you again? Ever.

Don't think like that. Doesn't help anything.

I'm gonna tell her.

What?

If I see her, I'm gonna tell her I'm sorry for taking her for granted. Sorry for not listening to her. She was right. I was wrong. I shouldn't've been so concerned with making money. I should've been listening to my muse, not my fear. She is my muse. I hope I can tell her. I should've listened to Mom more and Dad less. Ironically, I should've been out here with Dad more. I finally understand why he loved it so much.

Would Heather be willing to move here? Could she be happy living the small-town life? She would. She could. I know it. God, I hope I get the chance to ask her.

31

Now

"This is where he spent his last hours on earth," Heather says.

We have just left the outer edge of Remington's family's property, where the tiny dirt road ends near where Remington had parked that day, and are walking deeper into the woods that are only accessible by foot and ATV.

It's just the two of us. After putting Merrill through what I did this morning I just couldn't ask him to then come tromping through the swamp this afternoon. I told him we'd put off the boat ride down the river and the walk through the woods until tomorrow, then came out here anyway. Mainly to check on Heather.

"It's so beautiful and exotic, so dense and dangerous . . . and deadly. I love it out here. And hate it too, I guess."

She's exactly right about it. This land is breathtakingly beautiful, but deadly too. If you get too sentimental about it, it will kill you.

We're walking through a wooded area. The land here is higher and sandier than the lower, deeper, damper swamp ahead.

Since Remington had walked through here, the old-growth pines have been harvested and seedlings planted. The section of pine flats we're walking through is filled with rows of young, narrow trees some six feet tall.

"I feel closer to him out here," she says. "At least most of the time. Sometimes I can't feel anything at all. It's . . . surreal. All of it."

"Who owns this land now?" I ask.

"I guess I do," she says. "Hadn't really thought about that, but . . . this is my land now. Wow. That'll take some getting used to."

We are walking to where Remington's camera trap was found because she wants to show me something strange she noticed about it.

"I know I'm being foolish," she says. "I know I won't find anything out here looking like I have been. By myself. I . . . I just don't know what else to do. I try, but I can't stop."

"What if we narrow our focus and get some help?" I say. "Work on finding the other evidence Remington left behind and the burial site of the woman his camera traps captured getting murdered?"

"Have to be better than what I'm doin' now."

"I'll see who I can round up to help."

"Would you think I'm a complete nut case if I told you he actually talks to me sometimes when I'm out here?"

I shake my head. "I wouldn't."

"Not a complete one anyway?" she asks, looking over at me with a small smile.

"Not one at all," I say.

She looks back down, continuing to watch where she steps,

but as she does she shakes her head and frowns. "I can't believe the little shit we used to fight over, how much time we wasted on things that didn't matter the least little bit. Do you have someone?"

I nod. "I do. I'm one of the lucky ones who wound up with my dream someone. Took a while, but we finally got there."

"Don't waste a second," she says. "Don't argue over shit that doesn't matter. And don't deceive yourself about how much time you really have."

"Thank you. I try not to."

I'm overwhelmed with the desire to call Anna—even more than usual—but when I pull my phone out of my pocket I can see I have no service out here.

Suddenly sad and frustrated, I return the device to my pocket.

Once we're through the area of new-growth pines, the topography shifts suddenly.

Above us a thick canopy of laurel oak, bigleaf magnolia, Florida maple, loblolly pine, and American holly blocks out all but a small fraction of the afternoon sunlight, which dapples the dark dampening ground.

Scattered throughout the verdant forest are enormous oaks and pines well over one hundred feet tall, their thick, solid trunks as big around as any I've ever seen.

We wind around a thick midstory of smaller trees and palms, and over the ground cover of grass, shrubs, and herbs—but mostly the damp muck of wet, dark dirt.

Like a water-soaked jungle, every single species of tree and plant are connected, touching, growing in, on, and around each other. Twisting, wrapping, entangling. Thick vines like cables hang from and run along every tree. Kudzu creeps up every tree, crawls across every branch, covers every opening as if, like nature itself, it abhors a vacuum.

Mosquitoes buzz around us.

Overhead a Red-Shouldered Hawk circles and shrieks.

Other unseen insects and birds and squirrels and frogs

provide the soundtrack of the swamp. Their hums and buzzes and croaks and chirps and whistles so loud at the moment will, if we're out here long enough, eventually, inevitably, become as desultory as traffic and sirens and shouts of city streets to those in the apartments above them.

Though we both swat at the mosquitoes and continually look around us, it is the ground and in the vicinity of each step that our primary focus is on, our eyes scanning, darting, searching for rattlesnakes and moccasins, though both of us are wearing snake boots.

Heather's Chippewa snake boots are too big for her and have splatters of what looks like blood on them, and I wonder if they belonged to Remington.

She notices me looking at them again.

"Giving myself terrible blisters," she says, "but . . . I don't want to be out here without his boots on. I know it's silly, but . . . I can't help but believe his blood will protect me somehow."

"Not silly at all," I say.

"I miss him so fuckin' much," she says. "I regret every second we were apart when we didn't have to be."

I nod. "I'm so sorry."

Branches and limbs buffet us, striking and scratching us—mostly our hands as we press our way through them, and I can't tell whether the occasional stings are splinters, thorns, or mosquito bites.

She frowns and shakes her head. "Years have passed. Years. I miss him as much now as I did back then. *More.*"

I nod again, but don't say anything. I can tell there's more to come.

"We're virtual strangers," she says. "We're out here in the middle of nowhere. And I . . . I feel this overwhelming desire to tell you something I've never told anyone."

"You can tell me anything," I say. "And through your book about Remington you don't seem like a stranger to me."

"Never in my life . . . I mean not ever have I . . . even considered . . . not even the random thought of it, but . . . since . . . what happened . . . I can see the appeal of . . . suicide."

We both slow our pace though we don't stop walking. I look over at her, our eyes locking, and express all the acceptance and understanding I'm capable of.

"I don't mean—I'm not saying I'm suicidal. I'm not. I've never thought about actually doing it. Never made a plan or anything like that. But before . . . I never even—I couldn't even imagine having the thought."

"I understand," I say. "I really do. And I'm sorry. I'm so sorry for your loss. So sorry he's gone. So sorry you don't have more answers. Sorry—"

She stops walking and sort of flings herself over onto me, wrapping me up in a huge, tight hug.

I stop moving and hug her back.

She breaks down and begins to cry, and I hold her for a long moment while she cries.

Eventually, she pulls back, wiping her eyes, and says, "Thank you. You can't know what that did for me. To say it out loud like that."

I smile. "I know. I've experienced the release confession brings many, many times in my life. I get it. Telling our secrets is one of the best things we can ever do for ourselves."

Frederick Buechner's memoir *Telling Secrets* surfaces from my subconscious.

"One of my favorite spiritual writers, Frederick Buechner says, "I not only have my secrets. I am my secrets. And you are your secrets."

"It's so true."

I continue talking as she pulls herself together. "He writes about all of us having essentiality the same secrets, but how we keep them because, even though we want to be fully known in all our humanness, it is also the thing that scares us the most."

"Sounds like a book I need to read," she says.

"I highly, highly recommend all of his."

She nods. "Then I'll get them. Ready to push on? We're getting pretty close."

"Whenever you are."

We press farther in, inching our way toward where Remington's main camera trap was found.

More dank, damp swamp floor. More unwelcoming, unkind obstacles. More mosquitoes. More swamp soundtrack. More ancient trees. More hidden, haunted, harsh beauty few humans have ever seen.

Eventually we reach the small clearing where the equipment was found.

On the ground next to one of the trees is a wooden cross, dead bouquets, and faded cards.

"Did you leave those out here over the years?" I ask.

She shakes her head. "They were out here the first time I ever came out."

I find that interesting.

"Look at this area," she says.

I do.

"I'm not a photographer, but I picked up a good bit from Remington over the years, and I've studied the workings of camera traps since what happened. Remington was good. Knew what he was doing. No photographer worth his salt would set up a trap here. It's all wrong. There's no path. Animals don't even come by this way. There's no watering hole or feed trough or anything to draw them here or make them stay once they get here. Nothing. Plus the angle and light and space are all jacked. No way he set up here."

I think about that and what it might mean.

She pulls out her phone. "Look at these."

She extends her phone over to me and begins flipping through photographs of wildlife near a watering hole.

"He took these with his trap and sent them to me the week before he died. Anything around here look like the background of any of these photos to you?"

I look around some more and shake my head.

"And they're not from his other trap?" I ask.

She shakes her head. "It was where it was supposed to be and it matches the pictures he sent me from it. It's a smaller, secondary unit that's not nearly as good as this one. This was his main one and he did not set it up here."

"Unless doing so was a message," I say.

"If it was I can't figure out what it's supposed to be," she says. "And this area has been searched more than any other. There's nothing else here—no buried body, no memory card, no other evidence of any kind."

"So," I say, "someone else moved it because where it was is where the body or other evidence is?"

"I think so," she says. "We find where it was, we find the place where the woman was killed and buried."

32

Now

A lec Horn drives up from Miami toward Wewahitchka thinking about how much he hates North Florida.

Of course, he hates a lot of things. Lots and lots of things. Like his stupid nickname, which a football coach he hated at a high school he hated had given him. And it had stuck. Alec "the Hornet" Horn. Jesus. It's as imbecilic as it is obvious. He hates fuckin' traffic too. And people. God but he hates people.

His modest, unassuming vehicle is filled with a variety of weapons, but you'd never know it, nor would any cop who stopped him. They're hidden in specially made compartments and actually built into the car itself.

Like the car, the killer seems about as unassuming and nonthreatening as a grown man can. Middle-aged. Thinning hair gone to strands on top. Softish, pudgy build. Quick, corner-of-the-mouth smile. Hooded eyes that rarely make direct contact for more than a moment.

But when those small inset eyes do make and keep direct contact, it is to watch the life drain out of his victim's confused, frightened eyes.

He's lost count of how many times he's had that experience, but it's well over a hundred, maybe even as many as two.

He's killed as long as he can remember—going back to cats in childhood—but for the past three decades he's gotten well paid to do it.

He smiles as he thinks of that. His father, who beat and tortured and taunted him as if designed by a sadistic god specifically for that purpose, always said find something you'd do for free and get them to pay you for it.

Proud of me now, Daddy?

He's a proficient and prolific taker of lives, perhaps the best in the southeast, maybe the entire country. He can't know exactly. Not like there's a union or trade organization. And he doesn't care —doesn't have to be the best, doesn't have to have anyone know just how good he is. Just wants to do what he does and not attract attention to himself. Which is why he's operated at such a high level for as long as he has.

Of course, he doesn't just kill for money.

He killed a man a couple of hours ago at a rest stop on I-75 because he looked at him the wrong way. Nicked his femoral artery, slit his throat, and watched the light drain out of his eyes like the blood from his body. Look at me funny now. Left him sitting on the toilet inside the last stall on the left in the large, open, moist-tiled public facility.

Felt nothing then. Feels nothing now.

A juvie psyche specialist once told him he had two different disorders—each rare, both rarely seen together. He told him he suffered from paranoid personality disorder, or PPD, and antisocial personality disorder, or APD, but when he killed him he assured him he wasn't suffering from them at all. If there was any suffering related to them it was most certainly that of others, wouldn't he agree?

He's never killed a kid and only a handful or so of women.

One woman had asked him why God would make such a man as him as he was killing her. He had no answer for that and he told her so.

He had no answers for anything. At all.

He's not in the questions and answers business. Men who ought to know better run that sham.

He does have one burning question at the moment, though. Why the fuck did he ever agree to come to North Florida again? And a followup if he might. Does agreeing to do so, even for a huge sum of money, call into question his mental health?

He believes it just might. It just might at that.

33

Then

A s the engine cools, it begins to make a ticking sound.
Tick.
Tick.
Tick.

Remington's so close to the engine, he can't gauge how loud it really is or how close the others would need to be in order to hear it.

Rustling in the undergrowth nearby.

Radio off.

Movement.

Hands on the rifle, finger on the trigger. Ready.

Boots stamping on cold, hard ground.

Circling.

If he pulls back those branches are you going to shoot?

I can't. I can't do that again.

You'd rather die? Never see Heather again? Not be here to

take care of your mother?

No.

Then what? What if there's no third option?

I can't kill them all.

Why not?

I just can't. There're too many. Odds are too high against me. Even if I had the skills, I don't have the stomach or balls or whatever it is I'm lacking.

More steps.

More movement.

Swish of grass, scratch of branches.

Tick.

Tick.

Tick.

—I hear something, Tanner whispers.

—What is it? Gauge's voice responds from the radio.

—Not sure.

Pounding heart. Light head.

Blood blasting through veins.

Ears echoing an airy, spacious sound.

—Well where's it coming from?

—Not sure.

Tick.

Tick.

Tick.

—What's it sound like?

—Never mind. It was just a critter.

—Make sure.

—I will.

Tanner moves around the area a little more, then wanders off. Remington waits a while to make sure all the men have moved past him. Then waits a little longer to ensure they won't hear the four-wheeler.

Crawling out from beneath the machine, he lifts his head and scans the area.

No one.

Crouching, then standing, he continues to search for any sign of the men.

Nothing.

Quietly but quickly removing the branches, he puts the four-wheeler in neutral and pulls it out of the thicket.

Straining, he pushes the machine into the flats, and then about twenty feet more before starting it.

Key.

Ignition.

Gas.

Brake.

34

R acing.
       Lights off.
       Radio to his ear.
Listening.

Based on the conversations on the walkies, the men didn't hear him, don't know he's now racing toward the river swamp.

Unlike paper company-planted pines, the trees of the flats aren't in rows, but scattered throughout, roughly five feet apart. He flashes his lights occasionally to avoid crashing into one of the thick-bodied bases of the longleafs.

Crouching down, riding low on the seat in case he's wrong and one of them has him in his sights at this very moment, he drives as fast as he can, never overthrottling the engine, keeping the machine as consistent and quiet as possible.

In minutes, he is roughly halfway through the pines. You're gonna make it. Relax.

He lets out a sigh of relief, rolls his shoulders trying to release some of the tension from his body.

—You got past us, didn't you, killer? Gauge says. Impressive. Where are you now?

—You really think he's not here? Tanner asks.

—Then what the fuck we doin'? John says.

—He could still be here, Gauge says, but my gut tells me he's gone.

—Your gut's right again, a new voice says. He's on a four-wheeler in the flats.

—You got him?

No reply.

—Jeff?

Another one. Jeff. Makes six he knows of. Odds're growing worse all the time.

—I got him.

Remington turns to the left and begins heading north, zig-zagging, leaving his lights off as much as possible.

A round ricochets off the right front fender, and a moment later he hears the rifle blast.

He's on the eastern side, Remington thinks. Stay north. Get into the hardwoods.

Though not at the exact same spot, he's nearing the edge of the hardwoods where he had fallen asleep earlier. All of his efforts and he's no better off. Just as deep in the woods, miles from his truck, miles from the river.

But alive.

True.

Move about, but don't stop. Get into the hardwoods.

Another round flies by.

Come on.

And another.

Almost there.

The next round strikes his right front tire.

Blowout.

No steering.

Loss of control.

The handlebars whip left, and the ATV is airborne, flipping.

Remington feels himself flying through the air, centrifugal force momentarily keeping the machine beneath him.

Time slows, expands, elongates.

It's as if the whole event is happening to someone else, as if he's somehow witnessing the accident unfold in surreal slow motion.

Let go. Get away from the four-wheeler.

Tuck.

Roll.

He lets go of the handlebars, hits the ground hard, rolls a few feet, as the ATV sails into a fat pine, gashing a huge chunk of bark and chopping about halfway into the wood.

35

Now

When I get cell phone service again I see I have a missed call and message from the 305. It's from a DEA agent in the Miami office named Henrique Alvarez.

I listen to the message and return his call as I'm driving back toward town.

After a few moments of small talk and each of us saying what a good guy and agent Bryce Dyson is, we get down to it.

"How certain are you that large amounts of North Florida marijuana are winding up in Miami?" I ask.

"Certain," he says. "As certain as I can be. No doubt in my mind."

"And it's still happening?"

"Seized some today."

I nod and think about it though I know he can't see me.

"Dyson says you think it could be connected to the shooting you're investigating," he says.

I turn off the upper Dalkeith Road onto Highway 71 and head toward Wewa.

"Yeah, but I can't find any real evidence that it is," I say. "And in all this time, nothing has turned up—no drug busts, no crops found in the area where it happened. Nothing."

"May not be," he says. "The shit is coming from North Florida, but doesn't mean it's coming from your particular part of North Florida."

"True. And what happened in the woods that day might not have anything to do with drugs, but . . . I want to make sure before I move onto something else."

"Makes sense."

"And it's large amounts coming from up here?" I ask.

"Massive. And great quality too. People keep sayin' it's like Gainesville Green moved upstate a bit," he adds, referring to the legendary weed grown in Gainesville beginning in the 1970s.

"I'm assuming y'all looked for it, too," I say.

"Sure. Pot isn't the priority it once was and will probably be legal before long, but . . . yeah we've looked for it. Our people. I personally haven't been up there traipsing through the swamps. But we think it's more likely to be coming from a little more north of where you are. Like maybe in the Cottondale area. But that could be wrong. Hell, it probably is. We've looked all around there and never found anything there either. It was a long shot, tenuous connection anyway."

"Which was?"

"The logo. Grower uses a badass hornet and that's the school mascot up there."

"*Really*?" I say. "That's interesting."

I remember what Reggie had said about Robin coming from Cottondale where his dad coached football and how he made the mistake of wearing a CHS Hornets t-shirt when he first arrived.

"Yeah? Why's that?"

"*Hornet* has come up in the investigation of the cops who originally worked the case, the ones who were later killed. It's a stretch, but . . ."

"How so?"

I tell him.

"That could be it. We hit a wall with everything we looked at. Thought maybe it was completely unrelated to the school or the grower could've grown up there and be somewhere else now. Thought maybe it was random, like the grower had a hornets' nest on his farm and . . . I don't know, but I *do* know the shit is coming from somewhere up there, so . . ."

"But if it still is," I say, "means somebody besides the cops who were killed was involved and kept it going, or somebody took over the operation when they were killed."

"Maybe you'll find out who for us."

"Will do my best."

Passing through the intersection with Overstreet and coming into the city limits, I slow down a little.

"Let us know how we can help. Oh, and Bryce said to tell you there's one undercover female DEA agent missing. Her name is Cassandra Hitchens—Cassie. She worked out of the Gainesville office and has been missing the right amount of time to fit, so if you find the missing victim let us know. We've been looking for her for a while and it'd mean a great deal to us and her family to know what happened to her. Give me your email and I'll send you some information about her."

"Thanks," I say and give him my email address.

"I hope it's not her," he says. "But . . . in another way . . . Too much time has passed for us to find her alive, so now we just want to find her, you know?"

36

Now

When I get home I read Cassandra Hitchens' file and am immediately overcome with an urge to call and check on my girls.

I can't imagine what Cassandra's family is going through, what it must be like to not just lose a daughter but to have her missing with no answers.

Of course, the truth is I can imagine it all too well, which is why I'm calling to check on my girls.

A big part of what I do involves my imagination. I often put myself in the mind of victims, killers, other investigators through acts of imagination. In many ways that matter I have honed my imaginative skills to such an extent as to be able to torture myself with what ifs and dark possibilities.

I call Susan and talk to Johanna first.

Johanna is tired but enjoying their vacation and tries in between yawns to tell me about all she has been doing.

I call Anna next, and after a chat with Taylor, settle into a longer conversation with Anna while her mom gives Taylor a bath.

"How are you?" she asks.

"Lonely. Miss you so much. Never been in a sadder, quieter house."

"It's rarely quiet here and I get very little alone time, but I miss you more."

"Not possible. How are the wedding plans coming along?"

"Not as quickly or as smoothly as I'd like, but . . . they're coming along. What's happening with the case?"

I tell her.

"Tell me about Cassandra Hitchens," she says.

"Her older brother who she adored OD'd when she was in high school and she decided then to become a DEA agent. She became one of the best undercover operatives they ever had. She was smart and tough and could go right up to the edge of being strung out—so she had a lot of credibility. She was loaned out to the Miami office for an undercover job—they often do that to make sure no one recognizes the agents—and she went missing within a few weeks. Never seen or heard from again."

"You think she's the woman Remington saw Gauge kill?"

"Seems unlikely that she would wind up this far north, but . . . if our area is supplying Miami like they say, it's at least possible. Not sure. Just gonna follow everything as far as I can."

"Her poor parents," Anna says. "They've lost two children to drugs."

She's right. So much loss. So much grief. So much inhumanity and—

"How tired are you?" I ask. "Do y'all have plans tonight?"

"Not too and no. Why?"

"Want to meet in Marianna after you put Taylor down? Think your mom would listen out for her? We could get a room and . . ."

"Yes, yes, and *yes*."

W hile waiting to hear from Anna about what time to meet her in Marianna, I take Harvey Harrison out for a sandwich at Subway.

He's a large, muscular man who can barely fit into his side of the booth, with coarse, closely cropped gray hair and beard, dark eyes, and a dark complexion.

One of the more interesting people in town, he's funny and insightful, tough and courageous, and extremely entertaining.

The son of a Pentecostal preacher who tried to beat the gay out of him, he used to tend bar and perform in the drag show at the Fiesta before it closed. Now he runs several internet businesses, including a site specializing in gay porn from small towns, from the church his dad inadvertently left to him when he unexpectedly died.

He's a good friend of Merrick's and helped in his and Reggie's investigation into the death of Robin Wilson and the others.

"Honey, I hope you don't expect me to put out for a Subway sandwich," he says.

His low, gravelly voice sounds like his vocal cords have been worked over by a wood burner.

I smile and shake my head. "I certainly don't."

"Cool. I'll still put out. Just didn't want you thinkin' it was for the sandwich."

With very few dining options in Wewa, Subway stays consistently busy. We are at a table in the front corner, and though it's a little late for dinner, three other tables are occupied and there are two people in line.

"The kind of putting out I had in mind was of the informational variety," I say.

"Here for my mind and not my body?"

I nod.

"Shame, but . . . What kind of info are you after exactly?"

I tell him.

"Really thought Merrick and Reggie were going to solve those. They worked 'em hard enough. Even had my help, but . . . then it was like it all just stopped. Guess I always thought maybe they knew who it was but couldn't make a case. And it's not like anyone's mourning for those sadistic pricks."

"Who do you think did it?"

He shrugs. "Figured they were doin' it to themselves at first, but then when they all died. I figured it was Allen Maddox."

"Reggie's high school boyfriend?"

"He took her to prom. Don't think he was her boyfriend, but not sure. They were very interested in him back then. He was homeless and kept showing up around where the cops were being killed. Think he was stalkin' Reggie. He went missing after one of the murders—Robin's, I think—and they were like *we've got to find him*, but when I did, they had a short talk with him and lost interest."

"Do you remember what he said?"

"Not really. Something about seein' a kid in a hoodie leaving one of the crime scenes. Walking down Byrd Parker Drive from the landing where Donnie Ray Kemp's cop car was found, in a black hoodie with a big swath of white paint on it. I think. Not sure. Was only half listening."

"Allen Maddox still around?" I ask.

"Don't think so. Haven't seen him in a long time. Vaguely recall Reggie maybe helping him get in a program over at the Rescue Mission in Panama City."

"What do you know about the drug trade around here?" I ask.

"Meth heads mostly make it for themselves. Pills are the most popular. You can easily buy a little weed, crack, or coke if you know the right people."

"I was thinking more along the lines of serious producers shipping it way away from here. Heard of anyone called Hornet?"

He shakes his head. "But . . . it was rumored that—and this

was a long time ago, haven't heard anything about it in a while—that one of the main growers from the heyday of Gainesville Green moved up here with cuttings from those storied plants and started growing here. I had some one time a guy told me was from those cuttings. Had no way of knowing, but it was some damn good shit. Best I've ever had. But that was a long time ago, and when I asked him about getting some more . . . he said there was none, and that he had been bullshitting me about it being Gainesville Green."

"Who was it?"

His eyes widen. "I'll be damned. It was . . . one of Robin Wilson's boys—but he wasn't at the time. I mean . . . I guess he was still his boy, but he wasn't a cop at the time. I had forgotten he sold me that shit back in the day. If you hadn't brought it up . . . I may never have thought of it again."

"Who was it?"

"Dahl Rogers. First of Robin's men to die."

Anna and I meet in Marianna later that night.

We check into a room in a hotel out by the I-10 exit on Highway 71.

We are both horny and ravage each other like long-absent lovers, but most of our time is spent holding each other and talking, whispering between kisses and caresses, our naked bodies entwined beneath the cool sheets.

In the midst of our lovemaking and touching and holding and private exchanges I can't help but think of what Rumi said on the subject. It floats in and out of my mind while we're together, capturing the truth of what we're doing like only Rumi can. *Lovers find secret places inside this violent world where they make transactions with beauty.*

37

Then

Get up.
    Run.
Cover.
Get into the woods.
Radio?
Still got it.
Truck keys?
Gone.
Rifle?
Gone.
Leave them.
Camera?
Still in my bag. Probably broken.

He pauses for a moment to search for the rifle, but more rounds race by overhead, and he decides to leave it.

Aches.

Swelling.

Pain.

His entire body feels bruised and arthritic.

Moving as best he can, he pauses behind pines for cover along the way.

—You get him? Jeff?

—Not sure. Got the ATV for sure. Flipped it. Not sure about him. Could've clipped him. He's trying to get to the woods on the north side.

—Don't let him. You've got to stop him. We're too far away.

More shots.

Run.

I can't.

Do it or you die. Heather.

Hopping, limping, jogging as best he can, he reaches the woods, as bullets pierce bark and branches and buzz around him like dragonflies.

In the cover of hardwood.

Cold.

Sore.

Every joint aching.

Pausing.

You can't stop. Keep moving.

Breaking down over the destruction of his dad's Grizzly. He loved that four-wheeler so much.

He'd want you safe. That's all that would matter to him. Not the damned four-wheeler.

I know.

He loved it, but he's not here to ride it any longer.

How well I know.

He helped save your life.

He did.

Pull it together, you big sissy. You've got to keep moving. They're gonna be coming.

Moving.

Every step hurts.

This brings a quote to mind. What is it? A Native American saying. How does it . . . ?

How can the spirit of the earth like the White man? Everywhere the White man has touched it, it is sore.

Stumbling through the thick hardwood forest, he tries to think of another photograph, one to take his mind off the cold, off his circumstances, his hunger, his pain, but his mind won't cooperate.

—You a cop? Gauge asks.

Remington manages a small smile.

—Some of the guys think you might be a cop. Or maybe a soldier.

Furthest thing from, Remington thinks.

—I told 'em you're not a cop. You might be a hunter and know a lot about these woods, but I say you're no kind of bad ass.

—No kind, Remington says, unable to help himself.

—You still with us? Figured you might be somewhere bleeding out.

—Who says I'm not?

—You've lived a lot longer than any of us thought you would.

Remington doesn't respond.

—I could be wrong. You could be some kind of bad ass.

Remington wonders why the others remain silent. Are they sneaking up on him while Gauge distracts him?

Walk. Don't stop.

—What were you doing so far out here? You huntin' something exotic at that waterin' hole? By the way, sorry about your four-wheeler. It sure was nice. I know you hate to lose it.

Unable to help himself, Remington listens with interest, but he keeps moving as best he can, edging farther and farther into the woods, away from his truck, away from the river.

—They're taking bets on you now. You want in?

—What odds can I get?

Gauge laughs appreciatively.

—Not bad, actually, he says. Started at twenty to one, but now they're down to twelve to one.

—Yeah, I'll take some of that. Put me in for a hundred.

—You got it.

—Who do I collect from?

—Me.

—Okay.

38

Now

"What're we looking for exactly?" Hank Felty asks.

He's drinking a beer and driving the small boat from the back. Heather and I are sitting on a bench near the front.

We are riding down the Chipola River not far from the top of Cutoff Island where the Chipola flows back into the Apalachicola, near where Mother Earth had been found.

"Not sure," I say. "Anything. Everything. Just lookin'."

It had taken a lot of convincing for Hank to get off his barstool at the Saltshaker Lounge to bring his boat and expertise in all things river and marijuana in our search of where the shootout took place, but in the end a pretty woman—Heather—and a six pack of Busch in bottles had done it.

In the sunlight, the river looks watery like green tea, while in the shadow it takes on a darker green-gray-tan tint.

In the sunlight, Hank looks even worse than in the bar—red-purplish nose, bloodshot eyes, broken blood vessels, puffy face. Adding to his overall state of disrepair are his hacking smokers' cough, the tremor in his hands, and his unsteady step.

The banks lining the river, sloping down toward the surface of the always flowing waters, are a wet mixture of clay and sand, erosion exposing the root systems of oak, cypress, and pine trees that, though leaning, still cling to the more solid soil deeper in for stability.

Willow trees line large swaths of the river, the tips of their long flowing branches actually touching the top of the water.

Beyond the banks, the thick green and black swamp appears impenetrable and unwelcoming.

An egret stalks its prey in the shallows while nearby on a fallen log, a long row of turtles sun themselves.

At several spots along the river, homemade barges filled with bee boxes are tied off near large stands of tupelo trees. In other areas, the boxes are lined along wooden structures constructed farther up the hill. Bees buzz around both setups, and fly back and forth between the boxes and the blooming tupelo trees.

"See that?" Hank says.

I follow his gaze over toward the narrow overgrown entrance to a slough cutting into the state-managed land beyond.

"See that big spiderweb extending across the entrance?" he says. "That lets you know nobody's been up in there for a while. That's the kind of thing to look at when you're trying to find a place to plant your crop. If there's no web, somebody is probably already up in it so it's best to stay out."

I nod. "Did you ever grow in this area?"

He shakes his head. "I tried to avoid the swamps. I went for more hospitable areas. I preferred a pasture to having to deal with snakes and gators and snapping turtles, and mosquitoes the size of your fuckin' fist. But there's plenty who do—or used to. They like being up here 'cause not many people ever come here, let alone mess with your shit."

"You ever know anyone around here say they had cuttings from Gainesville Green?"

"Many, many years ago I heard somebody talkin' about rumors of something like that, but I never found anyone who said they had any. That was some good shit. I tried some in Gainesville back in the seventies. Some of the best shit I ever had—especially for the price. It was cheap for how good it was."

I look back toward the front again, studying the area around us as we make our way down river.

Everywhere you look, the interconnected vines and kudzu-covered trees, plants, and bushes are growing in the direction of the river, their green and brown and bark-covered bodies leaning, stretching, extending out to the slowly flowing tannic liquid making its way toward the bay in Apalachicola.

The signs of human life along the river are everywhere—houseboats, hunting dog cages, camps and cabins, bush hooks and trotlines, old abandoned hulls and stray blocks of styrofoam that have come loose from floating platforms.

"Those bush hooks and trotlines can be awfully dangerous," Hank says. "I've seen more than a few guys get hooked in the face as they rode along the river."

Bush hooks are fishing lines that hang from a tree branch down into the water, the bottoms of which have a baited hook on them. Trotlines are fishing lines that run across the waterway with a series of baited hooks hanging down into the water. People put both kinds out, then return in a day or two to gather up their catch.

Heather, who has been particularly quiet the entire trip, hasn't responded to anything that's been said for quite a while.

I lean over toward her. "You okay?"

She nods. "Yeah. Why?"

"You're so quiet."

"Just trying to concentrate on Remington, be open to any

direction he might give me, searching the banks for anything that might be a clue."

I nod. "Why don't I take this side and you take that one," I say.

"That's a good plan, but can we swap sides?"

"Of course. Tell you what. You just ease up a little bit and hold onto me and I'll slide under you."

She does and we're able to switch sides without rocking the boat or falling.

There's something sort of intimate about the maneuver and I wonder if it makes her as unportable as it does me.

"Thank you for all you're doing," she says. "I can't thank you enough for helping me the way you—"

I turn to follow her gaze. There, stretched out on the trunk of a fallen tree extending out into the water, is a small black and tan striped gator about three-and-a-half-feet long.

"Swamp lizard," Hank says. "Cute little thing. Just right for eating. Some fresh tender meat in that tail of his. Everybody wants to catch the big 'uns, but their meat is all tough and chewy. Wish I had my gig with me."

"I'm glad he doesn't," Heather whispers to me. "Didn't come out here to poach. Don't want to be a part of that."

As we near the log, the little gator glides into the dark water and disappears.

Hank revs the throttle and we continue down the winding river.

We each scan the banks and the woods beyond on our side of the boat. Hank isn't traveling particularly fast, still much of what whirs by is a blur.

We do this for quite a while, but see nothing, find nothing.

And then Heather thinks she sees something lodged in one of the willow limbs hanging down onto the water, but it's just a piece of trash.

We've only been traveling another few minutes when Heather jerks her head back.

"Wait," she says. "Turn around."

Hank eases off the throttle and the bow of the boat drops down into the water, the wake we have just created rushing under us and lifting the small craft.

Once the boat has slowed sufficiently and stopped bouncing, Hank turns the handle of the outboard motor and twists the throttle and turns us around, smoke from the engine drifting over us.

"Over there," she says. "That boat."

There in a web of cypress roots and small bushes, an abandoned boat, a huge hole in its hull, bobs as the wake from our boat reaches the bank.

Hank begins to slowly steer the boat toward it.

As we near the web of cypress roots, a thick-bodied water moccasin unfurls and slithers down one of the jagged wooden stems and drops into the water.

"Look at the top corner," she says. "That cloth. See it? I recognize it from the video Remington left me. It's faded but it's . . . you can tell it's from the tree stand he was in when he made the video message for me."

When we reach the beached boat, Hank cuts the motor and we drift into it. From the bow I reach out and keep us from slamming into it.

In another moment, Heather is beside me on the bow, looking into the abandoned boat, searching for anything Remington might have left behind.

There is nothing.

The boat is empty, only a hull with a hole in it, only river water inside.

"This has got to be it," she says. "He put that blanket on there to draw attention to it."

The shootout took place quite a ways from where we are now —across the Chipola and across Cutoff Island and on the banks of the Apalachicola, but maybe Remington came by this way first.

Maybe this is where he left the evidence of the crime he talked about in the video he made.

"Maybe he left something in it but it got washed out when the river rose."

She turns back to Hank. "Can you bring us around next to the bank? I want to get out and look around."

"Sure thing, Missy," he says, and then does as she requested.

I help her onto the bank and join her myself, holding the bowline in my hand as I do.

The sand of the bank is soft and wet and our shoes sink into it.

We look around. There's nothing here. Nothing obvious anyway that Remington could have left.

She takes a few steps inland toward the swamp beyond.

"Be careful," I say.

"See anything?" Hank says.

"Not yet," I yell back, "but—"

Heather steps on something, then bends over to pick it up.

When she holds it up I can see that it's a rusted old D battery.

"Here's another," she says.

Dropping to her hands and knees she begins searching around the ground and grass. I join her, but after several minutes the two batteries are still all we've found.

"What if it's just a coincidence?" Hank says. "The fabric on the boat just happens to be similar to the fabric in the video."

"It's not a coincidence," she says.

I step past her and search farther up the hill, deeper into the swamp.

Eventually she joins me.

We scan the area around us as we move about, but find nothing—no sign that a human being has ever even been here.

After a while, we turn and start back toward the river.

Through the trees and branches, I can see Hank having another beer in the back of the boat.

As we step out of the woods and back onto the sandy bank, Heather stops suddenly.

Closing her eyes, she mouths the words *help me*.

A moment later, she begins digging in the soggy soil, scooping it out the way a child building a sandcastle at the beach might.

I join in.

We dig for a while around the area next to the abandoned boat and close to where the batteries were found, but come up with nothing.

And then, just as I'm about to suggest that we come back with shovels and extra helpers tomorrow, my little finger hits something hard and I slide over and start digging in that direction.

Before long I've uncovered a flashlight that weighs too little to have batteries but has something inside the shaft that rattles around when it's moved about.

"That's it," she says.

I start to open it, but stop and hand it to Heather.

"Thank you," she says.

Wiping the wet sand off her hands onto her jeans, she unscrews the flashlight head and turns up the base.

A small memory card drops out into her hand.

39

Then

Got to stop.
Keep moving. You can rest when you get out of here.

His boot gets tangled in a bush, and he trips, falling to the ground and rolling. After he stops rolling, he just lies there resting, the bed of leaves soft, comfortable.

So weary.

So sleepy.

Stay like this, and they'll find you for sure.

Just a little rest.

Get up. Now.

I can't.

Then you're going to die.

Just a couple of minutes.

You won't wake up. You're too tired. At least hide.

I can do that.

With what seems like everything he has left, he pushes himself up into a sitting position, then begins looking around for a place to hide.

He sees two large cypress trees growing up next to each other, their wide bases nearly touching. One of them looks a little hollowed out. He could gather some leaves and branches and curl up in there and get some sleep without being seen.

Rolling over on his hands and knees, he pauses a moment, then pushes up, his entire body aching in the effort.

Padding over to the two trees, he bends over and begins to clear away the leaves and limbs between them.

Every joint seems swollen, every movement painful. As he lifts the last limb, his heart stops.

Spade head.

Blotchy black and brown.

Thick body.

Coiled.

Cottonmouth.

Mouth gaping white.

Remington slings himself back so violently that he hits the ground and flips over, his joints screaming in pain.

It's too cold for the snake to move much. So unless Remington had actually put his hand near its head, he probably wouldn't've been bitten, but just the shock. Just his phobia. His heart still bangs against his breastbone, skin clammy, fear pumping through him like a spike of pure speed.

He doesn't have to talk himself into getting up this time. He's happy to get away from this area, though it is probably no less safe than any other out here.

As he climbs to his feet, he notices a small structure high up in a laurel oak tree about twenty feet away.

Easing toward it, he studies what looks to be an enclosed home-made tree stand. Higher in the tree than most deer stands, it's extremely well camouflaged. Had he not been on the ground looking up at the exact angle, he never would've seen it.

As he reaches the tree, he sees a Cuddeback scouting camera like the ones his dad, now he, sells—probably sold this one— mounted about waist high. Removing it, he slides it in his sling pack.

At first he thinks the ladder is missing, but as he gets closer he sees that it's on the back side of the oak, that it starts way up on the tree, and that the branches of other trees hide it. It's so high, in fact, he can't reach the bottom rung.

Searching the area for something to stand on, he sees a chunk of oak tree several feet away—he suspects the hunter has it here for this purpose.

Rolling the heavy piece of wood over to the base of the laurel, he stands on it and is able to reach the rung. Kicking the stump away, he pulls himself painfully up, climbs the ladder to the top and into the tree stand.

Inside, he finds shelter from the cold, a blanket, room enough to lie down, two bottles of water, a bag of potato chips, some beef jerky, a couple of candy bars, a selection of hunting and girly magazines, a knife, a small signal mirror, a flashlight, and a field viewer for the scouting camera.

Twisting off the cap of the first bottle, he slings it aside, lifts the bottle to his mouth, tilts his head back, and drains it.

The liquid is as refreshing as any he's ever swallowed, rinsing the bad taste of vomit out of his mouth, soothing his parched throat, but he drinks too fast, gets choked and begins to gag. He stops drinking and swallows hard, trying to suppress the tide rising in his throat.

As soon as he stops gagging, he rips open the chips and jerky and begins eating them, reminding himself to go slow to keep from losing everything he's consuming.

Ordinarily not a huge fan of greasy potato chips or any form of jerky, Remington finds this junk food savory and delicious.

Within a few moments, he has consumed all the food and drink, wrapped up in the thick blanket, balled up on the small floor, and is attempting to fall asleep.

40

Now and Then

S oft, diffused light. Liquor-like glow. Late afternoon.
Humans.

Murder.

Handgun. Close range. Blood spray. Collapse.

Shovel. Dig. Dirt. Bury. Cover.

In flip-book fashion, the staccato images show two people appearing in the far right corner of the frame. The distance and angle lead to soft focus, the small screen adding to the difficulty of deciphering details. Based on size, carriage, movement, and mannerism, Remington believes he's looking at a man and a woman, but their camouflage jumpsuits and caps make it impossible to tell for sure.

Jittery, random pictures record the larger of the two figures raising a handgun, though a rifle is slung over his shoulder, and shooting the slightly smaller one in the back of the head. A spray of blood and the now-dead person falls to the ground like the leaves she lands on. The murderer then removes a small, folded camping shovel, kneels down and begins to dig. Hundreds of shots later, the larger person rolls the smaller into a shallow grave. Removing his jumpsuit, he drops it into the hole with his victim, douses both with liquid from a plastic bottle, drops a match, and steps back as the flames leap up out of the opening in the earth to dance in the dusk sky.

Flickering flames.

For a long time—over thirty images—the man stands adding accelerant to the holocaust hole at his feet, eventually dropping the bottle itself in and refilling the grave with dirt, covering the mound with dead leaves.

All the photographs had been taken in the afternoon light, preventing the strobe from flashing and alerting the murderer to the presence of the camera trap and the frame-by-frame chronicling of his crime.

It's early afternoon. The sun is high overhead, its beams piercing the thick canopy of trees and illuminating the forest floor below.

After giving the evidence to our crime scene specialist who also shared it with FDLE, Heather and I have assembled a ragtag band of reluctant searchers that includes Merrill, Carter Peak, Charles Masters, Hank Felty, Harvey Harrison, Mike Thomas and a couple of the men from one of his framing crews, and Clipper Jones, Jr.

Carter has a rare day off from emergency services, but his band, Mix Tape Effigies, has a gig tonight, so we won't have him long.

Glancing at our group I realize just how ragtag and misfit and ill-equipped our little gang really is. Standing next to each other, Carter Peak and Charles Masters resemble a giant and a small child. Harvey Harrison seems far too big and Mike, Clipper, and

Hank far too old to be able to walk to the edge of the swamp, let alone deep into it. Not to mention just how strong the smell of alcohol emanates from Hank—out of his mouth, through his pores.

In Hank we have a drunk, ex-con, former drug dealer, and in Mike we have the most respected and beloved county commissioner. And I'm grateful to have both of them.

In Clipper we have an elderly black man who'd rather be in a plane above us instead of entrenched in the swamp below.

Everyone has a few key pictures of the crime captured by Remington's camera trap on their phones and is here to help us find the location of the crime scene.

"Gauge's men must have moved Remington's camera trap away from where the victim was killed, buried, and burned," Heather says.

Towering over her, his long, curly hair gathered up but falling out of a bright yellow bandanna, Carter says, "They had to, 'cause I was among the first ones in from this side that day and that's where they were. I took video and pictures of them the moment I saw them."

"But now we know what the area looks like," she says, "so with your help we're going to find it."

We're all grouped together at the end of the dirt road near our vehicles, preparing to begin our search.

"Thank you all again for being here," Heather says to the group. "I can't tell you how much this means to me."

"All we need your help doing is finding the spot," I say. "As soon as we do, FDLE will send their crime scene techs to process it. It's extremely important not to touch or move anything. Just locate it. We'll go in teams of at least two, but most will have more. Every team will cover a single quadrant on the map, have a walkie-talkie, a flare, and a different color ribbon to mark the trail you take. It's easy to get lost or turned around out here. Go slow. Be careful. Stay together. Any questions?"

"I've got a question," Mike Thomas says, looking at me. "Why isn't the sheriff out here—or at least providing more deputies?"

His voice is soft and nonthreatening, though his words are pointed.

"I'm sure if I asked her—"

"Shouldn't have to ask her," he says. "Seems like some cases she doesn't want solved. I don't know. Anyway . . . Everyone be careful. Watch where you step. Stay hydrated. Try not to touch any poison. And look where you're walking. Try not to walk into a spiderweb."

"There's some mother of all snakes and spiders out here," Hank Felty adds. "We won't be able to search if we get bitten or stung so look out for each other. And have somebody check you for ticks when you're done—underneath your balls and everywhere. Little bastards love pubic and armpit hair."

"Take a good look at your quadrant on the map, make sure your equipment is working and that you have plenty of water, weapons, and supplies. We'll head out in five."

"I have a question, honey," Harvey says.

"What's that?"

"Do we get to pick our partner?" he asks, winking at Merrill.

"Sorry. Teams have already been determined," I say.

I hear a vehicle pulling down the dirt road and turn to see who it is.

To my surprise it's Reggie, and she has two deputies with her.

"'Bout damn time," Mike says.

"Mind if we join in?" she asks, as they get out of her black sheriff's SUV.

"Thanks so much for coming," I say.

When Reggie sees Harvey she does a double take. "Harvey? What're you doing out here?"

"Civic duty and all that shit, Sheriff," he says. "Feelin' butch as fuck about myself right now."

We split up into four teams: me, Merrill, and Heather; Mike

Thomas, his two men, and a deputy; Harvey Harrison, Charles Masters, Clipper Jones, Jr., and a deputy, and Reggie, Hank, and Carter Peak.

Clipper steps over to us and whispers to Merrill, "How I get stuck with the big queen and the midget? Either one of 'em pulls out a banjo and I'm outta here."

"I know we supposed to be lookin' for the watering hole from this picture," Merrill says, "but I'm havin' a hard time lookin' at anything other than my feet. Even with these damn snake boots on."

"Me too," Heather says.

"I'm sure we all are," I say. "Probably best if we pause every few feet or so and look in every direction."

"That's a good idea," Heather says, "but there's no need to do it until we're a lot farther in. He'd've set up his main trap as deep in the swamp as he could."

"Deep as he could," Merrill says. "*Great.*"

"I should've let everyone know not to waste time looking until they're pretty far in," she says.

"I'll radio and let them know," I say.

I use the walkie to tell the other groups what Heather said, get *10-4s* or *roger thats* from everyone and clip the walkie back to my belt.

"Even with four groups this shit could take weeks," Merrill says.

"Maybe we'll get lucky," I say.

"I'm counting on Remington guiding us," Heather says.

Merrill shoots me a wide-eyed *who-the-hell-you-got-me-out-in-these-woods-with* look.

When Heather begins to cry I wonder if she somehow saw Merrill's look, though I can't see how.

"You okay?" I ask.

She nods. "Just so . . . happy and relieved and . . . that we found the pictures, that Remington is vindicated. It was killing me for people to be accusing him of making it up."

"It *is* great," I say, "and he *is* vindicated, but *we* didn't find the pictures. *You* did."

"You send the best photo of the victim out to see if anyone recognizes her?" Merrill says.

"Yeah. But she's so far away from the camera, it's hard to see her. Henrique Alvarez says it could be Cassandra Hitchens, the missing DEA agent, but he can't be sure. No one else who has seen it so far seems to recognize her. No one from around here who was missing at the time fits even her general description, but Gauge was from Franklin County so we've sent it over there to see if they recognize her. Nothing so far."

41

We search nearly all afternoon to no avail.

A few areas look similar but upon closer inspection aren't the site we're looking for.

We're hot, wet, tired, frustrated, discouraged.

And then Harvey on the radio.

"I got the prize egg darlings," he says. "The prize egg. What do I win? What do I win? Do I get to pick? I want John's tall, dark, and handsome friend."

"Any idea where you are?" I ask.

Charles Masters voice comes across the walkie. "Best I can tell, we're almost dead center of our quadrant."

"Okay. Thanks. Great work. Stay put, but don't touch anything. I'm calling FDLE now and we'll join you over there shortly. Everyone else head back to your vehicles and thank you all very much. Back out and mark the area with your ribbon. What color are you?"

Harvey says, "Why pink, of course, honey."

42

Then

She messed up. Big time.

As usual, she was trying to do something nice, something kind and thoughtful, and it backfired on her. Why does it always do that?

She just loves him so much, just wanted to show him, to give him something to remind him of her during his long absences from her life. That's it. That's all.

She wasn't, as he accused her of, trying to brand him or claim him or control him. She wasn't trying to mark him or make him her property. None of that. Nothing like that. She's happy being his property. He doesn't have to be hers.

She had just made him a bracelet—one that looks a lot like the one she made herself, the one she loves so much. That's it. A gift to say I love you. A memento to say remember me, remember that I love you, that I would die for you.

What if my wife sees this? he said. What then?

She doesn't remind him that before that moment he had only called her his ex-wife, he had said it was only a matter of time until he moved out and took her with him.

She had cried so hard.

And it wasn't just that he had rejected her gift and accused her of trying to do something she wasn't. It was that she had spent every spare cent she had on it. She had skipped meals. A lot of them. Thankfully, Barbara and Nora had insisted she eat with them. Had they seen her picking scraps out of the trash? She didn't think anyone had. Maybe she just looked weak and skinny. She had skipped meals and gone without and was now short on the rent and he had hated it.

It woud've been bad enough if she had left it at that, if she had just accepted his rejection the way she had so many before him, but she couldn't. She's come undone. That's what he does to her.

To add insult to serious injury, to make sure her fuck up was not just run of the mill, but epic, she had actually called his house. She had found his home number—who has those anymore?—made up a story, and called him.

His wife answered the phone.

Stupid. Stupid. Stupid.

Why? Why did you cross this line? Why do you self-sabotage like you're trying to qualify for the Olympics in it?

What the fuck is wrong with you?

Too late now. Have to go through with it.

She pretends to be a co-worker.

Mercifully, he's not home.

Would you like to leave a message? the wife asks. He should be in shortly.

I'll just talk to him tomorrow at work. Should've waited "til then anyway. Sorry to disturb.

No problem.

She hangs up, absolutely certain he will know it was her. What she is less certain about is what he will do about it?

Stupid. Stupid. Stupid.

Then

He jerks and wakes up. Throws back the covers, looks for snakes by the light of his cell phone.

It was just a dream.

You need to go now. Keep moving.

Just a little more sleep.

He pulls the blanket back up over himself and closes his eyes. Sleep.

Dreams.

He wakes feeling stiff and sore, and when he sits up, his body screams in pain. Must be hurt more than I thought.

Check your cell phone.

I already have.

Do it again.

He does.

No signal.

Check your camera.

He does.

Seems fine. Still works.

What about the radio?

No way to know how much battery life is left. If it's a new battery, it could be days, if it's an old one, it could die at any minute. He looks at it. Seems old, strength weakening, but it's still working for the moment.

Check the Cuddeback. See what's on it.

The Cuddeback is a tree-mounted scouting camera hunters

use to record any activity near their tree stands or feed sites when they're not around. Used mostly to capture the number, size, and habits of deer, the unit captures anything that moves—other animals, trespassers. Equipped with both a still and a video camera, the Cuddeback takes color photos and video by day and infrared by night so as not to use a flash.

Unlike Remington's camera traps, the utilitarian Cuddeback isn't after art, just a record hunters can use in pursuit of their prey.

He removes the memory card, finds the viewer, pops it in, and starts watching.

Eerie, ghostly, infrared images of green-tinted deer with bright, glowing eyes fill the screen, each with a date and time stamp on the bottom left of the image and the Cuddeback logo on the right.

Color shots, mostly at dawn and dusk. Overexposed. Unbalanced color. Light. Faint. Serviceable. Usable. Deer. Fox. Coon. Squirrel. Bear. Boar.

Video clips much the same. Color. Infrared. Short. Jumpy. Jittery. Deer. Squirrel. Boar. Remington.

The clip shows his greenish, ghostly approach, glowing eyes glancing up, studying something above the frame.

Leave a message.

Erasing the clips currently on the unit, he prepares to leave a message for the hunter who will eventually come back and find it.

Think.

There's memory enough to record three clips, sixty seconds each. How to use them.

First, quickly tell about the murder and all you know about Gauge, Jackson, and the others. Second, leave a message for Mom. Third, one for Heather.

Take a few more moments to prepare. Got to be concise. He lights himself with the flashlight and huddles in the corner.

Holding the camera out as far as he can, he begins what may very well be his last will and testament.

Last words. Make them count.

When he's finished and preparing to depart, he wonders if he should leave the memory card with the murder on it.

No. The messages will be here. Don't leave them both. What if Gauge finds this place? He could, you know. Then he'd have them both. The Cuddeback stays here. Hide the camera trap memory card somewhere else.

43

Now

Under cover of darkness, the Hornet lies on the ground near a huge oak tree scoping the Jordans' house when John pulls into the driveway.

The oak is located between two houses across the street from John's, with an empty lot behind it and Main Street beyond. Several of its limbs actually hang down to touch the ground on this side. He couldn't have come up with a better blind if he had designed it himself.

The scope he's peering through is a Nightforce NXS 8-32x56 and is mounted to his Remington 300 win mag Model 700 Long Range rifle.

He hadn't planned on doing anything tonight but a bit of reconnaissance. The only reason he has the rifle with him at all is he wanted to use the scope.

But maybe now is as good a time as any.

No one is home. He's watched the house long enough to know that.

A simple, single shot. Half the job over before it really begins. Would only leave the girl. And she'll be the easier target by far— or so he thought. Hard to get much easier than this.

Small towns are the best. Very little traffic on Main Street. The house to his left is empty, the one to his right has two older people recently retired to bed.

Three options. When he gets out of the car, as he's walking to the door, or through the kitchen or dining room windows.

In the first option he's moving and it means he'll drop him on the fuckin' lawn. Will draw too much attention too quickly. Inside is better. Either option will work, but sitting at the dining table is the best option. If he even does that. How many guys sit alone at the kitchen table to eat when their family is gone? It'd be one thing if he were single and used to eating alone, but with them just away . . .

What the . . .

Before the first target even gets out of his car, the second target pulls into the driveway and parks behind him.

My lucky fuckin' night.

She here for dinner? Will they both sit at the dining table together?

Pop. Pop. Just like that. Take the second one out before she realizes the first was even hit.

Old bastards just thought they were overpaying me. Thought his ass was going to have to hunt them through the fuckin' jungle. But this . . . this is too easy. This means they're way, way over-paying me.

44

Now

I end the call with Reggie and get out of my car as Heather pulls into the driveway behind me.

She's so ecstatic that she practically bounces over to me.

"I still can't believe it," she says. "We found her. After all this time we found her."

Earlier when we found the memory card with the photographs on it was one level of vindication for Remington, but now that we've located the actual remains of the victim, it's another. It's a full and complete vindication and a major component in helping us solve the case.

"Let me help you," she says, taking one of the bags from me.

Before leaving Dalkeith, I had placed a to-go order from Tiki Grill and had picked it up on the way home. In a few minutes, Merrill and Reggie will be joining us for a late dinner and to discuss the case.

By the time we've put the food on plates and poured the drinks, Merrill and Reggie have arrived. Because each of their significant others is working—Merrick on a new podcast and Zaire at Sacred Heart Hospital—and because we all missed dinner while still in the swamp, neither of them hesitated when I asked them to join us for food and conversation.

We're all far more tired than we realized and spend the first several minutes eating and drinking in relative silence.

Eventually, our strength renewed, our bodies refreshed, we begin to talk and laugh and relive our experiences of today.

Reggie raises her glass to Heather. "To the woman of the hour," she says. "Doing our jobs for us out there today. Nice work, and with this drink I thee deputize."

"Hear, hear," I say, and we all raise a glass to her.

"I haven't felt anything like this in a—" Heather begins. "Haven't felt much of anything in a long time. And I've never felt anything quite like this. What a rush. Do you think it's the missing DEA agent?"

"We'll know soon enough," Reggie says. "Her dental records were waiting at the FDLE lab when the remains arrived."

Even with good food and good company, my house feels sad and empty without Anna here.

"I'd like to propose another toast," Heather says, raising her glass. "To the love of my life, one hell of a great photographer, and a very, very brave and courageous man, Remington."

"To Remington," we all say.

"I can see why you all do this," Heather says. "Feels so damn good. Finding the evidence. Vindicating Remington. Finding the crime scene, the victim's remains. What if, after all this time, Cassie's parents get to actually find out what happened to their daughter and give her a proper burial? I may need to change professions."

"Not many days like this," Reggie says. "It's mostly waiting and paperwork and being lied to and jumping down rabbit holes and one frustration after another."

"Which," I say, "is part of what makes a day like today all the more rewarding."

"Yes it does," Reggie says. "It certainly does."

45

Then

Climbing down the ladder into the cold, dark night, he wonders if he should stay in the tree stand.

You're just thinking that because you're hurt and it's cold.

Maybe, but this could be the safest place.

If they find you here, you're trapped.

Down here I could walk right into them.

Just be careful.

Oh, okay.

You're being sarcastic with a voice inside your head?

Why not? It's been a long night. You're all I've got to talk to.

You could radio Gauge.

He smiles at that.

Wonder why they've been so quiet? Are they out of range? Are we that far apart? What would that be? Two miles?

Probably switched to the other channel when they were all together.

He drops down from the bottom rung onto the ground, the shock shoving rods of pain up through his feet and legs and into his upper body.

How long 'til dawn?

The night is different now, the quality of light altered by the orbiting moon's movement across the night sky. The air and atmosphere have changed. It feels more like early morning than late night.

Is that just because that's what I want? How long did I sleep?

He switches between the two channels, listening for transmissions, something he should've been doing all along. Why hadn't he? He had been in shock from killing Jackson, focused on the conversations of the others, and running for his life. Probably hadn't been doing his best thinking. Still might not be.

Chances are slim anybody but Gauge and his guys are in range, but he has to try.

No idea where the others are, he moves slowly, carefully, quietly.

Should've stayed in the tree stand.

Where are you going to hide the memory card? He thinks about it. He has no idea.

How can he ensure it'll be protected and that he can find it again—or if something happens to him that someone will eventually find it? Preferably soon.

Boot banging into something. He stops and looks down.

It's a tall cypress knee.

He's standing in front of a small field of them. Hundreds. Most about two feet tall. He's never seen so many in one place before. They take up an area of about twenty square yards between a half-dozen cypress trees.

He walks in such a way as to minimize pain, holding himself just so, moving gingerly, but moving.

Where to hide the memory card.

He glances around. Everything looks the same.

Passing through a stand of bamboo, he emerges to see a small bog, water standing in it. Going around it, he climbs up the low incline on the other side and sees the remnants of an old moonshine still.

Bricks.

Broken blocks.

Rusted section of barrel.

Coil of copper, partially buried, twisting around dirt, grass, and leaves.

The things that have been done in these woods, he thinks. Wonder how many other bodies are buried out here? How many bones of indigenous people is this ground grave to? How many explorers? Missionaries? Settlers? Ridge runners? Turpentiners? Hunters? Victims?

One more if you don't keep moving. Time to turn toward the river.

He's walked north long enough. Now he needs to circle east, hopefully coming out at the banks of the Chipola much lower than Gauge and his men expect.

Exhausted.

Sore.

Sleepy.

Any benefit derived from the bottled water and junk food and sleep in the tree stand is gone now.

Got to be getting close to the river.

Stiffening with every step, his body begs for stillness, for horizontality. In the words of the old-timers around here, he is stove up.

Just a little further.

You've been saying that for a long time now. It's true this time. It's got to be.

—Killer? You still with us?

I'm actually glad to hear from him, he thinks. How sick is

that? It's like . . . what's it called? Stockholm. I've got some sort of loneliness-induced radio Stockholm syndrome.

—Won't be long 'fore these old batteries die, so I thought I'd say goodbye. Hell, yours may already be dead—well, Jackson's. It's pretty old. I may be talking to myself.

Remington doesn't say anything.

—If you're out there, I wanted to say congratulations.

Remington waits, but Gauge doesn't say anything else.

—For what? Remington asks.

—Well, Jesus Christ on a cross, he's still with us. How are you?

—For what? Remington asks again.

—What kind of shape're you in? You bleedin'?

—Congratulations for what?

—For making it through the night. Sun'll be up soon. You should be proud of yourself. Similar circumstances, others haven't lasted half as long.

—Do this a lot?

—Hardly ever. Only when we have to. But enough to know what we're doing. You now hold the record. And you won me some money.

—You bet on me?

—Up to a point. Now, I'm bettin' on me. By the way, I've got another battery for that walkie if you want it. Tell me where you are and I'll bring it to you.

—Even if I wanted to, I couldn't tell you where I am.

—Ah, come on now. You seem to know your way around these woods real good. He's quiet a moment before adding, They are big. And they all look pretty much the same. I'd hate to be out here without the right equipment. Know what I mean, Remington?

Gauge's use of his name shocks him, disturbing him more than anything else the man has said.

—I's real sorry to hear about your pops. He was a good man. I bought a good bit of stuff from him.

—How'd you . . .

—Your name? We finally broke into your truck. We were waiting, leaving it intact to get you to come back to it, but I reckon Arlington started shootin' a little too soon.

—Way too soon as far as I'm concerned.

Gauge laughs.

—Hey, killer, why don't you just come in? It's time for this to be over.

—Tempting, but—

—We know who you are, where you live and work. We won't stop. You did good. You did. But it's over now.

—You're right. Tell me where to—

—What is it?

Remington can't speak, can't comprehend what his eyes are reporting to his brain.

How can this be? There's no way.

Heart caving in as the center of him implodes.

—Remmy? You there? What happened?

He stands there speechless, radio hand dropped to his side, as he stares unbelievingly at the tree stand he had climbed out of just a few hours before. No closer to the river, to help, to a chance, he's made a full circle.

Not for the first time tonight, he's right back where he started from.

46

Now

He's got the shot. Well, he's got shots. Several shots. Hell, they're all sitting there in front of the big plate glass window like he's at a zoo or some shit like that. Be like shootin' fish in an aquarium.

But...

He's got no clean shot at the two targets.

Be tough to take all four out.

Miss the wrong one and he or she'll come running after him firing shots of their own.

Plus it'd make a big mess and a giant fuckin' scene.

Plus plus he's not getting paid to pop four, one of which is a sitting fuckin' sheriff, the other a big black mean-looking motherfucker.

Still...

It'd be a challenge.

And he's always lookin' for ways to challenge himself.

And god knows nothing else about this gig will be challenging.

But . . .

Never EVER pop somebody you're not gettin' paid for.

Plus the two targets are mostly blocked by the backs of the non-targets.

Still . . .

You could be headin' back home tonight, not even have to spend one night in this podunk piece of shit town. Be there when she wakes up.

But . . .

Never EVER pop somebody you're not gettin' paid for.

Plus which, between the glass and the non-targets you could miss.

Don't EVER take a highly visible shot and miss. Not EVER. Protect your reputation.

Still . . .

His thoughts are interrupted by his phone vibrating in his pocket.

He pulls it out to see that it's his daughter calling.

That settles it. Targets are temporarily saved by the bell.

He hops up, grabs his rifle, and answers the phone as he walks back toward the Methodist church where he parked.

"Hey, baby girl! Aren't you supposed to be in bed?"

47

Now

When Reggie's phone rings, she looks at it and says, "It's the lab."

She steps away from the table and into the living room to take it.

It's the news we've all been hoping to get tonight but didn't think we would.

Though we're all exhausted, we've lingered here, waiting for the long shot phone call, savoring the day, avoiding being alone.

"Still wonder what they were out there protecting," Merrill says. "And why we ain't found it."

I nod. "Me too. Plus where all the product's coming from. If they were protecting their crops and operation, why hasn't anyone found it? And who's really behind it or took it over when they were taken out?"

"I've got the rest of the week," Heather says. "Let's keep

lookin'. Let's cover as much of that damned ol' swamp as we can, answer as many questions as we can."

"You were talking about being an investigator earlier," I say. "That's the real thing that gets you."

"What's that?"

"The questions. The relentless unanswered and never-to-be-answered questions."

She nods and really seems to ponder what I'm saying.

"It's funny," I continue, "In many ways I went into both theology and criminology as attempts to solve mysteries, answer questions, and in both what I found was more questions and very, very few answers."

"That was your mistake," Merrill says. "You need to know something, just ask me."

"Being out there this week," Heather begins, "that deep in the swamp . . . I keep imagining what he went through in ways I never have before."

I nod. "Me too."

"It's a miracle he survived as long as he did," she says. "Well, a testament to his miraculous courage and resourcefulness. I kept thinking, *Did he step here? Did he hide here?* He had to be so scared, so . . . feel so utterly and completely alone. I just . . ."

A single tear rolls out of her right eye and down her cheek.

"He was a remarkable man," I say. "I look at his photographs . . . how dramatic and artistic they are . . . and I think how did an artist that sensitive survive as long as he did? How did he take on and take out that many armed men far more familiar with and comfortable in the swamp than he was?"

"Exactly," Heather says. "Cole took him out there a lot and taught him a lot about the land and hunting and surviving, but . . . he was no more a woodsman than we are."

"Hard to be less of one," Merrill says.

When Reggie returns to the table, she's shaking her head. "It's not her, not Cassandra Hitchens," she says. "They're certain. Used her dental records."

"Really?" Heather says. "Wow. I really thought it'd be her. I . . . thought for sure we had . . ."

We all find the news deflating, but no one more so than Heather. It seems to hit her particularly hard. Of course, it could just be the contrast from her earlier euphoria to this current letdown.

"The lab will collect DNA and submit it to see if she's a match to anyone already in the database, but that will take a while."

"So we're no closer than we were," Heather says.

"That's not true," Reggie says. "Today is still the single best day we've had on this case in years. Don't forget that. Don't get discouraged because we still don't know who the victim is. It was just a theory anyway."

"That's how this works," I say. "We develop theories and test them out. Abandon them when the evidence says they're wrong. Then develop another theory."

"Well, I'm'a take my black ass to the house so you can start workin' on your next theory," Merrill says.

"Yeah," Reggie says. "We should all get some rest. Pick up again in the morning."

Heather nods.

Everyone stands and begins to make preparations to leave.

"See you home?" Merrill says to Heather. "Where you staying?"

"With Mike and Jean Thomas," she says. "I was staying at Remington's parents' old place but got spooked."

"If it's okay with you, I'll follow you there, make sure you get in safe and sound."

"I'd really appreciate that."

As they leave I notice Reggie lingers, waiting back a little, and when they are both in their vehicles out of earshot, she turns to me and says, "Why was Harvey out there searching today?"

"I asked. He said yes."

"You know what I'm asking, John," she says. "Have you been talking to him about the Robin Wilson case?"

I nod. "Yeah. I spoke with him about it."

"After I told you to leave it alone and just concentrate on Remington's?"

I nod again. "Yeah."

"Why?" she says. "Why defy me like that? Why put me in this position?"

"What position in that?"

"Not being able to trust you," she says. "I've got to know when I give an order, it will be followed."

"Why don't you want me looking into that case?" I ask. "Because of your high school boyfriend or the fact that your son has a black hoodie with a swath of white paint on it?"

"How did you—"

"I've seen him wear it."

"No, not that," she says, and though she starts to say more, she stops.

"Does what happened to Wilson and his men have something to do with the secret drug trade around here or something that happened to your boyfriend back in high school?"

She shakes her head. "You're one hell of a great investigator," she says, "but I can't have someone working for me who just does what he wants to. I like you. Consider you a friend. I hate more than anything that you're putting me in this position, but . . . this just isn't working. And this isn't the first time you've done this— gone off the rez. I don't want to fire you, so I'll let you resign, but I want it on my desk in the morning."

"Firing me or making me quit won't stop me from looking into what really happened," I say.

"As a private citizen you're free to do anything that doesn't interfere with our official investigation."

"What investigation? There is no investigation. And for some reason you don't want there to be. Just tell me. Just be honest. You know I'll help you in any way I can."

"Night, John," she says, turning to leave and taking a few steps toward her vehicle. "It was great working with you. Don't forget. Have your resignation letter on my desk in the morning."

48

Then

B aying of bloodhounds.
Yelps. Whines. Barks.

Remington's pulse quickens when the first sounds of the distant howls reach his ears.

Everything's changed now.

He's now being tracked by man-trailing bloodhounds, but how? They don't have scent articles of mine to use. And then he remembers.

His truck.

They broke into his truck. It holds far more than they'd ever need—several shirts, a pair of old basketball shoes, a couple of caps, and a jacket.

He is being tracked. He will be found.

He'd heard enough talk around the pawn shop to know. If a scent article hasn't been contaminated, a relentless bloodhound will find his man—even at his own peril.

Handlers are key.

A good handler and a well-trained support team are vital for success with the animals. If loosed to chase down a scent, the animals who show no regard for their own safety often wind up injured or dead. Recently, one of the bloodhounds from the K-9 unit at the state prison just down the road ran out in front of a car while tracking an escaped inmate and was killed.

Bloodhounds also need a support team because of their disposition. They can find a man, but can't subdue him.

If the dogs tracking him right now are on leashes, leading Gauge and the others to him, he's dead. If they're on their own, he might stand a chance.

Run.

Get to the river—or even a slough or tributary—he tells himself. Cross a body of water—or just get in it. It's your only shot at making them lose your scent.

Run.

Running.

Maybe running is what they want me to do.

Most trained bloodhounds don't bark. The ones from the local prison's K-9 unit track quietly so as not to alert the person they're trailing. Barking warns the escapee—gives him time to set up an ambush.

Am I hearing beagles?

Beagles bark more and, unlike bloodhounds, don't track on a lead, but what he's hearing sounds like bloodhounds.

Some bloodhounds bark as they track. No telling who these dogs belong to or how well-trained they are.

Either way, they want me running. Don't mind if I know they're getting close.

But why do they want me to run? To panic? To get disoriented? Dehydrated? To hurt myself? So I'm easier to spot?

Should I stop running?

Can't.

F alse dawn fading.

     Just before daybreak.

Faint white light growing to orange glow.

Walking again. Too spent to run, too—walking's difficult enough. East toward the river. Follow the sun.

He smiles as he thinks, Walk toward the light.

If you can't find the river in the daylight, you deserve to die.

That's harsh.

I'm just saying. And find a place to hide the memory card.

I'm open to suggestions.

D awn.

     Damp ground.

Dewdrop-dotted landscape. Soft light. No warmth.

Whitetail deer darting through waking woods. Sunrise.

Birdsong.

Dogs still in the distance.

Renewed hope.

Rising temperature.

The morning, which he wasn't sure he'd see, is magical, and, unable to help himself, he spins his sling pack around, removes his camera, and begins to capture moments of it as he continues to pad east.

He has survived the long night. Has his mom?

Please let her have. And let me get through this and get home to take care of her. And see Heather. I want to see her so bad.

Then get to the river, get a ride, and get out of here.

That's what I'm doing.

Not fast enough.

49

Now

"Know how I had two jobs," I say.

"Yeah?" Anna says.

"Well a funny thing happened tonight. Now I only have half a job."

Keyed up and out of sorts, I am unable to sit down, so even as exhausted as I am, I'm stumbling through our dark, empty house as we talk on the phone.

"What happened?"

I tell her.

"I can't believe Reggie . . . of all people. I'm so disappointed in her."

Just hearing her voice makes me feel better, just being able to call her, just having her as my person, my partner, mitigates even the most challenging of moments.

"I'm in shock," I say. "I never thought it would come to this. I really didn't."

"It's like she's a different person," she says. "I mean when I think about her character, her integrity . . . For her to be . . . corrupt, to be . . . hiding something . . . covering up something . . . protecting herself or someone else."

"That's the thing," I say. "Given her character, her integrity. I've never seen her even bend a rule. This is so out of character . . . It has to be . . . she has to be doing it for someone else."

"Far more likely her son than an old high school boyfriend," she says.

"You're exactly right."

"You think Merrick knows?"

"Hard to see how he doesn't. He worked the case with her. They're . . . each other's move-a-body best friend."

"I just can't believe it. I really can't. But enough about that. Are you okay? I'm so sorry this happened. How do you feel?"

"Not much at the moment."

As true as that is, as numb as I am, I am already worried about providing for my family. It was one thing when it was just me, but now with Johanna and Anna and Taylor . . . I have to think about jobs and work and bills in a way I never have before.

"What can I do?" she says.

"Not worry," I say. "We're going to be okay. We'll figure it out. I don't want you worried about money."

You talking to her or yourself? Sounds like what you need to be telling yourself too.

"I'm not," she says. "I'm really not. Life is way too short for that. You know what they say, if you have problems money can fix you don't have problems. I know we'll be fine. I really do. And hey . . . we're together. What else matters? You don't think Heather would love it if she and Remington had some money problems right now?"

"Puts it into perspective."

"What're you gonna do?" she asks. "I mean your immediate plans."

"Keep investigating both cases. See if I can get my full-time position back at the prison. Not sure what else I can do."

"You could just take a few days off and come up here with us."

"I could," I say.

"But?" she says.

"But Heather will only be here a few more days and if it's okay, I'd like to help her keep searching her land. We made such great progress today. I feel like we're getting somewhere with the case finally."

"Do that and then come up here for the weekend."

"Sounds great," I say. "Perfect plan."

"Just be careful out there in that swamp," she says. "Stay safe and call me tomorrow afternoon when you come out. And don't you worry, either. Not about money. Not about anything. Night. Love you."

"Love you more."

"A mathematic impossibility," she says and hangs up before I can contradict her.

50

Then

Coming down an incline, he sees a small body of water, its black surface leaf-covered and death-still.

He stops before he reaches it, stands behind a water oak and surveys the open area.

The cypress trees around the water are sparse. It's a great place for an ambush.

When he's reasonably sure no one's set up, staring at him through a rifle scope, he continues moving toward sunrise, thirsty though he is, avoiding the watering hole.

Passing palmetto fronds, pushing aside hanging vines, stepping over fallen trees and around cypress knees, dead leaves crunching beneath his boots.

Stepping on long fallen branches, startling as their opposite ends rustle leaves a few feet away.

Ducking beneath low-lying limbs.

Cypress.

Oak.

Birch.

Magnolia.

Pine.

Bamboo.

The ever-emerging sun burns off the last wisps of fog, and begins to take the extreme chill out of the early morning air.

Still need to hide the memory card.

I know.

Well?

I'll do it at the river so I can mark and remember the spot.

What if you don't make it?

Then I'll have to hope the messages I recorded are found.

Climbing a small ridge, he crouches behind the wide, swollen base of a cypress stump, and searches the area.

Listen.

Anything?

Birds.

Breeze.

Swishing grass.

Clacking fronds.

Swaying trees.

Falling leaves.

Look.

Anyone?

Staring as far as he can see in every direction.

No one.

He walks along the ridge a ways, happy for the high vantage point.

Stay alert.

Eyes and ears.

Up ahead, where the ridge ends, he sees the bed of a dried-up slough. In his excitement, he runs over and jumps down into it, forgetting momentarily his injuries, quickly being reminded again when his feet hit the ground.

It's as if the pain is driven up through him with great force, every nerve jangling with it, every end, arcing.

Stupid.

Sorry.

You gotta be smarter than that. Keep your head. Shit like that'll get you killed.

Echoes of Cole in the conflicting voices inside his head.

Over twenty feet wide, the tree-lined dried-up slough bed is humid, drippy, soggy. Its damp ground caked with wet, black leaves and rotting limbs.

The trees that line it are long and large, stretching up from either side to touch each other, their tips forming a canopy, keeping the channel cool, moist, dank.

If the river were higher, if North Florida hadn't experienced such an extended drought, if those upstream weren't diverting so much water, if the Corps hadn't dredged so much, blocked so much, the area he's traveling would be under water.

How far inland it runs he can't tell, but he knows the eastern end runs all the way to the river. If the river weren't so low, this channel would be feeding water to the other tributaries throughout the swamp.

The river.

All he has to do is follow the slough bed.

Open and easy to traverse, he hobbles down it at a slow jog, his boots sinking into the soggy soil.

Thick vines hanging down from unseen limbs curl on the dank ground, and he has to be careful to avoid getting tangled up in them.

Twisting and turning, the water-hewn path snakes like a river, the exposed gnarled root systems of cypress trees growing along its banks.

Walking around the occasional small cypress tree growing in

the slough, and climbing over and ducking under large fallen oaks, he journeys slowly, but steadily.

As he progresses, he periodically scans the ground for any sign the other men have passed this way, but sees no evidence.

Stop.

Something running toward him.

To the left.

Get down. Find cover.

He searches the area.

Nothing.

Suddenly, two whitetail doe dart out of the trees, through the slough bed ten feet in front of him, and disappear into the woods on the other side.

Heart still thudding, he pushes himself up and continues to shuffle along.

After a while, he comes to a place where the leaves have been pushed back and the black dirt beneath is exposed.

A large circular impression of mud taking up about ten feet, the boar bog is fresh, and he glances about to make sure the wild hog isn't lurking about somewhere.

Confident the animal is gone, he continues east toward the sun now brandishing the tops of pine, oak, cypress, birch, and magnolia trees along the horizon.

You should walk along one of the banks. This is too open.

It's hard enough for me to travel down here.

A round from a rifle could rip through you before you even knew they were in the vicinity. The bullet could be in your body by the time you heard the report of the rifle.

Leaving the slough bed, he pulls himself up the small slope on the left bank, walks a few feet into the woods, then continues following the winding path toward the river that created it.

Progress doesn't come as easy on the bank as it did in the slough, but it's not nearly as thick as some parts of the forest he's had to negotiate over the past fifteen hours, most of the trees leaning away from him now, toward where the water used to be.

What's she doing right now?

Unbidden, but always welcome, Heather comes to mind.

Is she thinking of him? Angry or worried? Is she phoning his mom? The police? Or trying to convince herself it's really over, that she's better off without the inconsiderate prick?

It's been a while since he's heard from Gauge, and he wonders if his own radio is dead or if he's busy running the dogs.

Glancing down at the indicator light on his radio, he confirms it still has juice.

—You still out there, killer? Remington asks, doing his best impression of Gauge.

—That's pretty good, Remmy. For a minute, I thought it was me.

He's not out of breath, Remington thinks.

—Haven't heard from you in a while.

—Dealing with a fuckin' mutiny, Gauge says.

—That's good.

—Not as good for you as you might think.

—I guess that depends.

—On what?

—They refusing to take orders or actually leaving?

—All you need to know is that I'm not going anywhere.

—Never thought you were.

—Sounds like you're running. Dogs hot on your heels?

Barks. Bays. Yelps. Howls.

Closer now. Much.

The pawn shop had been a supporter of the sheriff's K-9 unit since its existence, and Remington had watched several tactical tracking exercises over the years. He pictures what is taking place not far behind him.

Big black snouts on the ground.

Ears and jowls flapping, drool dangling.

Nearly a yard tall, weight of an adult woman.

Running.

Remington's scent.

Relentless.

More moisture in the air.

More cypress trees.

Nearing the river now.

Good. Bloodhounds right behind.

Emerging from the woods, he stumbles down a shallow bank to a green, tree-filled tributary.

Narrow.

Still.

Craggy.

The small body of water, impassable by boat, is filled with the long, gnarled, bare limbs of fallen trees and the jagged stumps of dead cypresses.

Is it enough to lose the dogs?

Only chance.

Solitary.

Stately.

Sovereignly.

Across the way, near the bank on the other side, a lone great blue heron wades through the water stalking his prey.

Not sure where he is, this small slough could be part of the Chipola, the Fingers, or the Brothers. He just can't tell. He can't be sure how far he's come. Though he's traveled the river system here his whole life—from Lake Wimico to the Apalachicola Bay to the Dead Lakes—he's never entered from this direction on foot before. Thousands of tiny arteries like this one run through the flood plain of the Apalachicola River basin, every one indistinguishable from the next.

He's getting close.

This vein will lead him to a larger artery and eventually to help—tributary to slough to river.

Icy.

Hip-high water.

As cold as the water is, while he's in it all he can think about are snakes and gators—and the barking bloodhounds behind him. With every step, the soft, mucky tributary floor sucks at his boots, pulling them farther down, but he makes his way through, hands held high, protecting the camera, radio, and flashlight.

On the other side, he squats several times trying to squeeze the water out of his jeans, then shivering, follows the narrow body of water toward its source.

51

Now

Our search team is smaller today. No Reggie or deputies. No Harvey Harrison or Carter Peak. No Clipper Jones, Jr. And no Merrill, who's working security at a celebrity charity event on Panama City Beach that Carter's band is playing.

My dad and brother have joined us today. Charles Masters and Hank Felty have returned.

Mike Thomas is back, but he's not happy so few others are. "We find a body yesterday," he says, "an actual body buried in the ground and the sheriff and Fish and Game or FDLE, DEA, FBI doesn't have any people out here searching these swamps? Makes no damn sense at all. Just hold on. Tell you what I'm gonna do. I'm gonna shut down all my crews today and get them out here. Then I'm gonna move all the inmate work crews from town out here. I'll have thirty men out here in thirty minutes."

"Thank you," Heather says. "Thank you so much, Mike."

"Don't go thankin' me too much, girl. I feel guilty enough as it is. I hate to admit it, but I began to question what Remington said in his message over the past few years. And it's been eatin' me up inside. My best friend's boy, who I knew to be a good man, and I doubted him. I'm mighty sorry about that and ask your forgiveness."

"Nothing to forgive. I understand. I truly do."

We keep the same quadrants as yesterday, just have different people covering them.

Dad, Jake, and I take the first quadrant, Charles and Hank the second one, while Heather and Mike wait for his men to arrive.

Having disobeyed Reggie yet again, my resignation is not on her desk. I refuse to resign. If she wants me gone, she'll have to fire me, which I'm sure she will. But what she won't get me to do is quit.

As Dad, Jake, and I make our way through the swamp, I say, "Either of you ever heard of any drug producers or dealers known as the Hornet? Or bust anybody growing Gainesville Green?"

"The fuck you talkin' about?" Jake says. "Oh wait. Yeah. I did actually. Dad, you'll remember this. Think it was Halloween before last. May even have been three years back. Fight broke out at that party they were havin' at Potter Landing. Pretty sure we arrested the Green Hornet that night."

"That's helpful, Jake. Thanks."

Ignoring Jake, Dad shakes his head. "Don't think I have, Son. Why do you ask?"

I tell him.

"It being connected to Cottondale makes the most sense," he says. "Even if it was somebody who moved here, like Robin Wilson."

"Yeah," I say, "we've notified the sheriff's department up there. They're searching the area, asking their informants."

"Where's your gun and badge?" Jake asks. "First time I've seen you without them since you became an investigator over here. Don't tell me you've lost that job already."

Though I refuse to resign, I have left my badge and depart-ment-issued weapon locked in the glovebox of my car. Instead, I have only my own little sub nose .38 in an ankle holster.

I don't say anything right away.

Dad looks back at me and I give him a look and a frown.

"What happened?" he asks.

Jake turns serious and seems to feel bad for bringing it up.

I tell them.

"They just got rid of a corrupt sheriff over here," Dad says. "Can't believe they've already got another."

"Maybe that's not it," I say. "Maybe—"

"That's it and you know it."

"Yeah."

"You should run for sheriff," Jake says.

I wait for the joke, cut, or insult, but none comes.

"You'd make a great one," he says. "You really should. Or get the governor to appoint you when she's removed."

"Thanks, Jake," I say.

"You know . . . Nothing says thank you quite like a little nepo-tism. When you do become sheriff I could really use a job."

"You got it," I say, knowing I will never run for sheriff.

We search all morning without finding a single spec of evidence humans had ever been out here—let alone anything to do with criminal activity.

We all meet back at our vehicles for a late lunch provided by Jean Thomas, Mike's wife, and the supper club they're a part of.

On folding tables and chairs borrowed from their church, a group of about fifteen kind, funny, energetic, and spunky old ladies serve us some really, really good food—and a lot of it.

Feeding our entire search party, including Mike's construction crews and the county inmate work crews, a delicious but light lunch of garden and corn salad, cold cut sandwiches, fresh fruit, chips, cheese and crackers, and apple, strawberry, and key lime pie, these spry old ladies act as if nothing has given them greater pleasure in a very long time.

Toward the end of the meal, Heather stands up. "Mike, Jean, and everyone helping search or feed us—but especially Mike and Jean Thomas for going above and beyond in every way, thank you. Thank you all from the bottom of my heart. You renew my faith in humanity."

Jean, who is refilling one of the inmate's cups with tea, says, "It's our honor. These ladies and I just wish we could help search, but we're afraid before long y'all'd all have to be searching for us."

52

Then

E ventually, he reaches the Little River, though he has no idea
of his exact location on it.

Dogs in the distance, other direction. Lost.

The Chipola River begins at the Marianna Limestone Aquifer
known as Blue Springs Basin located just north of Marianna,
feeding ponds, sloughs, and creating swamps, and giving rise to a
variety of hardwood forests along its way. Its banks are lined with
oaks, magnolias, river birch, and dogwood trees. Joining the
Apalachicola twenty-five miles above the bay, the eighty-nine-
mile-long Chipola crosses three North Florida counties and
enters the Dead Lakes, its flow slowing its course, widening its
path as it spreads out among thousands of deadhead cypress
stumps.

The swampy banks of the Chipola are full of bald cypress,
tupelo, willow, black gum, and longleaf pine trees. The only place
in the world that supports enough tupelo trees for the commer-

cial production of tupelo honey, its banks are home to several bee apiaries and, inevitably, black bears.

As the Chipola flows out of the Dead Lakes, it connects with the Chipola Cutoff—a stretch of the river that flows down from the Apalachicola, creating Cutoff Island. On the west side of the narrow strip of land is the Chipola and on the east side is the Apalachicola.

Is that where I am? Got to be close.

What now?

Hide the memory card or take it with you. Wait for a boat or cross the river and the island to the Apalachicola.

Flowing unimpeded for 106 miles from Jim Woodruff Dam to the Gulf of Mexico, the Apalachicola River sends sixteen billion gallons of fresh water into Apalachicola Bay every single day. Falling some forty feet as it flows through the Gulf Coast Lowlands, the Apalachicola has a width ranging from several hundred feet when confined to its banks to nearly four and a half miles during high flows. Ranking twenty-first in magnitude among rivers in the continental United States, the Apalachicola is the largest in Florida, responsible for a full 35 percent of fresh-water flow on the state's western coast.

The Big River, as the Apalachicola is known, will have more traffic than the Little, as the Chipola is known, but crossing Cutoff Island isn't something he wants to do unless he has to.

While listening for the buzz of an approaching boat motor, he looks around for a landmark near which to hide the memory card.

That's it.

About a quarter mile down the bank to his left, an old abandoned boat, a large hole in its hull, sits atop a group of fallen trees. Left when the water was much higher, the boat now sits several feet back from the river's edge.

Racing down the sandy soil of the river bank, around exposed cypress root systems, over fallen trees, their long bodies extending ten to twenty feet into the greenish-gray waters, he glances over his shoulder, checking along the bank for Gauge and his men and in the river for an early morning fisherman.

Reaching the beached boat, he unscrews the head of the flashlight and tosses the batteries into the woods. Turning his sling pack around, he withdraws the camera, removes the memory card that had been in the camera trap and drops it into the base of the flashlight. He then places the original memory card back into the camera, snaps back the clasp and pulls the strap to return the sling pack to his back. Replacing the head of the flashlight onto the base, he drops to his knees and begins to dig.

The soggy sand is soft, the digging easy, and in a moment, he has dug a hole, buried the light, covered it up, and smoothed the surface. Next, he cuts a piece of the blanket from the tree stand and wraps it around a corner of the boat, then runs back up the bank so if Gauge and the others show up, they won't see him near the boat.

Once far enough away from the evidence, he finds a place along the bank to hide and wait for a passing boat. Beneath the swollen base of an enormous cypress tree, he hides among the tangle of exposed roots, giving him a view of the river and cover from anyone in the woods behind him or along the banks beside him. And he waits.

And waits.

And waits.

He thinks about where and how he's spent the night. He's always admired the beauty of the area he calls home, but now he has a new appreciation of this magical land and the majestic waters that surround it.

Suddenly, he's overcome by a profound sadness and sense of loss. Loss of life—a way of life on this land and its bodies of water. The transition from untouched treasure to turpentining, to timber logging, to tourism is destroying a place as sacred as any religion's holy land—and driving the poor from their home places as the rich raise property taxes by devouring the one thing no one can make more of for second and third vacation dwellings.

To occupy his mind while he waits, he thinks about what he likes best about Heather, his beautiful little flower.

Like the flower she's named for, she's a true Florida girl who grows best in full sun and needs to avoid cold winter winds. She's strong, but beautiful, just like the plant that is considered both weed and ornamental flower, and like the white and lavender species thought to bring luck and used to make honey, she brings nothing but sweetness and goodness to his life.

M other Earth.
    Even from a distance, he recognizes her.

An iconic figure in the area, Marshelle Mayhann, or Mother Earth as she is known, rides the rivers in her green seventeen-foot aluminum bateau, keeping watch over the water and land she so loves.

Radical tree hugger to some, river swamp savior to others, Mother Earth was an environmental activist before the term was coined.

Sunbaked skin.

Dark-tinted glasses.

Strings of mouse-gray hair dangling out of a faded camouflage bandana.

Dull black military boots.

Well-worn army fatigues.

Layering.

Long undershirt, flannel button down, dark camouflage hoody. Mother Earth looks like an elderly river rat, but has done more to preserve the rivers, land, and lifestyle of old North Florida than any other living person.

Originally meant as a dismissive, if lighthearted insult, the nickname stuck, and eventually Marshelle adopted it herself. Mother Earth stenciled on the side of her boat in bold black letters.

Growing in popularity over the years, Mother Earth eventually founded a not-for-profit organization named Friends of the Apalachicola. Its mission, to provide stewardship and advocacy for the protection of the Apalachicola River and Bay and all its tributaries, including the Chipola River.

Locked in a nearly lifelong battle with the U.S. Army Corps of Engineers over their dredging of the river, the creation of sand mountains, and their blockage of sloughs and tributaries, she has also fought against Georgia and Alabama's overuse and pollution, the loss of floodplain habitat, and explosive growth and development along Florida's once forgotten coast.

Often caught talking to the river and actually hugging the trees that line its banks, Mother Earth is as eccentric as she is effective.

He waits until the last possible moment, then stands and begins to jump up and down and wave his arms, attempting to catch her attention without alerting Gauge and his men to his whereabouts if they happen to be in the vicinity.

She doesn't see him.

Though the small outboard motor on her boat is not very loud, he doubts she could hear him even if he yelled.

Should I try anyway?

Risk revealing your position to Gauge when odds are she won't be able to hear you?

Yeah.

You stupid or just suicidal?

So you're saying not to?

Being a smartass with a voice inside your head makes you as crazy as Mother Earth.

She's not crazy. She's a hero.

Heroine. And I rest my case.

As she passes directly in front of him, he starts to yell to her, but reconsiders.

Looking along the banks to make sure he hasn't been seen by Gauge or his men, he quickly ducks back into the hole hewn out of the root system.

Depressed.

Disheartened.

And not just because he missed a great opportunity for rescue. He thinks about Mother Earth riding up and down the river, watching over, patrolling, helping, loving. All she's done. Dedicated her life to conserving one of the greatest rivers and bays in the world.

I've done so little. So little that matters with my life.

Hearing a boat motor approaching from the other direction, he looks up to see that Mother Earth is headed back toward him, this time much closer to his side of the river.

How appropriate, he thinks, that I should be rescued by a woman.

She's gonna pass by without seeing me again.

Maybe he had waited too long to motion for her like he had the first time. Maybe this time he needs to yell.

He starts to, but stops.

Looking up and down along the banks, he sees no one. Go ahead. Just hurry.

He tries, but just can't bring himself to do it.

As she's passing by directly in front of him, he thinks, You've done it again. Do you want to get killed, is that it?

But in another moment, she turns her head, as if catching a glimpse of something in her peripheral vision.

Decelerating quickly, the bow dropping down instantly, the small boat bobbing forward as its own wake catches up to it.

By the time she's turned around and approaching the bank, Remington is wading out into the water.

Placing his things in the boat, then pulling himself up the moment it's close enough, he doesn't wait for an invitation.

—Break down? she asks.

—Thank you so much.

—Sure, honey. It's no problem.

—No, I mean for all you do for the river.

—Ah, sugar, you're gonna make Mother cry. You're welcome. Thank you for thanking me. You get lost?

—We've got to get out of here as fast as possible.

—Why?

—I saw a game warden named Gauge kill a woman and now he and his friends are after me.

—What? I'm not . . . I know Gauge. He works over in Franklin County. Are you sure he—

—Please, let's just go.

—Okay. Don't fret. Mother'll get you out of this mess, but are you sure it was Gauge? I just can't believe—

—It was. I have proof. Pictures of him doing it. Please. Let's just go.

She shakes her head.

—Gauge. I just . . . it's just so . . .

As she whips the boat around and begins to head back down the river, he's flooded with such relief and emotion, he begins to cry.

—Let it out, baby. Let it all out. You're okay now. Everything's gonna be all right.

Saved by Mother Earth. He can't get over it.

Glancing back at her, he finds her weathered brown face beautiful, her camo do-rag, hoody, and fatigues stylish.

—What is it, honey? she yells over the whine of the engine and whish of the wind.

—I thought I was going to die.

53

Now

In the early afternoon, we lose the inmate county work crews, and a few hours after that, Mike's construction crews.

We're back at the vehicles to regroup and regather.

"I've been thinking," Mike Thomas says. "We're searching this area where it all happened, and that's great—hell, we found the crime scene and body and all—but what if Gauge and his men were over here—both to bury the body and then to hunt Remington because what they were actually protecting was somewhere else? I don't mean like a completely different place—just like farther east."

"It'd make sense that they wouldn't want to kill the victim and bury her where their crops were," I say.

"We've been focused on this area and the tip of the island because that's where the murder and chase and shootout were," Heather says, "but . . . you're right . . . it could easily be a little or a lot farther down."

"I'm not saying we've completely covered this area," Mike says, "but we have had a lot of people over it the past few days—and seen nothing. What if we expand our search to the east? We know there are houses and businesses to the west and south, so why not go a little north and east?"

"Especially since there's so few of us searching now," Hank Felty adds. "In fact, I think we should put a boat in and have one group look from the river side while the other searches from the land side. And that's not just me tryin' to get out of this fuckin' swamp. Truly ain't."

"Actually makes more sense to search from the river," Mike says. "If we find something, then we know approximately where to enter from the land."

"We could go farther down river by boat this afternoon and if we find anything, come in by land tomorrow," Hank says.

"Sounds like a plan," Heather says. "Let's do it."

Letting everyone else leave, Mike, Hank, Heather, and I board a boat at Douglas Landing and head down the Chipola River toward the tip of the island where the Chipola flows back into the Apalachicola, passing the swamp we've been searching through as we do.

When we reach the point where the Little River flows into the Big River, Hank slows the boat and rides much closer to the wet sand and clay bank along the right side.

"Hank, what do I have to pay you to not drink while you drive us down the river on this little trip?" Mike asks.

"They ain't made that much money," he says, raising his bottle of beer toward him.

"Why don't you let me drive, then?" Mike says.

"Just keep your seat and your panties on, old man. I drive better drinking than I do sober. That's a fact."

"If I had a dollar for every time I've heard a drunk say that," Mike says.

"Probably do, you rich bastard."

Though Mike seems serious in what he's saying, there's a playfulness and good-natured tone in the way both men are communicating.

"Everybody keep your eyes peeled," Hank says. "Look for any good-sized slough that cuts back up into the land high and wide enough to get a boat into it."

"River's high right now," Mike says. "Most of the sloughs and little tributaries should have plenty of water. We should be able to get back into them without much problem."

He's right.

We enter every one of any size that we come to.

And everyone is about the same. Canopy of branches overhead covering tannic water below filled with fallen trees, hanging vines, and low-hanging limbs.

Darker and more twisty than the river, each slough feels like a slow boat ride back into an ancient, untouched land time forgot.

Though the water is high, the narrow channels still have many trees and stumps just beneath the surface, the outboard motor hitting and popping up over each one, slowing our already slow progress.

Along the banks, trees, many with exposed root systems, lean out over the water, their trunks covered with thick vines, their branches host to Spanish moss and kudzu.

Beyond the shallow tree-lined banks, a thick, damp and dank jungle-like swamp extends toward an unseen infinity. Or so it seems.

In each slough we wind and twist our way around and beside and under jagged fallen tree trunks and hanging limbs and thick branches. Each time I think we will stop and turn around far sooner than we do, but somehow Hank manages to both fit the boat into impossibly small looking spots and get it out again.

About half a mile back in the fourth such slough, Hank cuts the engine and points to a huge gnarled cypress tree on the left side of the bank.

Heather, Mike, and I follow his extended arm, but can't make out what he's trying to direct our attention to.

"Six feet up," he says. "On the right side, just below that big knot right there."

We look again.

Just below the knot he's referring to is a barely visible notch, looked to have been made by a pocket knife in what might be the shape of a crude hornet—though I could be imagining that part.

"What is it?" Mike asks.

"Grower's mark," Hank says. "Been there a while, but . . . that's what it is. Y'all want to get out and have a look?"

"Of course," Heather says.

"How dangerous is it?" Mike asks. "Promised Miss Jean I'd make it home for dinner this evening."

"You never know," Hank says, "but my guess is nobody is up here. It may even be an old site. The mark looks pretty weathered."

We find the remnants of a once-major operation about half a mile walk in.

Cleared and tilled patches of land hidden beneath the ancient oaks and pines where rows and rows of post plants once thrived.

Stacks of plastic five-gallon buckets, hoes, rakes, and shovels. An irrigation system that pumped water out of the river.

Now it looks like an abandoned farming operation, but it's obvious that at one time it was a massive grow field.

"This is a very smart setup," Hank says. "See how they planted in patches—a little here, a little there. And how the trees hide it from airplanes or helicopters but the sun still reaches the rows."

"This has got to be it," Heather says. "It was massive. And it's on Cole's land."

Mike nods. "Has to be."

Hank says, "You think Cole was involved?"

"No," Heather says. "No way."

"To pay for his wife's illness," he adds.

"Absolutely not," Mike says. "You of all people should know growers always plant their crops on somebody else's land."

Hank stops walking suddenly and stares in the distance. "Look over there."

We follow his gaze but don't see anything but thick green forest.

"See that?"

"What?" Heather says. "I only see trees."

"Look closer. That's a greenhouse."

"Huh?" she says.

We follow him over to the area he's talking about and find a series of portable camouflaged buildings with military-looking green-and-camo netting covering them. Even a few feet away they are indistinguishable from the trees and underbrush surrounding them.

Gathering back the netting and finding a door, he pushes it open to creaks of protest and leads us inside.

Filled with wooden shelves, plastic pots, bags of potting soil and fertilizer, below a green-tinted skylight and a hanging PVC irrigation system, whatever once grew here is long gone, but the scope and sophistication of the operation is obvious.

"Pure genius," Hank says. "The whole set-up. And almost totally invisible. Bet they had generators out here, too. It's simple yet sophisticated. Water from the slough, light through the trees, hidden as hell. I'm not easily impressed, but this is . . . I'm impressed."

"Why abandon it?" Heather says.

Hank shrugs. "Not sure. I wouldn't if it were mine. Probably too much heat from the shootout or . . . maybe the boys who were killed were the ones running it."

Mike says, "But if it was theirs and they were killed and never got to come back to it, there'd still be plants all around—and the generators for the hothouses and the pump for the irrigation."

"True," he says. "Maybe somebody stumbled upon it and took everything. Maybe it has nothing to do with Gauge and the rest of them, but it'd be a wicked, ungodly coincidence if that's the case. Who knows?"

"If someone else was behind the operation and Gauge and the others just worked for them, it'd make sense that they'd keep it going. It might even make sense that they'd leave this site, but why leave so much behind?"

"Too much heat," Hank says. "Took what they could in one trip. Plants were the priority. I don't know. Just guessing."

"The more pressing question is where did they move it to?" I say. "How is such a massive operation still happening right under our noses?"

"Why do you think it is?" Mike says.

"We have it on good authority that North Florida is supplying a big part of South."

"Really?" he says. "Damn. That's hard to imagine."

"Think about how long this one must've run without anyone ever knowing," Hank says.

54

Then

The boat bounces, its front end bucking up and down, slapping the hard surface of the river. The spray from the water feels like tiny shards of ice pelting his face, the cold wind causing his eyes to water, then blowing the tears out on his temples.

—I thought we were closer to the foot of the island, he says.

—It's about another mile, mile and a half.

He nods.

—I want to join Friends of the Apalachicola.

—We'd love to have you. There's so much to be done. Right now the state refuses to give the Corps the permits they need to continue dredging, but they're fighting it—and we've got so much to undo from all the damage they've already done. Between them and what Alabama and Georgia're doing with pollution and damming, they're destroying an entire ecosystem.

He nods again.

—It's the way of the world, she continues. The folks downstream are always at the mercy of the people upstream. All this begins in north Georgia with the Chattahoochee. It has five major dams on it and supplies the water for metro Atlanta. Atlanta's polluting like a bastard, but they've decided to pay fines rather than fix their problems. That shouldn't be an option.

—How can I help?

—Well, first—

Her throat explodes, then the side of her head, and she slumps over dead in the bottom of the old bateau.

At first, he's so shocked he can't move, but as rounds continue to whiz by him and ricochet off the boat and the motor, he drops down into the hull, his frightened face inches from Mother Earth's lifeless one.

What have I done?

Terror.

Panic.

Futility.

Rounds continue to ricochet around him, but he doesn't move. He can't.

Numb.

Despondent.

Lost.

He can't think, can't move, can't—what?

Death.

Despair.

Distance.

He feels himself coming untethered again.

Adrift.

Are you going to die right here?

It looks like it.

Just give up? Give in? All you've survived and now you're just going to quit?

I can't . . .

You can. Come on. You've got to make Gauge pay for this. You can't let him get away with killing Mother Earth—he can't believe she's really dead—and who knows how many other people.

She's dead because of me. I got her killed.

And set back the environmental movement in ways you can't even comprehend.

Circles.

Without Mother's hand to guide it, the spinning propeller of the outboard motor has turned, and the boat is making large clockwise circles in the middle of the river.

How long before it spins around too fast and capsizes?

Bullets continue to pock the aluminum sides of the bateau, some of them piercing the hull, and the small craft begins to take on water.

You've got to make your move now. Wait much longer and it'll be too late.

Searching the boat as best he can in his prostrate position, he finds a small blued snub-nosed .38. Clicking open the cylinder, he sees it has all five rounds.

Shoving the handgun in his jacket pocket, he crawls toward the back of the boat, staying low to avoid getting shot, his body bumping up against Mother's.

Reaching the back of the bateau, his hands, face, and clothes wet, muddy, and smeared with blood, he lifts his hand just enough to grab the throttle and pivots the motor away from the gunfire and toward Cutoff Island.

Heading away from the shooters, fewer rounds come near the boat, and only the motor housing suffers any hits.

Crashing the boat into the bank, Remington crawls to the front, over the bow, dropping onto the mud and roots, and begins to run into the woods for cover.

More rounds.

Thwacking trees.

Splintering roots.

Splattering mud.

And just as he's about to make it into the thick swampy woods of the Cutoff, a round hits his right calf.

Searing.

Falling.

Rolling.

Dragging his injured leg, he claws his way up the incline and into the cover of ancient trees and thick understory.

Glancing back past the boat and across the river, he sees only two men with rifles standing there.

Is that all that's left?

Did the others leave?

Is one of them Gauge?

When he turns back around, he's staring at mud-covered snake boots not unlike his own.

—Hey, killer, Gauge says, a pleasant smile on his face.

55

Now

Patience.

People ask, what's the single most important ingredient to a successful hit?

It's patience.

You gotta wait—sometimes for hours—for a split second of work.

And that's exactly what the Hornet is doing, has been doing for a few hours now.

Waiting.

But not just waiting. Waiting patiently.

He's set up not far from their vehicles.

Ready.

It's late afternoon and he knows it's entirely possible they won't come out until near dark or dark, so he has his night vision equipment, too.

Prepared.

Preparation is important. But patience is more important.

Of course, the most important ingredient is sociopathology. You gotta not care about the killin'. You gotta be like there are over seven billion people on the planet, what's one less gonna matter? You gotta feel nothin', no empathy, no remorse, no nothin'. But that has to do with being able to do the job. Doin' the job itself requires patience. It's that simple.

Patience is more important than skill. It'll keep you alive. This is shit that, if you rush, will bite you in the ass. Hard. You rush, you miss, you make mistakes, eventually you get caught.

He reckons he's the most patient person on the planet. Still, he wishes they'd come on. They get out here and get this over with soon enough, he can be back in Miami by the time his daughter wakes up in the morning. He'd like that.

Pop. Pop. Two quick shots and he's out of here.

And here they come. Ahead of schedule. But not like he expects. They're coming not from the swamp, but down the little dirt road.

No matter. He doesn't ask why or wonder where they've been. He's an incurious man—another thing that makes him good at what he does.

Adjust.

He simply makes adjustments.

The only thing he's curious about—well, the two things are . . . how quickly will whoever's dropping them off leave, and will they stand around talkin' to each other long enough for a clear, open shot?

56

Then

—Took you long enough to get here, Gauge says. You came out a lot lower than we thought you would.

—Not low enough.

Pressure.

Unzipping his boot, Remington presses the gunshot wound in his leg with his hand, attempting to stop the bleeding.

—Just think, if she'd've taken you upriver instead of down, you'd've gotten away—for a little longer anyway.

Remington remains on the ground, Gauge hovering above him, looking down the barrel of the shotgun at him.

Throbbing.

His calf muscle feels like it's being stabbed with a serrated blade, then twisted, pulled out, and thrust back in again.

—You down to two men?

—Three. Sent one on an errand.

—What happened to—

—They retired.

—Bet a lot of people who work for you get early retirement.

He smiles.

—Before you retire me, you should know I have evidence against you and I've hidden it where it will be found.

—What sort of evidence?

Remington withdraws the small pocket knife from his jeans.

—You brought a knife to a gun fight? Gauge asks, smiling, amused, pleased with himself.

Opening his jacket, Remington cuts a strip of his T-shirt and wraps it around his leg over the wound, the pain spiking as he tightens it, then partially zips his boot up.

—Goin' to a lot of trouble for a man about to die.

Remington shrugs.

—Tell me about this alleged evidence.

Remington doesn't say anything.

—Let me rephrase, Gauge says, pumping his shotgun, jacking another round into the chamber.

A perfectly good round is ejected from the gun and falls on the ground not far from Remington's leg, and he realizes the action was only taken for dramatic affect.

—Photographs.

—Pictures of me out in the woods at night's not gonna be a problem.

—I have pictures of the murder.

—Bullshit.

—It's true.

—How?

Remington tells him about the images captured by the camera trap.

—Where is it?

—I also recorded a video message.

—Let's see what's in your bag.

Remington turns his sling pack around and opens it.

—Show me what's on the camera.

Turning it on, Remington sets it to display the images stored on the memory card, and hands it to him.

Without lowering his gun, Gauge holds the camera with one hand, thumbing through the pictures, his eyes moving back and forth between Remington and the small screen.

—These shots of the bears are fuckin' awesome.

—Thanks.

—Where're the rest of them? Arl told me he saw you take pictures of the fireflies when you was on the four-wheeler.

—Yeah. They're on the other memory card—the one that was in the camera trap. The one with you on it. I had taken it out of the trap and was viewing it in this camera when you showed up. It was in this camera until I took it out to hide it, so everything else I took last night is on it.

—Where'd you hide it?

Remington doesn't say anything.

—Suit yourself. Strip down. I'm gonna have to search you.

Remington nods and tries to stand, slowly turning his wounded leg several ways before giving up.

—Here, Gauge says, offering his hand.

Grabbing it with his left, Remington pulls himself up with Gauge's help, slipping his right hand into his jacket pocket in the process and coming out with Mother's .38.

Upright.

Continuing to hold Gauge's arm, Remington puts the barrel of the handgun to his temple.

—My my. What have we here? You're packin'?

—Borrowed it from a friend. Drop your shotgun.

He doesn't move.

—Do it or, poetically, you'll be killed by the gun of the woman you killed a few minutes ago.

—Poetically? Jesus.

—You don't think I'll do it?

—No, I've seen what you're capable of, killer.

—Then drop the goddamn gun.

He does.

—Now what?

—Walk.

—Where?

—To the Big River.

—Through the island?

—Yeah.

—What about your leg?

—Walk.

57

Now

Mike gives us a ride back from the landing in his white Platinum F-150 and insists that we join him and Jean for dinner tonight.

We left our vehicles where we had parked them for the search earlier in the day at the end of the dirt road on Cole's property where Remington had entered the woods that fateful day and had ridden to the landing with Mike.

"I know there's a few hours of daylight left, but don't even think about going back out there in those woods," he says.

He's looking at Heather.

"I'm just gonna go back in a little ways and say goodnight to Remington," she says. "No more searching today. I'll just be a few minutes. I'll be home in time for dinner."

He nods. "Okay. How about you, John? Will you join us?"

"Thank you. I'd love to. I'm going to wait here for Heather to say goodnight to Remington, then when I have cell service again I need to call in what we've found, but then I'll grab a quick shower and be over."

"See y'all then. I'll even invite ol' Hank. He deserves it after what he found today."

"Yes, he does," Heather says. "None of us would've ever found it."

As we climb out of the truck and Mike turns around to leave, I can see Reggie's black sheriff's SUV pulling down the dirt road.

"Don't feel like you have to wait for me," Heather says. "I'll be fine."

"I'm not going anywhere," I say. "I'll tell Reggie about what we found. Be here waiting when you get back. Tell Remington I said hello."

"Thank you, John."

Reggie and Mike wave to each other but don't stop and talk, and in another moment she's pulling up in front of me.

She cuts her engine and gets out.

"Where's she going?" she asks, looking after Heather who is disappearing into the woods.

"Have a little chat with Remington."

She nods and purses her lips as she continues to stare in Heather's direction.

"I was going to call you when I got service again," I say.

"That's why I'm out here," she says. "'Cause there's no damn service. I've tried callin' you several times today."

"What's up?" I say.

"You go first."

"We found what used to be a major growing operation," I say, and proceed to tell her about it.

"That's great. I'll let DEA know and y'all can take them to it tomorrow. So there was a massive operation over here and . . . what? After the shootout they moved it?"

I shrug. "Maybe."

"Where?"

"That's what we've got to find out."

"Up to Cottondale?" she says. "May not even be in our county any longer."

"May not be. What were you calling me about?"

"Noticed your gun and badge and resignation letter weren't on my desk this morning," she says.

I nod. "I'm not quitting. You'll have to fire me."

"I was glad it wasn't there," she says. "I regret what I said and did last night. Didn't sleep a wink. Was hoping to talk to you this morning when you came in, but you didn't. I'm sorry for how I acted. It was wrong."

I think about how, in general, women apologize more quickly and more often than men and wonder again what kind of a world it would be with far more women in key leadership positions— particularly women who didn't feel they had to masculinize themselves to get there.

"I'm not going to fire you," she says. "I'm asking you to trust me and let the Robin Wilson thing go, but if you won't . . . I won't try to stop you."

"You're asking for my trust but not telling me anything, not giving me anything to go on."

"Yes. That's what trust is. I had hoped we had built up enough trust so you would just . . . well, trust me. I've trusted you several times over this past year. In big ways. I've had your back. Taken heat for you. Thought we were far more than co-workers."

"We are."

"I'll say this and that's all," she says. "I swear to you on my word and the life of my child that neither Allen nor Rain did it and I'm satisfied justice was done in the case. Please, please let that be enough."

I don't say anything, just think about it.

"Please," she says again.

I continue to think about it, scanning the trees in the distance, the glint of something catching my eye.

"Can I ask you ... do you believe me?" she says. "Do you know that I'm telling you the truth about Allen and Rain?"

I nod. "I believe you. I'm ... I'll have to think about it. Give me a little while to process it. I won't do anything else on the case until I talk to you."

"That's all I can ask. Thanks."

58

Now

Goddammit!

The fuckin' sheriff again.

She cockblocked his play before, but not this time. She can die out here with the others today. Had enough of her stoppin' my fuckin' move. No more.

He looks through his scope again.

*Mother*fucker!

Not only is she cockblocking him, but her goddamn big black SUV is, too.

Is there a shot at all? Through the windows of her vehicle? Glass will alter the shot. Can he still make it?

Options?

Relocate. Move to a better position. But that takes time. More chance of being seen.

Take the shots from here. But the glass could alter the shot too much.

Wait. Hope the sheriff leaves before the other target comes back out of woods. What'd she go in there for by herself anyway? A nature call? If so, she'll be back soon.

Just start firing. Pin them down. Fire until you hit them. Draw Nature Calls Girl out of the woods. Move in on 'em to finish 'em if you have to.

Before he consciously realizes what he's done, he's made his decision. Or rather his trigger finger has.

59

Then

Branch and leaf canopy above.

Sun-dappled ground below.

Lacking the ridges of the woods on the other side of the Chipola, the island is flatter, its soil soggier.

Near the foot of the island, the walk across is around a mile, but with the pain from his calf shooting up to his knee and down to his foot, Remington's not sure he can do it.

—Movin' sort of slow there, aren't you, killer? You gonna make it?

—I'll make it.

Remaining no less than five feet behind Gauge at any time, Remington ensures that he can't just whip around and grab his gun before he can fire it.

—You might make it across the island, but you know you're not getting out of this, don't you?

—You better worry about yourself.

—I'm not saying I'll make it. You've got the drop on me. No doubt about it. I may be meetin' my maker today, but you definitely are. Even if you pop me, they'll still get you. They can't let you leave these woods alive.

—What will you say?

—Huh?

—To your maker. What will you say?

—About what?

—Your life. Killing people.

—All I've ever done is what I've had to. I've just tried to survive—just like you're doing now. It's a cold, cruel world. I didn't create it. I'm just existing in it. You see the way nature works. There's a food chain—predators and prey.

—Gauge? Where are you, man? What happened?

The words come from both radios simultaneously, creating a stereo sound with a split-second delay.

—Aren't you willing to shoot me? Gauge asks Remington.

—Only if I have to.

—To survive, right? That's all I'm saying. We've got to survive. That's our job.

—I think it's more than that.

—Gauge? Arlington says again.

—You want me to answer that?

—No.

—Tanner's on his way back with the package. Do we still need it?

—What's he talking about?

—Ask him.

—I'm asking you.

—And I'm saying ask him.

—Just keep walking.

60

Now

At first I think Reggie got stung by a wasp or yellow jacket. But as she turns to reach for the sting on her back, blood shows above her belt in the front and the round coming through her hits the front right tire of my car.

Though it only takes a fraction of a moment for me to realize she's been shot, everything seems like it's happening in slow motion.

My movements feel awkward and sluggish, like my reaction time is a step behind.

I tackle Reggie to the ground and pull her over to me, putting both of us behind the back passenger-side tire of her vehicle, as shots land all around us.

Divots of dirt pop up. Glass shatters. Rounds ricochet off metal, pierce plastic, puncture rubber.

Soon all three vehicles are shredded. Windows out. Engines shot up. Tires flat.

I've yet to hear a report or echo.

He's got a silencer on a long-range rifle.

The glint. The shots are coming from the area where I saw the glint earlier.

So stupid. Should have checked it out when I saw it. Instead, I thought it was a bottle or can or some other shiny discarded object left out here.

The guy is clearly a professional. Did Chris hire a hitman? Is he after me and Reggie was just in the wrong place at the wrong time? Or does he think Reggie is Anna?

Reggie's hit bad.

Blood everywhere. Pale, clammy face. Frightened eyes.

She's going into shock.

I apply pressure to the wound, to the front and back, her blood oozing out through my fingers.

"They raped me," she says.

Her voice is soft and dry.

"What? Who?"

"The night of our prom. Robin and his boys."

"I'm so sorry," I say, "but don't worry about that right now."

"I moved back to make them pay. Knew they were dirty. Knew I could get them. Legally. My mom found out what they did and . . . she was dying or . . . thought she was. She . . . took them out one by one for what they did to me and . . . to my niece. Feeble old lady . . . they never saw her coming. Please . . . don't hurt her. Please let her . . . She doesn't have long."

Her eyes close.

"Reggie? Reggie?"

Without opening her eyes she says, "Save Heather. Don't let her die out here like Remington did."

"We'll save her," I say. "Together. I need your help. We'll—"

Just then a round sears white hot through my right quadriceps.

61

Then

Blood loss.
Lightheaded.
Stiffness.
His leg hurts so bad he figures there must be nerve damage.
Cold sweat.
Clammy skin.
—You don't look so good, Gauge says.
—Keep moving.
Thirst.
Hunger.
—Donnie Paul's a hell of a tracker. Not that he'd have to be to follow the blood drops trailing after you. They'll be coming. Catch up to us quick, as slow as we're moving.
—Whatever happens, you get shot first.
—You're a stubborn sumbitch, I'll give you that, but goddamn.
—You sure talk a lot.

—Rather walk in silence? Fine by me. Just trying to pass the time until you die.

—Or you.

—More likely you.

—No doubt, but right now you're the one on the wrong side of this little revolver.

—I told you, having the drop on me doesn't get you anywhere. They can't let you live any more than I can. You're outnumbered, outgunned, almost out of time.

—And yet I'm still here.

—Oh, you've done good. I'll give you that, but making it through the night and making it out of the swamp are two very different goddamn things.

—Well, if what you say is true, Remington says, grant a dying man his wish and shut the fuck up.

—You got it, killer.

62

Now

Both hit.

No way to tell how bad.

But both are down.

Keep firing. Keep them pinned down.

Keep checking woods.

When the other target comes out of the woods, she'll be confused, will try to help. One shot to the head.

But got to finish these other two off first. Now.

He looks for any part of the two on the ground, scanning the area around them with his scope.

Continuing to fire rounds, trying to get them to move.

He's never been more ready to be finished with a job and far away from a place.

He really wants to be home when his daughter wakes up in the morning. Besides, how long is it before he's bitten by a snake or spider or a mosquito carrying the fuckin' Zika virus?

Shoot the shit out of them and get the fuck out of here.

63

Now

I fall down onto Reggie. She doesn't even open her eyes.

The pain is immediate and excruciating and I can only imagine what Reggie is feeling, hoping that she's feeling anything at all.

With rounds still flying around us, I pull off Reggie's coat and belt. Wrap the coat around her wound and fasten the belt around it, as tight as it will go.

As soon as I finish with her, I pull my own belt off and tighten it around the wound in my leg.

Got to get Heather. Got to get us out of here.

Awkwardly, I pull myself up by the tire, careful to stay bent over so the SUV is between me and the shooter.

With no weight on my right leg, I lean over, grab the door handle and pull the door open, nearly falling down several times during the simple process.

Gotta be quick. Can't be exposed for even a second longer than you have to or he'll put one in your head.

Create a diversion.

Reaching down, I pull off one of Reggie's boots.

Then gathering her up to me as best I can, I toss the boot out toward the front of the vehicle and drag and pull her with me around the door and inside her SUV, staying below the driver's side window as I do.

With her crumpled in the passenger's side—partially on the seat, partially on the floorboard—I pull the door closed and crawl into the driver's side.

Reaching back over and digging the keys out of her pocket, I return to crouching down in the driver's seat, insert the key, start the engine, pull down the gear shifter, and stomp on the gas.

Without looking where I'm going, I head straight. Or as straight as I can without being able to see and on four flat tires that resist rolling, let alone turning.

I drive toward the spot in the trees where Heather entered the woods, hoping to block her from the sniper shots when she returns.

64

Then

Mouth dry.
      Leg feverish and swollen.
Seeping.
Steady drip.
He's got to get to the river and out of the swamp soon. Think of Heather and keep walking.
If you get out of here, you'll owe her your life.
I plan on giving it to her—if she'll have it.
You know she will. She was never ambiguous about what she wanted.
Stumbling.
Shuffling.
Dragging his right leg.
Think of her.
—Huh?
—Where'd you go, killer?

—What'd you say?

—I said, why are you doing all this?

—A woman. Why else?

—Your mom?

—Okay. Two women. Let's stop here and rest a minute.

—Gauge, if you can hear us, we wanted to let you know we're coming to get you. Me and Arlington are behind you, and Tanner's on the other side.

It's the first time the radio has sounded in a while.

The two men sit five feet apart, Remington leaning against the base of a birch, elbow resting on the ground, gun held up, pointed directly at his prisoner.

—Who was the girl? Remington asks. Why'd you kill her?

—You'll die without ever knowin'.

—Or maybe I'll kill you and find out from the investigators.

—She's gone. Doesn't matter to her anymore. Why should it to you?

—When I first entered the woods last night I saw a gaunt old man. I think he was a poacher. Shot a black bear. Did you kill him?

He smiles.

—Not for shooting no damn bear, he says.

Rustling.

Padding.

Light footfalls on leaves.

Remington lifts his arm and extends the gun toward Gauge.

—Slide over here.

Gauge doesn't move.

Remington thumbs back the hammer.

—I'm coming. I'm coming.

—Hands behind your back. Back toward me.

When Gauge is close enough, Remington wraps his left arm around his throat, places the gun to his temple, and waits.

A moment passes.

Then another.

And then a young hunting dog with a tracking collar walks out of the underbrush. Moving too slowly to be after them, he's most likely lost.

Tilting his head, his eyes questioning, the dog seems to look at the two men for guidance.

—He doesn't belong to us, Gauge says.

About two feet tall, the Redbone coonhound's solid short hair is the color of rust in water. Floppy ears. Long tail. Black nose at the end of a long muzzle. Amber-colored eyes.

Remington releases Gauge and pushes him. He slides back to his previous position a few feet away.

Remington whistles.

—You lost, boy? Come here.

He does, wagging his tail, whimpering.

—That's a good boy, Remington says, as he pats and rubs him. You got a name?

Searching the collar beneath the tracking device, Remington smiles and shakes his head when he reads it.

—What's his name? Gauge asks.

—Killer.

He laughs a lot at that, his face showing genuine amusement.

—Now that you've got some company, can I go?

Remington shakes his head.

—Let's go. Time to move.

Using the tree for support, Remington manages to get upright again.

—Need a hand? Gauge asks, smiling.

—Walk.

He does, and Remington falls in a few feet behind him, whistling for the hound to join them, which he does for a short while before veering off into the woods and disappearing.

Leg worse.

Much worse.

Swollen.

Stiff.

Nearly unusable.

His dragging boot leaves a smooth flat track smeared with blood in the soft dirt.

—We're almost to the other side, Gauge says. You gonna make it? I'd hate for you to miss the surprise.

—I'm gonna make it—all the way out of here.

—Man needs a dream.

Remington steps closer, holds the .38 down low, aims, and shoots Gauge in the right calf.

His leg buckles and he falls down, rolling, grabbing his leg.

—Fuck.

Breathing fast and heavy. Pain contorting his face.

—What the fuck? What was . . . ? That was . . . unexpected.

Once the initial pain has passed and his breathing's under control, Gauge begins to laugh.

—Goddamn. I've got to meet this girl of yours.

—You never will. Now get up and let's go.

65

Now

He's almost out of rounds for the rifle.

Never intended to shoot everything to shit like this. Never done this before. Usually it's one round to the head or chest, but this . . . this . . . He's a fuckin' one man war zone.

Why? Why so unprofessional? Why so imprecise? Why so fuckin' impatient?

He knows why.

His daughter.

Never planned to have a kid. She was a complete accident. When he couldn't get her mother to abort her, he seriously considered popping the bitch, but . . . she was too closely connected to him. He's a consummate professional—or used to be. He couldn't take out someone he'd had that much intimate contact with.

And later he was glad he didn't. He was glad she had kept the kid.

He likes having a kid. Likes it a lot. Doesn't exactly love her. At least he doesn't think he does. He's not sure what that even is or if there is such a thing, but . . .

She's who has changed everything for him, has him acting like it's fuckin' amateur hour out here.

He wants to be done with this shit so he can get back to Miami to see her.

Well, so what if he does? There are worse reasons.

So get on with it. Bet there's a police radio in that SUV. Bet the fucker is callin' in backup right now.

Of course, maybe it doesn't have signal out in this godforsaken hell hole.

You better find out. Better see how much time you have left and what you have to do to get out of here safely. Your ass may have to go through the fuckin' swamp, steal a boat, go down river, find a car. Goddamn but you've screwed the pooch on this one. Well, can't be undone now, so just get the fuck to fixin' it.

What're you waiting for?

Out of ammo for the rifle. Gonna have to do this one up close and personal.

More trouble. More effort. More aggravation.

But one big consolation.

He can make them look at him when he does it and watch the light go out of their shocked and frightened little eyes.

66

Now

Heather is emerging from the woods. I can hear her.

I stop the vehicle and quickly rise up enough to see out of the front window.

"John? John? What's going on?"

"Get behind the base of a big tree," I yell. "Hurry. Now. We're being shot at. Reggie and I are both hit."

"Oh my God. Are y'all okay?"

"We've got to get Reggie to a hospital," I say.

I pick up the mic of Reggie's mobile radio and let dispatch know what's going on, requesting backup, SWAT, emergency services, and anyone else they can find, warning them we have an active shooter situation.

A year ago when I first started with the department I wouldn't have been able to radio in, but we recently switched over to a new service that works nearly everywhere in the county—even out here.

"What do you want me to do?" Heather asks.

I check the side mirror. It has been shot out and isn't usable.

I realize the shots aren't hitting around us anymore and I wonder if the shooter is out or merely relocating for a better vantage point.

"Can you get down low, move from tree to tree directly behind the SUV and make your way over here? It's very important that you don't leave yourself exposed. He's a great shot and has a high-powered rifle."

"I can make it," she says.

"Be careful. Stay low. Move quickly between the trees."

I turn in the seat and quickly rise up and look back down the dirt road. I do this several times. Up. Look. Down. Up. Look. Down. Think about what I've seen.

My department-issued car is shot to shreds. Heather's car is too. But no sign of the shooter. No sign of anything else.

I glance at Reggie in the seat next to me. She's lost a lot of blood and her breathing is raspy and ragged, but she is breathing.

Got to get her to a hospital.

Heather. Got to save Heather for Remington. Got to get her out of here. Can't let her die out here like this.

"Know what," I say to Heather. "On second thought, just stay behind the biggest tree you can find and don't move. Help is on the way."

"But if I come to you we can get Reggie to help sooner," she says.

"Yeah, that's what I had been thinking, but . . ."

"I can make it," she says. "I—"

I hear the unmistakable wet thump sound of her getting hit with a round and then the hard dry thwack of the same round hitting a tree behind her.

"Heather," I yell. "Heather. Are you okay? Can you hear me?"

"I'm . . . I've been hit. I'm . . ."

"Where?"

She doesn't respond.

"Heather?"

Still no response.

I jam the shifter in Park.

"Stay alive, Reggie," I say. "Help is on the way. I'm going to get Heather and then we're going to ride out of here. Just fight. Fight for Rain. For your mom. For Merrick. Stay alive for them."

Taking the small .38 out of my ankle holster and tucking it into the waistband of my jeans, I take a deep breath, let it out, and say a quick prayer.

As quickly as I can, I sling the door open, hop out of it, and run as fast as I can, dragging my right leg as I do.

67

Then

—Let me bandage my leg, Gauge says.

　　—Now, Remington says.

—Okay. Okay. Don't shoot.

He smiles. Holds his hands up.

It's as if Gauge is actually enjoying himself. He's having fun, Remington thinks. He's not afraid of dying. He doesn't feel anything, doesn't have normal reactions.

Stumbling onto his one good leg, he begins to hop unsteadily toward the river.

Moving more slowly now, the two men look like lost and wounded soldiers attempting to return to their platoon.

—They'll catch up to us fast now.

—If they're still out here. They may've gone home.

—They're here.

World spinning around him.

Dizzy.

Unsteady.

Weak.

Gauge could easily overpower him if he tried. He doubted he could even get a shot off or hit him if he did. He's been through too much, too tired, too banged up from the wreck, lost too much blood from the bullet hole in his leg.

But Gauge has his own problems.

Limping.

Hobbling.

Trailing blood.

—Still can't believe you shot me.

—Probably won't be the only time today.

Gauge laughs.

—I'm beginning to think none of us're gonna make it out of here. This whole thing's just fucked.

—Even if you walk out of here—

A round hits the tree next to his head, splintering a piece of the bark off and hurtling it toward his face.

Ducking as best he can, he lunges for Gauge, grabbing him around the throat, jamming the gun into his ear, and spinning him around toward the gunfire.

Covered from the back by a thick oak and in the front by Gauge, Remington is protected for the moment.

—Tell them to stop shooting—unless they're trying to hit you.

—Hold your fire, Gauge yells.

Another round rings out, sails by.

—Stop shooting, goddamn it.

The shooting stops.

In the silence that follows, Remington can hear the river. So close. Almost there.

—How the hell he get the drop on you? Donnie Paul yells.

—I'm shot.

—Tell them to come out where I can see them, hands in the air.

—They won't—

—Tell them I'll kill you right here and now if they don't.

—Come on out, guys. He'll shoot me if you don't.

—No, he won't. You're the only leverage he's got.

—Let us walk to the river, Gauge says. No harm in that.

—I know what you're saying, Arlington says, but I ain't coming out where he can shoot at me.

Remington thumbs back the hammer of the gun, jamming the barrel harder into Gauge's ear.

—We're both bleeding pretty bad, Remington yells. Y'all keep telling me I'm not going to make it out of here alive, so what've I got to lose? At least there'll be one less sociopath in the world. Besides, I drop him, I think my chances are still pretty good to make it to the river and get help. Made it this far.

—Listen to him, Gauge says. Come out.

—Right now, Remington says, or I swear to Christ I'll put a bullet in his ear.

—Goddamn it, Arlington, Donnie Paul. Get your asses out here right now.

The two men step out of the woods and slowly begin to walk toward them.

When they are within twenty feet, Remington motions for them to stop.

—Put down your weapons and start walking in the opposite direction.

—Fuck that.

—Hell no.

—Just do it, Gauge says. You know this ain't over.

The two men carefully set their rifles on the ground.

—Now start jogging back the way you came and if I see you again, I'm not going to negotiate or count or hesitate. I'm just going to put a bullet into the reptilian brain inside this skull.

—Go, Gauge says. What're you waiting for? Run.

They turn and begin to walk slowly away.

—I said jog.

They pick up the pace a bit, but don't actually do anything that could be misconstrued as jogging.

When they are no longer visible, Remington shoves Gauge toward their guns, and they begin to stumble over to them.

Close.

Ten feet away. Five.

As they reach the weapons, Arlington steps out of the woods beside them and starts firing with a semiautomatic of some kind, 9 millimeter or .45.

Without releasing Gauge, Remington swings the small .38 around, takes a quick breath, aims, squeezes off a round.

Then another.

And another.

The third hits Arlington in the right cheek above his mouth. He falls and doesn't get up.

—Goddamn, Gauge says. That's impressive. Pretty slick, there, slick. Nice and cool, Cool Hand Luke. Somebody shootin' at them from close range, most men panic.

Numb.

—Shut the fuck up, Remington says.

You did what you had to, son, comes Cole's voice. Don't waste time worrying about it. Just keep moving.

—Donnie Paul, Gauge yells, if you're around here, don't do anything stupid. Get out of here. I got this. Everything is under control. Go on now. Get. You're just gonna get one of us killed.

Releasing Gauge, but still keeping the handgun trained on him, Remington bends down and picks up the rifles, slinging the strap of each over an arm.

—Let's go, he says, pointing toward the river with the revolver.

Walking.

Shuffling.

Limping.

—That's four shots, Gauge says.

—Huh?

—Four shots. One in my leg. Two misses. One in Arlington's face. You shot the poor bastard in the face. Reckon that'll be a closed casket service. Anyway, that's four rounds. Snub-nose like that holds five, so if it was full to begin with, you only have one shot left.

—It was, and one is all I need.

The river.

All roads have led here.

It is both destiny and journey.

As he searches the area for Tanner or any of the others that might still be out here, he gives thanks for the river.

—You're here. You made it. Time to let me go.

—We're gonna leave here together.

—Never gonna happen.

—Me and my three guns beg to differ.

—You're gonna let me go. Just wait.

Walking down the muddy bank to the river's edge, Remington backs up against a cypress tree and pulls Gauge in front of him.

Leaning against the tree, Remington lifts his right leg slightly to take the pressure off the wound.

Just flag down a passing boat and get out of here. That's all I have to do. Call the cops and an ambulance. I'm gonna make it. Get Gauge in custody. Check on Mom. Get treated. Bring investigators back out here.

Shooting pain.

Gasp.

—How long you think before you pass out from losin' all that blood? Gauge asks.

—You better hope a long time. I feel myself about to go, I'm gonna shoot you before I do.

—Killer, you know I wish you only the very best, Gauge says with a smile. Always have.

—You're leaking a good bit of oil yourself.

—Not even a quart low yet.

Withdrawing the knife from his pocket, Remington opens the blade, turns slightly, and begins to carve MM into the bark of the tree.

—Hell you doin'? Gauge asks.

Remington doesn't respond.

—Who's MM? That your girl?

Remington shakes his head.

—Then who?

—Not who, what.

—Then what?

—Stands for Memento Mori.

—For what?

—Ancient Romans used to write it on everything.

—What's it mean?

—Just a reminder.

—Of what?

—Mortality. It means remember that you're mortal. Remember you'll die.

—We really need a reminder? Hard to forget out here today.

68

Now

I duck behind the first tree I come to and search for Heather.

As I do, I realize there are no rounds buzzing about.

What's he waiting for? Did he move? Is he firing from a different angle now?

I spot Heather some fifteen yards away. She's lying flat on her back, a smear of blood on her face and across the right side of her shirt.

Ducking down and moving as fast as I am capable of, I zigzag my way over to her, behind and between the trees, dragging my leg and feeling like an awkward fool as I do.

I trip and fall a few times and struggle to get up, each time expecting my head or chest to explode.

When I finally make it over to Heather, I fall down on the ground beside her.

After a moment of gathering myself, I crouch over her awkwardly and check on her.

The smear of blood on her face is just that—a smear. She must have touched the wound in her shoulder and then rubbed her face.

"Don't you die on me," I say.

"I wouldn't mind so much," she says. "Out here where he did."

"You're gonna have to settle for having your ashes scattered out here one day decades from now. None of us are dying out here today."

"I can live with that too," she says.

"Good. Okay. Let's g—"

I feel the barrel of a gun in the back of my head.

69

Then

White of an approaching boat motor. Sound of salvation.
Remington scans the woods around him and down
the banks beside him for any signs of Tanner or Donnie Paul.
Sees none.

—Help me flag the boat down, Remington says.

—Gladly.

—Try anything and I squeeze the trigger. Got no reason not
to now.

—I ain't gonna try anything.

As the boat draws closer, Remington nudges Gauge forward,
and the two men step down to the water.

—See if you can get their attention, Remington says.

Gauge does as he's told.

Still a good ways away, the driver throttles down the engine
and the boat slows, its bow angling toward them.

—It's almost as if they were looking for us, Gauge says with a smile.

Remington's stomach sinks.

—Back up, he says.

He does.

Wrapping his arm around Gauge's throat and pressing the gun against his temple, the two men resume their previous position in front of the large cypress tree.

—Anything happens, Remington says, you die first.

—Fine with me if we just stand here until you pass out or bleed to death, but you're gonna let me go.

—That you jumping up and down and waving your hands, big G? Tanner asks.

Releasing his grip around Gauge's throat, Remington removes the radio from his pocket.

—Pull the boat up to the bank and get out or Gauge gets a bullet to the head.

—Almost there.

A good bit bigger than Mother Earth's boat, Tanner stands behind a windshield and steers the boat ashore. As the bow touches the bank, Tanner cuts the engine, opens the center section of glass, and steps through it into the front part of the boat.

When he squats down to lift something from the bottom of the boat, Remington thumbs back the hammer.

—What're you doin'? Remington says. Get up.

—Wait for it, Gauge says.

—Don't shoot, Tanner says. Just gettin' somethin' you need to see.

In another moment, Tanner is helping Caroline James up, her frail body looking even more vulnerable out here. As if a mirror reflection of Remington and Gauge, Tanner holds Caroline in front of himself and points a gun to her head.

—Mom, Remington says in that way that only a child speaking to his mother can.

—Told ya you'd let me go, Gauge says.

—Remington, are you all right?

His mom is still in her pink pajamas and robe.

—Got your address from the truck, Gauge says.

—I'm fine, Mom. You okay?

—You gonna lie to your mother? Gauge whispers.

—I'm okay, honey. Don't worry about me. What's all this about?

—My camera trap took pictures of them killing a woman.

—We're not the only ones who've killed out here, Gauge says. There used to be more of us. Your son shot a man in the face just a few minutes ago.

—That true?

—Yes, ma'am.

—I'm so sorry you had to do that, she says.

—They weren't none too happy about it neither, Gauge says.

—That one's got a smart mouth on him, doesn't he?

—Yes, ma'am.

—Yeah. Yeah. I'm just a psychopathic smartass.

Rustling leaves.

Snapping twigs.

Swishing grass and weeds.

Donnie Paul steps out of the woods not far from the tree Remington is propped against.

—He fuckin' shot Arlington in the fuckin' face. You see that?

—I saw it, Gauge says. What took you so long?

He looks at Remington.

—I'll have my rifle back now.

—Not just now, Remington replies.

—Honey, did you get anything before all this started?

—Yes, ma'am. The most amazing shots of black bears and bats and fireflies. I can't wait to show you.

—I can't wait to see them.

—I know now this is what I'm supposed to do.

—Well, you just keep on doing it. Don't let anything stop you. Anything.

Is she saying what I think she is? I can't let her die.

—Remington, look at me. Anything.

—I hate to intrude on the last conversation between a mother and her son and all, but we're standing here bleeding. I mean, for fuck sake. All Jesus said was Woman, behold thy son. You'd think you could be a little less verbose.

—I love you, Mom.

—That's more like it, Gauge says.

—I love you, honey.

—I wish there could be a happy ending in this for us, but there's just not one.

—No there's not.

—They're going to kill us either way.

—I know.

—But in one way, we can take a few of them with us, he says. She nods.

Gauge shakes his head.

—What'd I just say about being so verbose? Now look, you let me go and tell me where you hid the memory card, we'll let your mom live. You have my word.

—Your what?

—You heard me. I don't want to cap some old woman in her pink pajamas. But I will. And I'll make it hurt like a son of a bitch if you don't let me go right now and tell me where you hid the evidence.

—Do it, his mom says.

—Do it?

—It. I'm so ready to see your dad again.

—I can't.

—Of course he can't, Gauge says. You're asking him to kill his own mother.

—He's right, Remington says.

—Look at how I live, she says. Well, not live, exist. Think about how much I miss your dad.

She's right, he thinks.

—Don't let him get away, she continues. Don't take a chance on him leaving the swamp and killing again.

—I told you, Gauge says, there's no—

With that, Remington squeezes the trigger and the left side of Gauge's head explodes, spraying his final thoughts onto a nearby oak tree.

Telegraphing.

Slow motion.

As if watching from outside himself.

Dropping the empty handgun.

Shoving Gauge's empty body aside.

Grabbing the rifle hanging on his right shoulder.

Spinning.

Flipping.

Dropping.

Aiming.

Firing.

One knee.

From a crouching position, he aims for Tanner first, even though the other man comes up with a handgun and begins to rush him, firing as he does.

Pop.

Echo.

Crack.

Echo.

Thump.

Thwack.

Crack.

Echo.

Boom.

Echo.

His mom's still alive.

He's got a shot.

Breathe.

Aim.

Thank you, Dad, for teaching me how to shoot.

Squeeze don't pull.

Fire.

But before he can, one of Donnie Paul's running rounds finds him, shattering the bone of his right elbow.

Ignore the pain.

Take the shot.

Save your mom.

Cole's voice. You can do it.

Now.

Take the shot.

He does.

Blood splatter on pink silk. Not her blood. Tanner crumples.

Another round hits him. This one in the thigh. Excruciating pain.

It takes all he can do, but he manages to turn toward Donnie Paul.

Close now. Round after round. Semiautomatic. Empty. Eject. New clip. Several more rounds. Lots of shots. Donnie Paul, going for quantity of rounds over quality of shots. Playing the odds.

Another one finds its mark.

Remington's chest explodes.

Get off a shot.

One last shot.

Now.

Now or never.

If you don't get him, he'll kill your mother.

Squeeze.

Heart.

Hole.

Blood.

Falling.

Dead.

Saved Mom.

Dropping rifle.

Death be not proud, though some have called thee mighty and dreadful, for, thou art not ...

Falling over.

Shock.

Got Gauge.

Saved Mom.

Love Heather.

Ready?

Ready.

Really?

I really am. Don't want to go, but not afraid.

Numb.

Nothing.

70

Now

"Did you radio backup?" a surprisingly soft voice says. "How long do I have? Tell me the truth and I'll let the sheriff live."

"I'll tell you the truth," I say. "Under three conditions."

I slip the little .38 out of my waistband and put it in Heather's hand.

When I glance back at her, she looks as if something has just dawned on her, like she's just received a revelation or insight about something. Odd how that happens in the strangest of moments.

Heather can smell the man standing behind John—the coffee and country club aftershave that takes her back to that frightened, helpless moment when she was being held at gunpoint while Caroline was being groped and molested.

The empty gallery. The feeble, childless widow in her wheelchair. The smell of the man whispering threats into her ear. The voice. The threats. Caroline wetting herself. It all comes rushing back as if it has just happened.

"Oh yeah?" the man behind me is saying. "You're in no position to bargain, but humor me by telling me your conditions."

"Let me stand up and look at you when you shoot me, tell me why you're doing this and who's behind it, and let Heather live."

He laughs. "Stand up and look at me," he says. "Slowly. Was gonna have you do that anyway."

I push myself up off of Heather.

As I do, he takes a step back, and Heather lifts the .38 and fires all five rounds at him, hitting him with at least three.

But not before he gets off a round of his own.

Fortunately, it hits the ground next to Heather. Three inches to the left and it would have hit her in the head.

I jump down on him and grab the rifle, and toss it away.

He doesn't offer much resistance. Shot in the hand, chest, and throat, he's in no shape to offer much resistance to anything.

"Who hired you?" I ask.

He mumbles something I can't make out.

He doesn't have long.

"What?" I ask. "Who hired you? Why're you doing this?"

He shakes his head. "Got . . . no . . . answers . . . for you. I'm . . . not in the . . . answer . . . There are . . . no . . . answers."

Blood gurgles out of the hole in the side of his neck.

He says something else but I can't make it out.

"What?" I ask again.

"Tell my . . . daughter . . . I . . ."

71

Then

Days pass.
        Then some more.
    Then some more.

Heather holds the Cuddeback camera viewer as if a holy object, as if a reliquarium, as if it somehow houses Remington's soul.

Upon returning to his tree stand to check his scouting camera, Jefferson Lanier had discovered Remington's recordings, retrieved the hidden memory card and turned everything over to FDLE. After transferring the video from Lanier's Cuddeback unit, the agency had returned the camera to him. He had then taken it directly to Heather, making a gift of it to her.

The gift, Remington's final words.

Cheating death. Like a message sent back in time from beyond the grave.

How many times has she watched the messages? Hundreds?

Thousands? She's not sure. She no longer needs to watch it. She has every word, every pause, every breath, every expression, every inflection etched in her brain, continually playing on the memory card viewer of her mind. When she's awake, when she sleeps. But she watches it anyway. It gives her something to hold, a tactile bond, her hands where his hands had been, creates a stronger link, a more direct connection.

Huddled in the corner, holding the camera away from himself with one hand, lighting himself with a flashlight with the other, he talks to her, his dry voice and weary face unwittingly revealing his pain, shock, fatigue, fear, but also his heroism—is that a word?—and bravery.

—My name is Remington James. My camera trap captured images of a game warden named Gauge killing a woman deep in the woods between William's Lake and the Chipola River. She is buried not far from a watering hole on the back edge of the James hunting lease. Gauge and his friends are trying to kill me—probably succeeded if you're watching this. I'm trying to make it to the river—either the Chipola or across Cutoff Island to the Apalachicola—to flag down a passing boat.

He holds up a corner of the blanket.

—I'll hide the memory stick somewhere near an easily recognizable landmark—manmade, a tree stand like this one, a houseboat, if I can find one—probably in the ground, and I'll cut off a piece of this blanket to flag the spot.

—I hope you find it. Hell, I hope I survive and can take you back to it, but . . . These are dangerous, soulless men who need to be stopped.

Which is exactly what you did, she thinks.

—Mom, I'm sorry I didn't make it home last night—or at all, I guess, if you're watching this. I really tried. But more than anything else, I'm sorry for letting you down. You entrusted me with your camera, you charged me with taking the pictures you no longer could, and I stopped. I let making money—money of all things—get in the way of what I was meant to do. You and Heather were right.

—Anyway, I wanted to let you know that I realize that now and that I took some amazing shots tonight that I hope you somehow get to see. I really think you'll like them. Sorry I didn't bring you more, but I'm just glad I rediscovered what I was meant to do—even if I don't make it out of here. A little late, but I did it.

—You and Dad were the best parents any kid could have. Thanks for all you did for me—in spite of being sick and fighting so hard just to survive. I'm fighting hard to survive tonight. I learned that from you.

—I love you so much.

—Dear sweet Heather, I'm so sorry for everything. You were right. I was wrong—about virtually everything, but especially how I had gotten off my path. See my message to Mom about that.

—If I get through the night, it will be because of you. I can't stop thinking of you. I love you so much. Everything about you. Everything. You've been with me tonight in ways you can't imagine. I'm reliving our all-too-brief time together.

—I took some extraordinary shots tonight, but my favorite photographs will always be the ones I took of you, my lovely, sweet, good, beautiful girl.

—I'm sorry I wasn't a better husband. You deserved me to be. Don't mourn for me long. Find someone who will be as good to you as you deserve.

—I finally love you like you should be, and I'm afraid I won't be able to tell you in person.

Tears.

Thick voice.

—Just know my final thoughts will be of you.

Each time she cries as if hearing his words for the first time.

Each time she caresses the camera and viewer, then holds them close to her heart.

72

Now

The only request Heather made from her hospital bed was to have the old Cuddeback camera viewer with Remington's messages on it, which Mike and Jean Thomas found in her things in their guest bedroom and promptly brought to her.

She lies clutching it to herself now in her hospital room at Bay Medical Center in Panama City, a Gulf County deputy on guard just outside.

Reggie is still in surgery, and we haven't received an update lately.

I'm lying in a hospital bed of my own, after having had x-rays to ensure what I and the ER doctor suspected—that the projectile that pierced my leg hit only muscle and not bone during its short pass through my quadriceps.

I'm on the phone with Anna, and though there is a Gulf County deputy posted outside my door, Merrill is seated in a chair next to my bed, his hand never far from his holstered .45.

"He was just a hired gun," I say.

"I don't care," Anna says.

I've already told her what happened and that I'm okay. Now I'm trying to convince her not to come home early.

"Whoever hired him is still here. We haven't gotten him or her or them yet."

"I realize that, but there's no way I'm not coming home to check on you, be with you."

"Give me just a little longer," I say. "I want it to be safe for you and Taylor. And it's not yet."

"Then it's not safe for you."

"Merrill's here," I say. "There are cops everywhere. I'll be okay. Promise. But between Chris and whoever's behind this, I'd feel better about you and Taylor and Johanna being far away from here right now."

She doesn't say anything at first, but then, "Are you saying not only are we safer up here, but you are, too, because you don't have to worry about protecting us?"

"I just want you safe and this is almost over. I can tell we're close."

She sighs. "I'll stay but only because it makes you safer."

"I love you."

"We'll get to that in a minute," she says. "Let me speak to Merrill."

I hand him the phone.

They talk for a few minutes, during which he confirms for her everything I've told her about my wound and assures her he's not leaving my side until we catch whoever's behind all this.

He hands the phone back to me.

"Okay," she says. "Now, listen to me. I don't care what's going on, it's not worth your life. It's not. Not even close. Don't forget that. Don't do anything to . . . Just take care of yourself. Stay safe. Promise me you will."

"I promise."

"Are you sure Chris didn't hire him?" she asks.

"Yeah. I thought he might have at first, but the guy, Alec Horn, was easy to identify. He's a professional from Miami—where the drugs from here are going—and Heather recognized him as one of the men who threatened her and Caroline in the gallery after the opening of Remington's show."

"Okay. Now you can tell me you love me."

I do.

"I love *you*," she says. "More than anything. Don't make me a widow before I'm officially and legally your wife."

"Y ou really close?" Merrill asks. "Or just tell her that so she stay put?"

"I really think we are. There's something flittering just at the edges of my consciousness."

"You figure out Wilson's involvement?"

"I didn't, but Reggie did," I say. "He and his men weren't involved in what happened to Remington. They were probably getting skim from the operation and probably didn't conduct a thorough investigation, but didn't have direct involvement in Remington's death."

He nods, but doesn't say anything.

"Knowing that helps," I say. "Less to think about, can focus more on . . . other things like . . . where did the massive operation we found go? And how the product is being transported out of here to South Florida and other places. That's the one I think I'm close to like a word on the tip of my tongue I . . . just . . . can't . . . quite . . . get."

"Well, you just lay there and have one of your little thinks on it," he says. "All this shit out here is under control."

I do.

While Merrill is so still and quiet it's like he's not even there, I think about everything we've uncovered so far, everything we've learned, but all that we haven't found, all that we didn't uncover.

We haven't found any drugs. None. Just a site where they used to be produced.

Where are they being produced now?

And how are they getting to Miami and other places?

Growing and shipping and killing for pot—who, how, where, why? Over and over I roll it around.

Think about where it was being grown—up that slough, back in the swamp.

Of course.

It's being transported by boat on the river.

Has to be.

The river isn't really patrolled, isn't really watched like highways. A handful of game wardens aren't able to do much—and they're looking more for wildlife violations than anything else.

Traffic along the river is rarely stopped or checked.

That's it.

They boat it down the river to Apalachicola Bay and load it onto ships that then take it to Central and South Florida.

I fall asleep.

I dream of drugs.

When I wake, I feel like maybe another element of the solution was in my dreams, but I can't remember what it was.

I feel slow and sluggish, thick and groggy.

And my leg hurts like hell.

Through the window I can see that it's daylight. I only intended to have a think, maybe take a nap. I slept through the night.

I look over at Merrill. "Would you find me some crutches?"

"She already did," he says, nodding toward the other side of the bed.

I turn to see Anna in a chair on the opposite side, a pair of crutches leaning against the wall next to her.

"I couldn't stay away," she says. "Sorry."

"Don't ever be sorry for that."

"I left Taylor with Mom, so . . . she's safe, but I had to see you."

"Come here," I say, lifting my arms.

She stands up, takes a step, and then leans down over the bed. We embrace for a long moment.

When we finally let go, Merrill says, "We leaving?"

I nod. "Yes we are. I can't take another minute of this place."

73

Then

S pring.
    North Florida.
Gallery.
Hardwood floors. Squeaking.
Hushed crowd. Awe. Reverence.
Wine. Cheese.
Opening night. Posthumous show.
Last Night in the Woods by Remington James.
Enormous prints. Framed photographs. Color.
Incandescent.
Luminous.
Radiant rain.
Arcing sparks.
Falling drops of fire.
Field of fireflies.
Black and white.

High contrast.

Palmettos, hanging vines, fallen trees, untouched undergrowth, unspoiled woodlands.

Bounding. Loping. Barreling.

Black as nothingness.

Buckskin muzzle bursting out of a forest of fur, chest ablaze.

Shy eyes.

Florida black bears.

Looking up from a small slough, rivulets of water around large, sharp teeth, dripping, suspended in midair.

Heather, teary. Caroline in a wheelchair at her side, wiping tears of her own.

—He could've lived a long life and never taken any shots better than these, Heather says.

—I keep thinking about what Ansel Adams said, Caroline says. Sometimes I get to places when God is ready to have someone click the shutter.

—Exactly, Heather says. That's it exactly.

They are quiet a moment, each looking around the large room at all the people who've come out to see Remington's work.

Every shot, every single one draws intense interest, but none more than the stunning, seemingly impossible images of the Florida panther captured by Remington's second camera trap—the one discovered by two hunters a week after his death.

Sleek.

Dark, tawny coat.

Flattened forehead, prominent nose.

Spotted cub.

Crouching.

Red tongue lapping dark water.

Playful cub pouncing about.

—He did it, Heather says. He did what so few of us do. He became who he was supposed to be.

—I know it had to be unimaginable for him, but he managed

to live a lifetime and do some real good in the world by surviving the night, stopping those men, saving these images, Caroline says.

Heather nods.

—He did what so few of us ever do—found out the meaning of his life, rediscovered real passion, purpose, rededicated himself to love.

—He did, Heather says, nodding. You're exactly right. It's . . . I'm . . . I just wish he could be here.

Caroline looks around the room, her trained eyes taking in each astonishing image with the peerless pride of a mother.

—He is.

Beyond the women, on the far wall behind them, hangs the only image not taken by Remington or one of his traps. Just a snapshot, but one that, in its way, completes the exhibit.

Taken by a grieving, but grateful mother, with a son's new camera, just before being rescued by a passing fisherman, the image is that of a cypress tree trunk on the bank of the Apalachicola River, the letters MM carved into its bark.

A monument.

A memorial.

A remembrance.

The artist, by his own hand, reminding his many admirers to make preparations, for they, too, will soon experience their own dark night of the soul, waking to the full weight of their mortality, journeying to the undiscovered country from whose bourn no traveler returns.

74

Now

"Any word on the victim found at the crime scene?" Anna asks.

We're coming into Wewa. Anna is driving. Merrill is in the passenger seat beside her holding a shotgun. I'm stretched out in the backseat, my bad leg extended out, the crutches lying across both floorboards.

I shake my head. "Not much. Only that she wasn't Cassandra Hitchens, the missing DEA agent."

"So we're no closer to knowing who she really was."

"I'd say we're closer than we were this time last week," I say.

"What happens if there's no DNA match?" she asks.

I shrug. "Usually they try to use clothes, jewelry, anything personal buried with her," I say. "But in this case it's all too deteriorated to be useful. All except part of a tarnished silver bracelet. It's charred and part of it is missing, but it's a very distinctive pattern, may even be one of a kind. It's got a pattern etched into the flat piece and three short, narrow prongs that stick out."

"I want to see it," Anna says. "See if I can help identify it or locate who made it."

"Sure," I say. "We'll have it back from the lab soon. But it's going to be tough. It's in very, very bad shape."

"Some questions never get answered, do they?" she says. "Some identities never identified."

"Far too many," I say, shaking my head. "I hope this isn't one of them."

"Remington died without knowing, didn't he?"

"I'm pretty sure. Based on what he said to his mom out in the swamp that morning."

Before we left the hospital, we checked on Heather and Reggie. Reggie is in critical but stable condition. Her chief deputy or undersheriff, Langston Costin, is in charge of the department. Heather should be able to go home in a couple of days.

Anna is driving slowly, cautiously, though there is very little traffic—a few cars, a few pickups, some pulling boats, log trucks, most of them loaded and headed to the mill, others returning empty, a couple of flatbeds pulling trailers, both the trucks and trailers loaded down with bee boxes.

"Heard it was a terrible tupelo season," Anna says.

"We had no winter this year," Merrill says. "Blooms were confused as fuck. Opened early. Closed. Opened again. Closed too soon. Climate change fuckin' with our ability to have biscuits and honey."

I think of Charles Masters and his family's bee business and wonder how they're going to make it.

And then it hits me. Hard.

"You okay?" Anna asks, glancing at me in the rearview mirror. "Wait, I know that look."

Merrill turns in the seat toward me. "Whatcha got?"

"A little theory I want to test."

"Yeah? What's that?"

"We're gonna need a boat."

"Not a problem. What's the theory?"

"What is it, honey?" Anna asks, her eyes quickly searching mine in the rearview.

"That the drugs are being shipped down the river to Apalach and put on boats to be sent to South Florida."

They both nod. Merrill says, "Makes sense."

"It's obvious, I know," I say, "but . . . what if the grower's logo isn't a hornet and has nothing to do with Cottondale or Wilson or Alec Horn? What if it's a bee, and they're hiding their product beneath bee boxes on the barges and shipping it down river that way?"

"*Mo-ther*-fucker," Merrill says. "That's brilliant."

Anna smiles at me.

"I feel slow for not thinking of it before now," I say.

"How you think that makes us who still haven't thought of it feel?" Merrill says with a wide smile.

"If they're hiding it in empty bee boxes beneath a top row of boxes with actual hives in them . . ." I say.

"Nobody gonna mess around with them," Merrill says.

"If it's not how they're doing it," Anna says, "it should be. Blend in. Be protected. It's genius."

"*She-it*. Nobody gonna mess with them. Scared of gettin' they ass stung to death. Damn. Damn. Damn."

"Still don't know where they're growing it," I say, "but if we figure out how they're shipping it maybe we will."

"Then," Merrill says, "let's take a boat ride."

75

Now

We enlist the help of Charles Masters, who brings his full beekeeper suit and smoke, and Carter Peak, who brings EpiPens and a big boat he borrowed from Search and Rescue.

Of course the boat would have to be big just to accommodate Peak, whose tall, big, thick body looks out of place in it.

The five of us launch the boat at Lister's Landing, not far from where Reggie, Heather, and I were shot, and head down river.

Anna is on the bench seat beside me. My right leg is propped up on one of Carter's Yeti coolers, my crutches lying on the bottom of the boat beside me.

Carter is driving. Charles is in the front with his gear. Merrill is in the very back, shotgun at the ready.

The overcast morning is gray, wisps of fog still clinging to spots along the banks.

The river is empty. Particularly this far down, and though there were two other trucks with empty boat trailers parked at the landing, we haven't seen another human since we've been out here.

When we reach the first barge with bee boxes stacked on it, Carter slows and brings the boat alongside it.

Bees are buzzing about, flying to and returning from the swamp behind the bank the barge is moored to, and swarming all around us.

"What am I looking for?" Charles asks, as he suits up and climbs aboard.

"Just lift the lid off several of the boxes and look inside," I say. "It's okay to be quick. If everything looks okay, move to the next one. We want to check as many as we can. Especially in the bottom middle."

He gets his smoker started and squeezes out several puffs of smoke around us, letting it drift back over us, to keep us from being stung.

Smoke calms bees and masks their alarm pheromones.

"That'll keep 'em off of you for a few," he says, "but you may want to back away and wait for me to finish before coming back to get me."

"Cool with me," Carter says. "Bees freak me the fuck out."

Once Charles is on the barge, Carter reverses the motor and backs far enough away for the bees not to follow.

Charles goes to work, first laying a thick layer of smoke around the hives he's close to, then lifting and looking, returning and re-stacking.

"We lookin' for signs of poisoning, John?" Charles yells over. "'Cause these hives look good and healthy."

"Good," I say. "Just make sure you search all the way down—check the boxes sitting on the deck and in the center of the stacks."

"Okay."

He does. And only finds boxes filled with bee hives.

When he's finished, we pull back up and pick him up, as he squeezes smoke around us again.

We repeat this process for two more barges and one set of boxes up on the hill above the banks, but it isn't until the fourth barge that we find what, unbeknownst to Charles, we've been searching for.

"Son of a bitch," he exclaims.

"What is it?" I yell from the boat about twenty feet away.

"Is this what we're out here lookin' for?" he says.

"Depends on what it is."

"Dope," he yells. "Lots and lots of it. Packed in boxes beneath the boxes with the bees in them. We're talkin' a shit ton."

"That's it," I say. "Any idea whose barge it is?"

He shakes his head, his beekeeper's hat shaking about.

I turn toward Carter. "You do, don't you?"

Anna studies me for a second, then turns toward Carter, too.

"I do what?" he asks, his voice rising in nervousness and surprise.

"Know whose barge it is."

"No. Why would I?"

He looks around a little like he's trying to figure out a move— grab a weapon, hit the throttle, something. As he does his long curly hair waves about.

Behind him, Merrill jacks a shell in the chamber of the shotgun even though to do so ejected the one that was already in it. A small price to pay for a dramatic warning.

Carter stops moving. "Easy," he says. "Why would you think I know who the barge belongs to?"

"You play this right and you can live to play with Mix Tape Effigies another day," I say. "You don't want to be making music in a prison chapel somewhere for the rest of your life."

"Prison? Rest of my life? The fuck you talkin' about, John?" His voice climbs even higher this time. "I save lives. I'm the fuckin' emergency services director. I save lives and make music. That's my life."

"You were the first on the scene after everyone was shot," I say. "You came from the land side, not the river. You moved Remington's camera trap. Gauge and all his men were dead. They hunted Remington all night. Never had a chance to go back to the trap. You moved it. You were the only one who could have. Then later to really sell it, you put cards and flowers at the spot to memorialize it."

He shakes his head but doesn't say anything.

"We're not just talkin' obstruction or producing and selling large amounts of an illegal substance," I say. "We're talking murder and attempted murder. You really want to go down for all that?"

"This is worth a shit ton of money," Charles yells from the barge.

"Even more in Miami," I say.

"I told those old fucks the cards and flowers and shit was too much," Carter says. "But . . . any egotistical idiots who're gonna put a damn logo on pot . . . are gonna find other ways to fuck up, too."

"I don't know," I say. "Y'all've operated a long time without getting caught."

He shrugs. "Not long enough."

"Whose barge is it?" I say.

"The barge, the bees, or the Gulf County Green?" he says. "'Cause the Green belongs to all of us, but the barge and the bees belong to two different individuals—the big bosses. You want them, I want immunity in writing from the state's attorney."

76

Now

"Boy, do I have a story for y'all," I say.

Heather, Anna, and I are in Reggie's hospital room, Heather still in the wheelchair we used to bring her over in.

Reggie, who is still very weak, widens her eyes and in a soft voice says, "Let's hear it."

"You know the old man Remington saw out in the woods?" I say. "Who was later killed by one of Gauge's men? Randal Collins. He moved up here from Central Florida with Gainesville Green cuttings because two of his old acquaintances told him they could make a fortune together up here growing good, cheap weed in the swamp and shipping it other places where it sold for more— like Miami. And Gulf County Green was born."

"Who were the two men?" Heather asks.

"An old grower recently out of prison and a respected businessman and county commissioner," I say.

"Hank Felty," Reggie says.

"And *Mike Thomas?*" Heather asks. "Really?"

I nod.

"No," she says. "No."

"He's sitting in the Gulf County jail right now," I say. "I'm sorry."

"He and Cole were such good friends for so long."

"It was his idea to grow on Cole's land," I say. "He knew Cole wouldn't be doing anything like that on it and that he only hunted part of it part of the year, so . . ."

She shakes her head. "I still can't believe it. He's behind what happened to Remington."

"Says he had nothing to do with that," I say. "Says that was all Gauge, that he didn't even know about it until it was over and he had to scramble to clean up the mess and change their operation. And I'm inclined to believe him because he never would have approved of Gauge killing and burying his victim out there, not that close to where they were growing. And he wouldn't have had them kill Randal. They didn't even know who he was. Just thought he was a witness like Remington."

"Why would Gauge take her out there then?" Heather asks.

"I think he knew about the operation, think he was being paid off to keep quiet about it, maybe even run some interference once they got it down near Apalach to transfer and ship out. I think they thought it was a safe place to do it, that because of the operation, it was being guarded and that even if she was discovered, they wouldn't want any attention drawn to them, so they wouldn't do anything. But that's a guess. We don't really know what Gauge was thinking or why he was doing what he did. He may have asked for a bigger payout and was refused and that was his way of retaliating—bury a body on the land near where they had this huge operation going. Just don't know for sure."

"Whose idea was the bee boxes and barges?" Reggie asks.

"Hank Felty's. It came to him while he was in prison."

"Had a lot of time to think," Anna says. "Put it to good use."

"This is all coming from Carter Peak," I say. "From his statement and interview. So far Felty and Thomas are saying very little."

"Mike tried to have us killed," Heather says. "Almost did. Does Jean know?"

"Not sure. I don't think so, but . . . She was involved in the operation, so she knew all about it, but . . ."

"Wait until you hear about the operation," Anna says. "It's as genius as transporting the stuff on the bee barges."

"Let's hear it," Reggie says.

"Know how only too happy Mike and Hank were willing to show us their old grow site?" I say. "Well, it wasn't just because they had moved their new site farther downstream and inland. That's now the smallest part of how they grow. Don't get me wrong, it's still huge, but they have a whole new system that works better than . . . perhaps any anywhere."

"What is it?" Heather says.

"Old people," Anna says. "Carter Peak kept saying he was doing it for his grandparents."

"They use retired seniors to grow the crops in their homes," I say. "Spare bedrooms of elderly couples all over north Gulf County are filled with pot plants. Not just any pot plants. Gulf County Green. Carter says they treat them like grandchildren— just the right amount of TLC and UV and several of our senior citizens are supplementing their meager retirements and social security by producing some of the best weed around— completely under the radar."

Heather's eyes widen. "That goddamn dinner club," she says.

"Exactly," I say. "They actually came out and served us lunch while we were looking for them, for their crops."

"It really is brilliant," Anna says. "Even if they happened to get busted, it looks like one small operation—an elderly couple growing to help with their own medical needs or to supplement their income. And they're old. No jury is going to be very punitive with them. And that's even if it gets to court. It probably won't. What prosecutor's gonna put grandma and grandpa on trial? Plus, pot has such a low priority now. Be legal soon. Everybody's concentrating on the opioid epidemic."

Reggie shakes her head slowly. "It's true. I know *our* department is. It's a brilliant operation. No wonder they've gotten away with it for so long."

"It's diabolical," Heather says. "Growing and selling pot is one thing. Killing people and trying to kill people is another."

We all nod.

"So what role did the previous sheriff play?" Heather asks. "Wilson and his men who were killed with their own guns. Did Mike and Hank hire this same guy to take them out too?"

Even in her weakened state, I can see Reggie tense up and prepare herself for what's coming next.

I look at her, our eyes locking.

"No," I say, "shaking my head. "That case has nothing to do with this one. I was wrong to think it did."

"So who killed them?" she asks.

"I can't say, but it wasn't related to what happened to Remington or what happened to us yesterday. The truth is . . . with that level of corruption, it could have been anyone. My guess is they crossed the wrong person, but . . . I doubt it will ever come out. But . . . who knows? Given the type of men they were, what happened to them may have been in its own way a certain type of justice."

Reggie blinks back tears and nods at me, her eyes filling with pure appreciation.

"So what happened to Remington wasn't directly connected to Sheriff Wilson and was only tangentially connected to the drug operation," Heather says. "So it all comes down to the woman Gauge murdered and we're still no closer to knowing who she was than we were. Who was she? Why was she out there with him? Why did he kill her, bury and burn her?"

"Remember what we said about most days as an investigator yielding far more frustrating questions than any kind of answers," Reggie says. "We'll keep working on finding those answers, but . . . it's possible we may never know."

"I can't accept that," Heather says.

"We can't either," I say. "It's why we do what we do. We won't stop."

Now

Q uestions.
Obsessive, relentlessly repeated questions nagging
mercilessly at the edges of everything else.

Open wounds.

Seeping, susceptible-to-infection lacerations incapable of
healing without intense treatment.

They haunt me.

Who was she? Why did she die like that? Why did Gauge kill
her that way? Because he was a sociopath like Alec Horn or for
some other reason? Where was she from? Why does no one miss
her? Why isn't her DNA in the database? What am I missing?
What am I doing wrong? Will we ever know who she is and why
she was where she was when the light went out of her eyes?

And those are just the questions about that case? What about
just a few of the others?

Where is Daniel? Is he okay? Where is Randa Raffield? What

is she up to? What is the best way forward with Chris? How serious a threat is he to our family? What could I have done differently to stop Sam from getting shot? Who really killed all the children in Atlanta? How many victims did Bundy really have? How many are still out there somewhere? Did I do the right thing with the Stone Cold Killer? Who really killed JonBenet? Should I be spending less time investigating and more time ministering or more time investigating and less time ministering? How can I prevent more suffering? So much suffering. How can I protect Anna and Johanna and Taylor?

And on and on and on.

These relentless questions and my obsession with them is in conflict with life itself.

The thing about life is how rarely there are answers.

Life is a mystery. It is filled with both general unknowns and specific unknowables.

We know and understand so little. We ask, but we seldom get answers.

There is very, very little that is certain—nearly nothing. And that which is—death, say—isn't particularly comforting, and brings with it a whole new set of questions.

But comfort with questions, with not knowing, with ambiguity and uncertainty, is essential for serenity, for a peaceful and positive life.

Not knowing, having far more questions than answers, is so maddening that we too often accept shallow, incomplete, even erroneous answers in an attempt to silence the questions. And unfortunately we far too often succeed.

As a member of the human race I have accepted uncertainty, embraced not knowing, but as an investigator I can't.

I am a seeker of truth. A finder of facts. A solver of puzzles. An answerer of questions. A collector of unsolved cases. This is not just what I do, but who I am.

Open and unsolved cases come with the territory, but I don't have to like it. Don't have to accept it. So I have found a way to both accept them and refuse to at the same time. I accept that they are, but I refuse to accept that they have to remain that way. I have found a not insignificant amount of peace by accepting what is while still working to change what will be.

Remington died without knowing who Gauge killed or why. Will I? Will Heather?

78

Now

I spend the next several weeks searching for Gauge's victim.

Merrill, Anna, Heather, Merrick, and a host of other people help.

All we have to go on is part of a bracelet—a charred, partially burned bracelet that spent the past few years tarnishing, corroding, degrading underground.

We hunt for it online and in jewelry stores, but can't find anything exactly like it. We post pictures of it and drawings of what we think it may have looked like at one time, but nothing comes of any of it.

Anna and I spend our free time in Apalach and Eastpoint, since that was the area where Gauge lived, going from store to store and door to door, asking anyone who will let us if they've ever seen the bracelet or the woman who used to wear it.

Nothing comes of it.

Nothing comes of anything we try.

While in the area, we had also looked for Daniel, following up on a couple of leads we had come across recently. Nothing had come of them either, and I'm beginning to wonder if anything ever will.

On the drive back I actually wondered which, if either, case we'd close first. I had no idea I'd find out so soon.

Ironically, as is so often the case, I find what I'm looking for in a moment when I'm not looking for it.

Anna and I are on our way back home from a day of knocking on doors in Apalach when we stop in the No Name Café in Port St. Joe for coffee and books.

The No Name is a book and gift shop with a deli and coffee bar. Passing puzzles and trinkets for tourists, while Nora, the young woman behind the counter concocts our usual coffees, Anna and I browse the books, each of us picking out a few that we hope to read as we lie beside each other in bed tonight.

When Barbara Radcliff, the owner, rings us up, I pull some cash out of my pocket to pay. As I do, the plastic evidence bag with the bracelet remains comes out with the random wad of bills.

"What is—Let me see that," she says.

I hand it to her.

"Do you recognize it?" Anna asks.

Barbara examines it closely and carefully through the clear plastic wrapping around it.

"Where did you get this?" she asks. "Why does this say evidence?"

"Have you seen it before?" I ask. "Do you know who it belongs to?"

"Belongs or belonged?" she says.

She turns to one of the other two women behind the counter and asks her to take over at the register, then asks the other one to join the three of us in the back.

When the young woman, a part-time employee named Nora,

joins Anna, Barbara, and myself in the back corner of the store, Barbara hands her the bracelet.

As she takes it and sees what it is, her eyes grow alarmed. She glances at Barbara, then me, then begins to cry.

"It's hers, isn't it?" Barbara says.

Nora nods.

"Whose?" I ask.

"April's," Nora says. "Did something happen to her? Is she . . ."

"April Bennett," Barbara says. "She worked here for a short while. Just sort of passing through. Something I think she did pretty much everywhere. Sweet but sad girl. She and Nora got pretty close though."

"When you can," I say to Nora, "will you tell us all about her?"

"Is she . . . dead?"

"Are you sure this is her bracelet?"

She nods. "It's a one of a kind. She wore it as a sort of joke, you know. It's an antique silver spoon she made into a cuff bracelet. That's why it's open like that. It was an old tea spoon from like 1911 or something. That's why it's so small. She twisted and hammered it. That Old Colony pattern is unmistakable. It's hers all right. She was always making things—mostly to sell."

"Why was it a sort of joke?" Anna asks.

"A silver spoon," she says. "April was an orphan, grew up in the system. Never had anything. Definitely not born with a silver spoon."

Barbara says, "She had a very rough life—abuse, sexual and otherwise from foster dads, bullying from other foster kids, neglect, you name it—but . . . she was so kind, such a good person. Never complained or made an excuse about anything. Hardworking. Grateful for everything she ever got, grateful for every day. Meek. Mild. Sweet. Only two ways you could tell she was . . . that she had the kind of life she did was how . . . sad her eyes were and how insecure in general she was."

I look back at Nora. "How long since you've heard from her?"

"She met a guy who was gonna love her like she finally deserved," she says. "Who was gonna take care of her and give her the best of everything. He was leaving his wife and child for her. They were running away together. She swore not to tell anyone his name and she didn't. She said she would contact me after she got set up in their new place far away, and that she'd come see me when they came back for his kid eventually. Last time I saw her was the last day she worked here. Never heard from her again. She was supposed to leave with him the next day. I . . . I had hoped she'd gotten a good life finally and just forgot about me, but I knew that's not what happened. I thought the best case scenario was that he stood her up or left her after a while of being together and she was too embarrassed to reach out to me. But I knew better. I knew not to ask around either. She said he was some kind of cop. Is she really dead? Is it possible her life was that bad all the way through?"

It *is* possible. More than possible. It's *probable*. But I don't tell her that. I don't tell her how the innocent suffer and the evil are rarely punished—and almost never like they deserve or in any kind of timely fashion. Instead I join her in grieving for a mild, kind soul who gave life far more than it ever gave her, who suffered more in her short life than most do in lives three times as long, who was brutally murdered, burned, and buried and left by herself all this time in an unmarked grave, and who was missed by nearly no one.

"Who killed her?" Nora asks. "Was it the man she was supposed to run away with?"

I nod. "His name was Gauge. He was a game warden in Franklin County. Remember the shootout on Cutoff Island?"

Nora shrugs, but Barbara nods.

"He was killed that day. Lived less than fifteen hours longer than April did."

"Good," Nora says. "Thank God for that."

79

Then

Her things are packed, but they're not going with her.
He told her to leave everything behind.

All of it, he had said, is part of your old, sad, lonely life. Leave it all behind—your old things and your old self.

Something she's only too happy to do. Well, except for the silver spoon bracelet she had made herself. For some reason she can't part with it. Reaching down and touching it with her other hand, she thinks, Surely he won't mind if I keep this one small memento. Probably won't even notice.

Can this really be happening? Is she finally going to get a happy ending? She hadn't believed the unlucky ones like herself ever really did.

We're starting a new life together, he had said. Way away from here. Just the two of us. We'll go where nobody knows our names and be happier than either of us ever imagined.

That won't take much for her. She's never imagined being

particularly happy. The best she's ever hoped for is pretty modest —to be safe, to have food, to have shelter.

Can she really add to be loved to that list?

I'm gonna love you like you never been loved, he had said. To care for you like you've always deserved.

Will he? Will he really do all that for me?

He said he would. Has said it over and over. And she mostly believes him. And what has she got to lose?

What's the worst that can happen? That he doesn't show? That he doesn't come and pick her up and take her away from her old life and self? Or that he does, that he takes her somewhere far away and decides, after he's been with her for a while, that he doesn't love her after all and leaves her? She'll just start over in a new town. Like she's done so many times before.

A knock at the door of her tiny home—little more than a shed she rents behind someone's real home—and Goodwill is here to pick up the boxes containing all the worldly possessions of her old life.

She was hoping he would arrive before Goodwill did, so she would really know he's coming, but . . . it's not like she's giving up much even if he doesn't show. The truth is, if Goodwill knew what these old cardboard boxes contained they wouldn't be here. Wouldn't bother at all.

She opens the door wearing the pretty new outfit he bought her and gives her bravest smile to the young black men in the blue Goodwill shirts.

—Just these three boxes here, she says. Thank you.

She starts to rip the bracelet off her wrist and toss it into one of the boxes, but she just can't bring herself to do it.

—Need a receipt? the taller of the two asks.

She shakes her head.

As they leave with everything she has amassed in her sad little life, she wipes at unexpected tears and tries to pull herself together. Can't be crying when Gauge arrives.

There were several times when she didn't think this was really going to happen—and part of her still doesn't—like the time he seemed to be having doubts about leaving his baby boy.

What if we take him with us? she had said. Instead of coming back for him.

She still remembers the way he had shaken his head and looked at her.

She had panicked inside, felt everything she ever wanted slipping away, and made her biggest blunder of their entire relationship. She had always been so careful. So cautious. Tried too hard to tiptoe atop the eggshells to keep him happy. But this time . . .

She hadn't meant it the way he took it, but she shouldn't have said anything at all.

Maybe I should talk to your wife, she had said before she realized what she was saying, before she realized words were coming out of her stupid, stupid mouth.

She could tell instantly he thought she meant it as a threat, that she would expose him, reveal their affair, but she hadn't meant that at all. She meant so Casey could see that she was a good person and they could talk woman to woman about caring for the son the three of them would share.

Stupid. Stupid. Stupid.

He hadn't hit her like she expected him to.

What he did was far worse.

He—or rather something inside him—had shifted. As mysterious and unknowable as he had been before, he was now the Iceman. She shivers now just thinking about it.

She tried to explain what she meant right then and there—and several times since—but the change in him wasn't a temporary reaction to a misunderstanding. Something she hopes will change when they get to the new town and their new life together far, far away from here.

I wasn't threatening you. I didn't mean . . . I'm not a threat to . . . anyone. I'm just a silly girl. I love you. I'd never do anything to hurt you. Not ever. Even if you leave me. Even if you . . . no matter what you do . . . I'll never do anything to hurt you. Not ever.

Had he believed her? She can't be sure. Can't be sure about anything with him. But she doesn't believe he did.

So why is he still leaving with her?

Maybe he's not. He's not here yet, is he?

True.

And then suddenly, miraculously, he's here.

Her prince. Her white knight. Her hope at happiness has arrived.

—They already come and get all your stuff?

She nods. –Just a little while ago.

—Did you erase your phone and give it to them too?

—Did everything just like you said to. Everything. You sure you still want to do this?

—Absolutely. Just have to make a quick stop first.

Does she dare ask where or why?

—Oh yeah? she asks, unable to help herself.

Stupid. Stupid. Stupid.

—Yeah. For us. For our future.

—Where's that?

—I buried some fresh-start funds—a lot of them—out in the swamp not too far from the river in Wewa. We've got to go by, dig them up, and then we're home free. You willing to help me dig a hole out in the swamp if our future is in it?

80

Now

Anna and I are cooking dinner together when the doorbell rings.

It's the first of two times it will ring tonight and the far less shocking of the two.

We're making fresh field peas, fried green tomatoes, cornbread, garlic-crusted chicken breasts, and new potatoes.

Sam will be home tomorrow and Anna is also baking a cake to celebrate her return.

I'm saddened again to think about Sam's improvement and the fact that Daniel isn't here to see it—and might not be ever again.

To be more accurate and honest, Anna is cooking. I am mostly watching, helping with little things here and there, though she keeps insisting I sit down over at the table by Taylor and prop my leg up.

"I'm even more in the way on crutches?" I ask. "Or is it not possible for me to be more in the way than I normally am?"

"The only difference I can discern is you're groping and fondling me less than you normally do."

"I'm so sorry," I say. "I bet I can balance on one crutch and still have a hand free to explore your beauty while you work."

"You could at least try," she says. "Let a girl know she's still fondle-worthy in the kitchen."

Before I can try to let a girl know she is most certainly still fondle-worthy and always will be, the doorbell rings.

"Hey, Hopalong," Anna says, "you wanna hop over and get that while I stick this in the oven?"

When I open the door and see that it's Heather, I say, "Howdy pardner."

She looks confused .

"Come on in."

She does so slowly, gingerly moving through our galley kitchen and taking a seat on a high stool at the tall cypress table.

"Sorry to interrupt dinner," she says.

"You're not," Anna says. "Just starting on it, really. Please stay and eat with us. How're you feeling?"

"Mostly like a fool," she says. "Can't believe I trusted the bastards all these years." She then glances over at Taylor who is eating Cheerios off her highchair tray and says, "Sorry."

"Which bastards in particular?" I say.

"Mike and Jean Thomas."

"Least you didn't marry him," Anna says.

"Huh?"

"When I make a statement like *I can't believe I trusted the bastard,* I'm actually referring to my ex-husband, so . . . it could be worse."

"Oh."

The kitchen smells of garlic and other seasonings that make me both hungry and happy. And though I wish Johanna were here, having Anna and Taylor make this fifty-year-old brick ranch feel like home.

I sit down across from Heather, putting aside the notebook with the draft of the letter I am writing to let Alec Horn's daughter know his final thought was of her.

"Don't feel like you have to sit here with me," she says.

"No, please keep him over there," Anna says.

"Off his leg?"

"Away from dinner."

She laughs, and in another few moments Anna joins us at the table with glasses and a pitcher of sweet tea. Without asking if we want any, she pours each of us a glass, offering and adding lemon to Heather's before sliding it over in front of her.

We are quiet for a few moments, sipping on our tea.

"I want to thank you again for all you did," Heather says. "Both of you."

"Our pleasure," I say.

"I didn't do much," Anna says, "but was honored to be involved."

"I so wish Caroline was here to see it," Heather says. "She had such a hard life toward the end, but to . . . actually see her son shot like that . . . killed right in front of her. Her only child riddled with bullet holes while she watched."

Anna and I both glance at Taylor and I think about Johanna.

"I can't even fathom," Anna says.

I can, but wish I couldn't.

"She said she wanted to die right then and there," Heather says. "That she came so close to picking up one of the guns and shooting herself in her broken heart. Actually lifted the gun from where it had fallen inside the boat, but . . . felt like she had to tell everyone what had happened, what he did, how very brave he was. Wanted to be the one to tell me, to grieve with me."

I think about April Bennett again. And Remington. And Martin Fisher. And Nicole Caldwell. And Lamarcus Williams.

And Angel Diaz. And Stacy Andrews. And so many other innocent victims, lambs led to the slaughter by wicked, violent men,
and I am overwhelmed with sadness and pain and despair.

"I think I can't be any more grief-stricken and distraught,"
Heather says, "and then I imagine actually seeing him being shot
the way Caroline did and I think . . . there are levels of despair I
know not of."

I look over at her, then to Anna, and realize all three of us
have tears in our eyes.

"I actually came by because I have good news," Heather says,
wiping at her eyes.

"Talk about burying the lede," Anna says with an attempt at a
smile.

Taylor tosses a Cheerio onto the table. When I pick it up and
eat it, she throws another at me.

Anna tells both of us to stop then asks Heather what her
news is.

"I finally know what I'm going to do with the land,"
Heather says.

"Oh yeah?" I say. "What's that?"

"Make a memorial to Remington and April," she says. "Make
a wildlife sanctuary named after and in honor of them, create a
park, a place of contemplation and connection with the wild
beauty of this area and even to take pictures—though none will
be as exquisite as those Remington took."

"No, they won't," I say. "That's a beautiful and brilliant idea. I
love it. It's perfect."

"I also plan to set up camera traps throughout with still
cameras and live video feeds that can be watched online from
anywhere in the world."

"Nice," Anna says, "I like that."

"I'm going to sell part of the land to pay for everything and to
create a not-for-profit for the prevention of child and domestic
abuse. The April Bennett Foundation."

"That's . . . incredible . . ." I say. "Just so, very generous and kind of you. And so restorative in a way. It's things like that that mean evil won't win, that darkness won't overtake the light."

"Restores people's faith in humanity," Anna adds.

"I'm glad y'all think so," she says, "'cause I want y'all to help me with it."

"Absolutely," I say. "In any way we can."

"We'd be honored," Anna says. "Thank you for asking."

"Could I make one suggestion?" I say.

"Thought you said it was perfect?"

"Guess I meant it was almost perfect."

"How can I make it more perfecter?" she asks with a smile.

"Include Mother Earth in the memorial."

Her eyes widen and her mouth falls open. "I can't believe I didn't think of that. You're right. She has to be a part of it. We'll have to create something that honors her down by the river."

"Perfect," I say.

Heather is about to say something else when the doorbell rings again.

"I'll get it," I say.

But Anna's already moving toward it. "Save your hops," she says. "I got it."

Ignoring her, I climb up on my crutches and hop along after her, just in case it's Chris or Randa or some other possible threat.

And I'm glad I do.

Because when she opens the door, Daniel Davis falls onto the floor inside.

Anna screams and dives onto the floor beside him.

Lying awkwardly after a straight fall and hard landing, he's not moving, doesn't even appear to be breathing.

"Is he alive?" I ask.

Dropping my crutches, I hop on one leg the rest of the way. Pulling my weapon, I look through the open door, searching the area outside.

"Daniel?" Anna is saying. "Daniel?"

I turn toward Heather. "Call an ambulance."

Anna looks up at me, her face a mask of sadness, pain, and confusion.

"Is he breathing?" I say. "Anna? Anna? *Is he breathing?*"

ALSO BY MICHAEL LISTER

Join Michael's Readers' Group and receive 4 FREE Books!

Books by Michael Lister

Sign up for Michael's newsletter by clicking here or go to
www.MichaelLister.com and receive a free book.

(John Jordan Novels)

Power in the Blood

Blood of the Lamb

Flesh and Blood

(Special Introduction by Margaret Coel)

The Body and the Blood

Blood Sacrifice

Rivers to Blood

Innocent Blood

(Special Introduction by Michael Connelly)

Blood Money Blood Moon

Blood Cries

Blood Oath

Blood Work

Cold Blood

Blood Betrayal

Blood Shot

(Jimmy "Soldier" Riley Novels)

The Big Goodbye

The Big Beyond

The Big Hello

The Big Bout

The Big Blast

In a Spider's Web (short story)

The Big Book of Noir

(Merrick McKnight / Reggie Summers Novels)

Thunder Beach

A Certain Retribution

(Remington James Novels)

Double Exposure

(includes intro by Michael Connelly)

Separation Anxiety

Blood Shot

(Sam Michaels / Daniel Davis Novels)

Burnt Offerings

Separation Anxiety

Blood Oath

Blood Shot

(Love Stories)

Carrie's Gift

(Short Story Collections)

North Florida Noir

Florida Heat Wave

Delta Blues

Another Quiet Night in Desperation

(The Meaning Series)

Meaning Every Moment

The Meaning of Life in Movies

Sign up for Michael's newsletter by clicking <u>here</u> or go to www.MichaelLister.com and receive a free book.

CPSIA information can be obtained
at www.ICGtesting.com
Printed in the USA
LVOW12s0137170518
577513LV00001B/144/P